Wyld Wynd Unleashed

Book Three of the Wyld Wynd Series

Peter Sandor

Wyld Wynd Unleashed, 3rd Edition.

Rev. 17, 05-13-25

ISBN 978-0-9917954-7-5

Read other books by Peter Sandor

<u>The Wyld Wynd Trilogy</u>

Book 1 – Wyld Wynd The Rising

Book 2 – Wyld Wynd The Unrest

<u>The Wall Plug Boys</u>, a hilarious adult comedy

The Talus 3 Series

Book 1 – Arctic EMP

Book 2 – Galactic Illusions

Book 3 – Forsaken Drifter

Book 4 – Time Undone

Paperbacks, hardcovers and ebooks are available from Amazon.

Contents

Chapter 1

Iswan. The name rolled off Nolan's tongue with a natural harmony that would give people the impression a world so called was calm and beautiful. However, here he was, huddled in a half-covered scallop cut into the rock, giving partial protection from the vicious winds howling over his head. To make matters worse, the tormented air carried fine particles of dirt and sand, pelting anyone who would brave the surrounding open, seemingly endless plain. *Great,* Nolan thought. He had hopped from a world of red haze only to find himself on a world with a similar environment, differentiated only by the color of the dust.

The scalloped floor of the den was really nothing more than a wide, thirty-foot-long ditch dug ten feet below the level of the surrounding plain. Behind him, the displaced rock from the floor was piled high in a rough wall, providing an essential, twenty-foot-high windbreak. Considering the tool marks along the ditch's floor and the odd placement of rocks in the windbreak, it was obvious the protection was man-made. His silent thoughts were between a curse and a prayer—a prayer for whoever built the depression, and a curse for the same man for conceiving the notion in the first place.

Nolan was lost in thought as his gaze focused on the flames coming from the odd fire pit in front of him. The flattened stone ledge was surrounded by a black, fire-hardened cylinder of metal. There were louvers cut into the side to control both the amount of air entering and the heat retreating. He sat by one of the side louvers, across from Daniel who held his hands out to the louver on the opposite side.

Through the persistent wind, Nolan looked up at his friend as he held his hand up, letting the wind-carried sand pelt his palm. "Why here?" he said. "This is as god-forsaken a place as I've ever seen."

Daniel's leather hat was pulled low over his forehead. He tilted his brow up with his light-blue gaze just visible under the brim. "Iswan is a word from one of the old tongues. The closest literal translation is *River World.*"

Nolan's guffaw cut the older man off. "River World!" He rolled his eyes. "That's a little freaking ironic, don't you think?"

Daniel shifted his weight on the rock while pointing a crooked finger at Nolan. "Sometimes you let your good sense go by the wayside. Remember, there are more than a few people who want your head, including General Treve and Julian Morenz of Kaezzar, not to mention the rogue group of Akkadians we just escaped from. Also, keep in mind the list has grown with many in Bailemor thinking you and I are spies. It is unlikely any of them will find us here. At this point in time, it would not be advisable for the three of us to walk up to one of the comfortable inn's dotting the many waterways of this world and request accommodations."

Nolan opened his mouth and was about to respond when Ranaa came into view. She had cleaned herself of the red dust using the water from a deep-cut well on the far side of the ditch. Now that she was free of the grime, the color of her skin, still barely covered by her scant clothing, could be seen as quite fair—almost lily-white. Without saying a word, she circumvented Daniel and sat on a rock next to Nolan. The wind was warm, but the water droplets evaporating on her skin caused her to shiver.

Nolan pulled off his jacket and offered it to her. "Put this on. It'll keep you warm."

She looked twice at the jacket, still covered in a thin layer of red dust. Finally, she reached out her hand and took it, draping it over her shoulders. "Thank you," she said in a low, soft voice.

Daniel turned his eyes to her. Things happened quickly during the pursuit in Bailemor, so this was the first opportunity to question the girl. "You were lucky we were there to save you. Who were those men chasing you?"

She looked from Daniel to Nolan. Her face was drawn from fatigue, but also sadness. "Yes, it was fortunate you were there to save me. As for those men…" She shrugged. "I don't know exactly who they were—someone who paid to hunt us I suppose."

"Who were the men with you?" Nolan asked.

She kept her eyes downcast. "Others who were raised for *The Hunt*."

His eyes opening wide, Nolan turned to her. "You mean you've been captive since you were a child?"

Her sad eyes turned up to him. "I was born in captivity. I know nothing

2

of the world other than the walled village we were kept in and the knowledge that, one day, I would be killed in The Hunt. I know nothing of you or him." She pointed her finger at Daniel. "All I do know is you saved my life, and no matter how horrible this world looks, it is better than death, and I feel protected."

Nolan was at a loss for words. Ranaa's words quickly brought the vision of Deahna back to his mind. He'd failed to protect her, and now this woman needed the same.

Thankfully, the uncomfortable silence was interrupted by an unusual sight. Off to their left, the sand and dust was being deflected around an invisible barrier, and a moment later, they saw the familiar ripples of someone hopping in. Daniel put his hand on the hilt of the long knife at his waist, but his grip relaxed as he saw the familiar sight of Germaine. Germaine's long, black hair, tied behind his head in a ponytail, was buffeted by the wind. He saw the three travelers huddled by the fire and made his way over to the bottom of the scallop and the minimal protection offered by the rock wall.

There were warm hugs of welcome amongst the men and a quick introduction of Ranaa, whereby Germaine looked at her with a dubious gaze. Never at a loss for words, he said what first came to his mind. "Although luck has been good to us so far, we have a long road ahead of us here on Iswan. The woman will not keep up." His last words were spoken as if she was a commodity.

Nolan was about to speak, but he was stopped by Ranaa's soft fingers on his knee. Her eyes were no longer downcast. Rather, the golden gaze was directly aimed at Germaine. "I have lived most of my life looking after myself. My parents were taken from me when I was very young, so I have learned two things. First, I've learned I can keep up just fine. In the camp, failure to do so meant death. Second, if for some reason I cannot keep up, then I will not put others at risk for my sake."

Nolan looked down and smiled. The girl had a hidden spirit and a common-sense approach. He also remembered how fast she ran from the mounted trosks, leading both her unfortunate companions in the foot race. Although he was beginning to feel her words held truth, he had every intention of leaving her in the safety of the first settlement they came to.

Ranaa was not finished as she held Germaine's gaze. "What of you? Can you say the same?"

"I don't follow you," Germaine replied.

Ranaa took a quick breath, then exhaled as if impatient with Germaine's lack of understanding. "I mean, if *you* slow us down, will you let us move on without you?"

Germaine's eyes went dark with anger. "I'll not hold up the group. You do not know me at all!" His voice rose over the wind whipping above them.

Ranaa suppressed the fullness of her smile, but there was enough there to show her little victory. "Exactly! Just as you, who only met me a few moments ago, don't know my abilities. It would be just as foolish for me to judge you a burden without knowing who you are," she concluded in a soft, but matter-of-fact tone.

Germaine jumped to his feet without consideration for the sand and dust pelting his face. "Foolish—burden!" He had difficulty spitting out the words. "I'm a leader of 100, and I've earned my silver band on the world of Crann Bith.

Raising his hand and slapping his forehead while he shook his head from side to side, Nolan muttered through his chuckle, "The woman has a quick tongue. Unfortunately, now we'll have to listen to Germaine's history."

"Look—there!" Daniel yelled over Germaine's babble and the wind.

They all turned to the wall of rock behind them, where a man had just appeared. Nolan turned just in time to see the shimmer of another planer hop disappear. He looked at the newly arrived man suspiciously until he saw the smiles on the faces of both Daniel and Germaine. Daniel sprung to his feet before his quick pace took him over to the man, where their arms locked in greeting. There were smiles of familiarity on both their faces.

The newcomer was dressed in loose fitting clothes made of a leathery material. The pants were dark, but as the two drew nearer to the fire, Nolan could see they were, more accurately, a dark-green. The tunic was a light-green while the short, loose-fitting jacket, hanging down almost to his knees, was of the same color as the pants.

As the pair drew close to the fire, Germaine jumped up and shook the newcomer's arm, then Daniel turned to Nolan. "This is the one I have spoken to you of. This is Nolan Harrison of Earth." Daniel's smile turned to Nolan as his arm opened toward the stranger. "This is Garawin, Prince of Rivenloc."

Holding out his arm, Nolan expected the same greeting as offered to Daniel, but instead, Garawin slid his palm against Nolan's, placing his other hand against the back of Nolan's hand.

Garawin's face was handsome and long, matching his approximate six-foot-four-inch frame. His honest, brown eyes, framed by black hair streaked with silver, looked upon Nolan for the first time. "So, you are the one."

In the dim firelight none could see Nolan blush as he opened his mouth, unsure how to respond.

Garawin pulled his feet formally together and tipped down from the waist. Still with a grasp on Nolan's hand, he said, "I Garawin, Prince of Rivenloc, second in succession, give my oath to support you as long as there is breath in my lungs and the power in my body to do so."

Nolan pulled back his hand uncomfortably. The revelation of his powers, and what it could well mean, was still fresh in his mind. He knew he would find it awkward for some time yet to come, but at the same time, there were things happening in life that gave cause for a man to rise up and accept who he is and what his purpose will be. Even though he was still unsure of exactly what purpose it was, he knew people were counting on him. His friends were foremost in his mind when the thought passed over him. He didn't want to let down any more people, and in the back of his mind, he wanted, one day, to go back and visit his father with Daniel.

Nolan knew it was time for him to step up and be counted. He put his hand on Garawin's shoulder, relieving the confused look on the taller man's face. "I accept your allegiance, and I'm proud to have Garawin, Prince of Rivenloc, with us."

Garawin gave a momentary, bright smile, but his face quickly changed to a look of concern as he brought his attention to the woman who was close by Nolan's side. Nolan introduced her while explaining her circumstances.

Garawin frowned as he rubbed his chin, reviewing her petite frame "A woman—well, we had best find you a place—" He caught Germaine's movements out of the corner of his eye. Half hidden beside his knee, the warrior was frantically waving his index finger to and fro. At the same time, Germaine, combing the fingers of his other hand through his hair, shook his head back and forth while his eyes gave Garawin a stern look of warning. Garawin's words continued after the short pause. "—a place to get into some clean clothes." His eyebrows were raised as he looked for approval from Germaine.

Nolan looked at Ranaa who still wore the two rags barely covering her body. Even he was still devoid of the shirt he'd ripped to rags to protect himself from the red haze on Crann Bith.

When Nolan turned his eyes back toward Garawin, it was to see him dematerializing and then he was gone. He turned to Daniel with a raised finger, "He can't do that—two transpositions in such a short time."

"You are correct," Daniel replied. "But then, he did not transposition. It was teleportation. Garawin is an Anasazi."

There was a grinding noise from the wall of rocks and dirt. One of the larger boulders was slowly shifting. Behind it was a dark cavern leading downward. Within it was a spark. The oil-soaked tinder in the lantern caught, illuminating Garawin's face. With his free hand, the prince motioned them to follow as he backed into the darkness.

Daniel opened the louvers on the metal fire pit. The wind flowing fully through it almost doused the fire with its strength. Germaine threw several handfuls of dirt on the remaining flickers of flame that were stubbornly refusing to die. Finally, the dirt suffocated the last embers, and they shifted their focus to the glow from the cavern. Daniel led the way as Nolan grasped Ranaa's hand, pulling her along. Germaine, as they would find out, took his normal position, bringing up the rear of the group.

Once inside the cavern, Nolan realized they were on an outcropping of rock overlooking a long tunnel snaking off into the distance in both directions. There were other crags of sharp rock. Some were smaller, some larger, but for the most part, the walls were smooth. Garawin pulled a lever within a recess in the rock face. As he did so, the boulder that had just moved aside, groaned as it reversed its direction, moving back to cover the entrance to the cavern.

Nolan was aware of the silence as the howling wind, which had been a constant for several hours, was now gone. Here it was quiet except for the sound of water droplets falling from the roof, passing through the 30 feet to the base of the tunnel below. As he looked back from the edge of the precipice to the others, he saw dust-covered, wooden shelves with cupboards against the far rock wall. Close beside it was a barrel filled with water where Germaine and Daniel were already cleaning themselves of the layer of grime having accumulated.

Nolan moved over beside them and dunked his head fully into the barrel of water, turning his head from side to side where the motion sent waves of water splashing over the side. Whipping his head back, his hair, having grown longer, sent a spray of water through the darkness behind him. He cleaned his arms and chest just before a dry towel thudded into his chest, thrown to him by Germaine. Daniel was still burrowing through the cupboards where he had found the towels, and was now pulling out pants, shirts and jackets. He inspected each, and those with holes were thrown back in. Having found enough for all of them, he pushed the drawers closed with a wooden thud as dust was thrown into the air, signifying the extended time since they had last been pulled open.

Germaine, not having been exposed to the elements for as long, shook out his clothes and put them back on, but Daniel and Nolan's clothes could not be salvaged.

Ranaa, for all observations, could be best described as not having clothes in the first place. She was the first to select, moving the shirts about until she found a smaller, light-blue one. She did the same with the slacks, finding a dark-blue pair. She lifted these along with a pair of soft boots and turned from the table.

Nolan, without even really looking, picked up a brown shirt. He felt Ranaa pull the shirt from his hand before turning back to the table where she was now rummaging through the remaining clothes. She handed Nolan a silver shirt with a black, narrow, upright collar and a pair of black pants. "Silver will suit you better," was all she said before walking into the shadows at the edge of the outcropping of rock where she could get dressed privately.

Daniel and Garawin chuckled. Even the more stoic Germaine joined with a wide smile as Daniel and Nolan quickly donned the clean clothes and leather boots. Ranaa came back into the lamplight. She had dressed and handed Nolan's jacket back to him, having cleaned it of most of the dust and grime. Pulling it over his shoulders, Nolan tied the belt. It brought back memories of those he left behind on Crann Bith, and he wondered, *would he ever see Lukas again or even the Gypsy King?* Pulling his mind back to the present, he surveyed the group. They were five—five who would need to come together and trust each other explicitly if they were to survive. Daniel was right in what he had said. There were many groups who now wanted them dead. He felt a weight come over him as he realized it wasn't *them* they wanted at all. It was *he* they wanted. These others were all here willing to sacrifice themselves—at least that's what it would seem. He looked to each in turn: the warrior, the so far mysterious prince, the old man who was not so old and the woman who he couldn't figure out—yet. He could not read her, but she seemed to have a strong spirit that he liked.

Then he considered himself. The girl was right. He looked good in the silver shirt. He felt as if he was in a constant state of shock, but through it, he realized his position was as their leader. Unready as he was, he was being thrown to the task, and he decided in his mind and heart to accept it even though he didn't think he had many other options. He felt foolish as he considered he knew very little. He didn't know why they were on Iswan, nor did he know how Garawin fit in, although it was simple to decide he was here for a reason.

"So, does someone want to tell me what's going on?" Nolan asked as his curiosity won out over his sense of foolishness.

Daniel turned to Garawin. "How long do we have?"

"We have an hour before we must leave to avoid the water," the prince replied.

Daniel motioned to the long table sitting between two benches. "Let's sit for a few minutes then. There are some things we all need to know before we start."

Everyone took a spot on the benches. Nolan sat at the end, and Ranaa pushed her way beside him, forcing Germaine to the side.

Daniel turned to Garawin. "Nolan has already asked why we are here on Iswan. Perhaps you can explain since this world is your home."

Garawin leaned forward, resting his palms on the wooden table. "Iswan is an old world. It is in Anasazi control, although it has not always been this way. Many thousands of years ago this was an Ionian world. Of all the pureblood races, the Ionians were the engineers of the group. They searched for answers to life and death in the technology and science that consumed their time. They had the technology to make them a formidable foe, and as such, they survived the ongoing wars. However, they also tired of the war. The logic which science bred into them told them the war and associated death was pointless. There was no point to the war. It was just fighting for the sake of fighting.

Eventually their efforts for peace grew, and they invited the Anasazi, one of the less fervent fighting races, to join them on Iswan. My people accepted. We lived together for many years along with the growing scull population, but the war continued around them, and, from time to time, hit directly on this world.

Then there was a morning when the people of this world awoke to find there wasn't an Ionian to be found. Every last one of them had left, and no one knows exactly where they went. Many surmised they became so disillusioned with humanity, they just decided to leave for an endless corner of the Athar, hoping never to be found. Another just as plausible theory was that, with technology, they found a way to hide their existence." Garawin chuckled. "Some say they are still here on Iswan, and they have discovered a way to keep themselves out of phase with the rest of us while only becoming visible when they choose to do so. Consequently, they are the roots of our ghost stories here on Iswan."

"It sounds similar to what Daniel told me happened to the Ionians on Earth—without the ghost stories though," Nolan whispered.

"Tell us of the Three Keys." Daniel urged Garawin on.

The prince took a moment. The flickering light from the lantern in the center of the table reflected in his eyes as, in turn, he looked to each of those who listened to his words. In his gaze each of them knew the unspoken message about to be revealed. This was important and the atmosphere at the table had turned reverent—almost spiritual.

Garawin continued just as a slight breeze came from the unknown darkness of the tunnel, curling around the table and brushing against the flame in the lantern. Ranaa shivered, scooting closer to Nolan as she wrapped her fingers under his arm. The brightness of the flame increased, bathing Garawin's face in an eerie glow as his words told the story. "This world was chosen by the Ionians as the location to experiment on the blood of the races. The difference in our bloodlines is the root of our wars, and we fight because we are different. The Ionians knew they needed three things to prove to the other races that coexistence between the bloodlines was possible. The three items had to be created in unison as they were closely related. They needed a sample of blood that was a mixture of all the seven pureblood races. This was a larger feat than one would first think. You see," Garawin pointed his finger above the table, "two of the races were already extinct." The Ionians had the foresight to save samples of the DNA that flowed through their long-lost blood, so the sample of mixed blood, including those of the lost races, is in fact the Third Key."

Daniel and Germaine heard the story before, but even so, they leaned forward in interest as Garawin continued. "The blood in itself was not enough. It needed to be reproducible, and for that the genetic formula was required. Consequently, the Ionians decided to manufacture a hammer—a hammer worthy of the builders who were their ancestors. It had a stout wooden handle tempered to an extreme hardness by special chemicals known only to the Ionians. On the handle was embossed the symbol of the Ionian builders—those long ago known as the Soichaint. The emblem was a full circle overlaid with a crossed hammer and sword. The emblem has passed the test of time and lives on with more of us each and every day. Attached to the sacred handle was a stone head that was six inches long and three inches around."

Garawin slammed his fist down on the table as his voice rose, causing all those seated around the table to jump. His passionate words continued. "It was a mighty hammer, and if you looked closely you could see the seven lines that circled the head. Each held the genetic formula of a bloodline, chemically engrained in the stone. The hammer was the Second Key."

The prince's voice lowered again. "That leaves the First Key. The samples of blood and the genetic formulas are strong keys needed to show the races had the potential to survive, retaining their powers even though their blood was mixed. The final proof required was a sample. Less clinically put, they needed a pureblood who had the mixed blood flowing through his or her veins. This being would then have the powers of all the great races. The Ionian scientists knew any two keys without the third was pointless. They spent many hours on the human element, and sadly, more than a few humans were sacrificed for the better good of the peace movement.

Eventually, they succeeded, or so the lore goes. Long ago, the war was in its feverish height. The Ionians knew it was not the time to reveal the Three Keys, and instead, they hid them. Rumor has it the Second and Third Keys are hidden somewhere here on Iswan. The human who was the First Key was sent out and hidden in the expanse of the Athar. The Ionian scientists knew the secret must remain just that until more people were swayed toward the peace movement.

A chemical was injected into the being's blood to suppress his powers. It was a DNA time bomb set for hundreds of years in the future. By then the First Key would be dead, but it would live on in his ancestors. One day a child would become a boy who would become a man, and the powers would rise to the surface, hopefully found by members of a growing Soichaint movement."

Garawin settled back in his position on the bench. His voice lowered, but the intense passion was still there. "The ancestor of the First Key is found, and he is here in our midst." His eyes were moist, turning up to look squarely at Nolan. "You are the First Key."

Chapter 2

The head of Intelligence for the Sillian Alliance stood on the raised podium located near the west edge of the crowded amphitheater. He was the sixth speaker of the day at the Annual Toltec Security Congress. His voice was deep, feeding through the microphone to the speakers, spreading it evenly through the acoustically perfect venue.

Julian listened from the third row of the Kaezzar delegation's section. Nothing he heard today was of significance. His interest was focused only by the fact this was his very first Congress. Only the heads of State within the Toltec Athar and their senior officials were allowed to attend. He looked around the low-lit amphitheater, noting the other six sections reserved for the representatives from the other planes that collectively made up the greater Toltec nation. With curiosity, he considered each group, all Toltec, yet all culturally and visually distinct.

The Sillian delegation sat next to the Kaezzar. They were characterized by their features, beginning with their long, narrow faces, accentuated by the large rings hanging from their ears. Julian had been told, as children, the earrings were actually weights, stretching the lobes until they almost reached the base of their necks. He didn't understand it, but apparently the longer the facial appearance of the Sillians, the more attractive they were considered by the opposite sex. Amplifying their hallowed appearances were the shaved heads of each of the 35 delegates listening attentively to their representative on the podium.

The Sillian administrator was almost finished. "Extensive effort has come from our people in working to squash the rebellious peace movement. Intelligence has been slow in coming, but we finally have a breakthrough. We have discovered the name of the group." He paused momentarily for dramatic effect. "The peace activists call themselves the Soichaint."

A murmur arose in the amphitheater. This was the first piece of shared information that bore significance. As the Sillian stepped from the podium, Julian clapped politely, putting the name of the peace movement to memory. There was a stir from the Prime box where the heads of State of each of the seven represented Toltec worlds sat. They were in an arc of comfortable chairs facing the podium in front of the raised general seating that angled up behind them.

The vice-prime of the Kre Alliance of Worlds rose to his feet. The sound of his movements passed through the completely empty Kre delegate area before echoing off the curved perimeter walls of the structure. Julian considered the Kre politician who appeared more warrior than statesman. The observation did not surprise him. The Kre worlds were known to be a loose collection of brutally violent clans who warred just as well against anyone who was willing to stand in their way. Be it by sculls, Anasazi, Celtae or even other Toltec's, the Kre were feared throughout the Athar. Consequently, they were given a wide berth and sizeable leeway. It was this leeway that prompted the Congress officials to overlook the general insult of not sending a formal and full delegation. The Congress did send a silent message by canceling the Kre vice-prime's speech in the opening ceremonies, replacing it with a few short words when time permitted in the schedule.

Now, on the second day of the conference, the time had come. The Kre warrior stepped proudly out of the Prime box and moved toward the podium. There were metallic clinks as he walked. Although Congress officials had taken away his weapons at the entrance to the hotel housing the amphitheater, as they had for all those who entered through the tight security, he retained his suit of metal-knit clothes. An unusual metal breastplate that hugged his form and shone bright-silver, covered it. His left arm was gone below the elbow, and the left side of his face was mottled from a long-past burn. A long, black tail of hair hung from his otherwise shaven head, completing his barbaric appearance.

As he stepped up into the brighter light on the podium, Julian could not help but admire the man. He had dark, intelligent eyes and strong facial features, exuding strength of mind, body and character. Even though his body was scarred, the Kre was ruggedly handsome. *In some ways, this was a man he could aspire to become,* Julian thought.

The Kre warrior raised the microphone to his tall frame. "For those who don't know me, my name is Theron. I'm second of the Kre Alliance. I'm also a man of very few words, so I'll get to the message I was sent here to give."

The other six world leaders shifted uneasily in their seats. Of the seven worlds in this larger alliance, the Kre were the strongest. Fear of them was only abated because the other six member nations knew, if they remained united, the Kre would not attack. Rather, they would choose easier prey in the Celtae or Anasazi worlds.

"It's obvious I came to this conference alone. A delegation was not sent since every man of Kre is a warrior when need be, and we don't have warriors to waste on this Congress."

The Sillian king jumped to his feet. "You dare to insult this Congress? Your prime swore an oath to it."

Theron's face remained emotionless. "I don't agree. The Prime of Kre swore an oath to the Constitution of this Congress, not the Congress itself." He turned to the banner hanging on the wall to his left, reading the large letters aloud. "War is our way. War is our life until we are one." Underneath, in smaller letters, he read, "This will be accomplished by ridding the Athar of other pureblood lines that would mingle and degrade our one true blood."

The Kaezzar prime stood. The congress was being held on his world, and as such, he felt compelled to speak. "That's what we speak of, Theron. We speak of our continued existence."

The Kre smiled wide. Through it, he said, "Not at all. You speak and focus all your time on some insignificant, obscure peace movement. While we sit here in comfort, the Celtae, and even the Anasazi, build their empires. Our intelligence indicates their exploratory missions grow in leaps and bounds while every day they bring more worlds into their confines. It's much more than can be said for the weak reports which were given by the heads of your own exploratory departments on the first day of this Congress."

"The peace movement is a greater threat than you think," the Kaezzar prime added.

The Kre's brow furrowed with irritation. "On our world, as it is on many worlds, there's a wide variety of animal life, and they all have mechanisms for survival. From the smallest rodents to the ferocious tigers, they all have their place in the order of life. Consider the small rodents. They move into our homes and become a nuisance. We spend some of our time finding them and removing them from existence, primarily to stop the whining of our women." He looked stone-faced at each of the six officials in the Prime box. Then the veins at his temples creased the skin while his voice rose higher with each sure word. "However, we remember the rodents are a *small* problem. We don't discuss them at our Councils of War while the tigers run free to hunt!" His fist slammed into the wooden table in front of him on his last word, and he stalked confidently off the podium. As he walked by the Prime box, heading for the exit, he said to the leaders, "The Kre will return when this Congress for War is once again a Congress *for* War." His strong steps took him out the doors at the rear of the amphitheater as the rumble of voices that had begun as he slammed his fist, became a crescendo of noise.

The delegates were all on their feet, cueing off the energy of the Kre leader. There was yelling from delegation to delegation as members spread their unbridled opinions. The Congress had degraded into an uncontrolled, uproarious mob, leaving the Congress officials unsure what to do. They looked to Julian, who was the last scheduled speaker for the day. Julian looked back and shrugged. *I'll let them decide what to do*, he thought. However, one of the officials finally came over to his seat and pulled him to his feet, herding him up onto the podium.

No one even noticed.

The Congress official who stood close by said, "Do something, for god's sake. Get their attention."

Julian pulled the cue cards for his speech from his pocket and laid them on the table.

Tapping the microphone with his finger, he said, "Excuse me. Your attention please."

It went unnoticed. The noise level had increased, and several of the groups looked like they were ready for a physical confrontation.

Julian smiled. Luck was an unusual thing. Sometimes good fortune can come from bad. Right now, that shit of a Kre had stolen the spotlight, and his speech would be forgotten if he ever got the opportunity to deliver it. He put the speech back in his pocket and tapped the microphone again. "I know where they are," he said.

There was no reaction. They weren't listening.

His dark eyes filled with anger as his fingers grasped the base of the microphone. He lowered his lips to it, yelling, "Stop! I know where the Soichaint are!"

This time they heard, and their faces turned to the podium with interest while the noise level decreased immediately.

The Kaezzar prime took his hand off the Sillian's shoulder and turned to Julian. "What did you say?"

Julian cleared his throat and repeated, "I know where the Soichaint are."

Row by row, the delegates took their seats.

"Can someone put a map of the Athar on the screen, please?" Julian asked.

The leaders looked to each other and the Kaezzar prime nodded his approval to one of the Congress officials. He went scurrying off through a curtained opening behind the podium, and it didn't take long for the screen to fill with the image of the Athar and its familiar red and yellow dots.

Julian turned to the official who had returned. "Please magnify Sector One."

The official lifted the remote, pressed a button and Sector One was displayed.

"Magnify Zone 32."

Just as a cube can be turned while sitting on its bottom face, the view on the screen rotated 90 degrees.

One of the seated delegates yelled out, "That's Anasazi territory!"

Julian ignored the outburst. "Drill in to the TaaSha region."

The view on the screen moved into the side of the cube, speeding past markers. This lasted only a minute until the movement slowed, then stopped. There was a refocus and a slight shift, centering the view on the region.

"The TaaSha region is a grouping of 28 populated planes." Julian turned from the screen and looked at the leaders in the Prime box. "Our very reliable intelligence group reports the leaders of the Soichaint are located in this region on one of those planes."

"Which one?" the Sillian leader blurted.

"Our agents are still working on that."

The Kaezzar prime turned and glared at the senator for war who sat behind him. After a moment, he turned back to Julian. "We should have been given immediate notice of this breakthrough."

"My apologies, but the information is fresh. In fact, it could change at any moment as my agents scour the region, isolating the rebel's exact location."

The Kaezzar prime looked down at the paper on his desk, running his fingers along its length. He tapped his finger on the page near the bottom and held it there. His eyes turned back up to Julian. "Very well done, Commander Morenz. This is indeed a breakthrough, and in spite of the efforts of some of our distinguished members, it allows us to bring the Congress to an end on a high note." He turned to the assembly with a wide political smile on his round face. "As Kaezzar prime, leader of the host nation, I call this Congress to a close!"

As the delegates rose to their feet and clapped, Julian had a smug grin on his face. He had saved the day. The Kre, in his roughshod abandon, had almost left him out of the spotlight. However, he would now be the center of attention. His name would be repeated, over and over, across this world and many others. His quick thinking made him instantly famous. He felt a tug on his coat sleeve, and immediately he recognized the aide to the Kaezzar prime. He stooped, bringing his face close.

"You will give a detailed report to the Kaezzar prime in the morning. The senator for war will also be present." The aide handed Julian a card with the time of the meeting written on it.

"Of course," Julian replied.

The aide looked at him with disdain as he considered Julian's words a waste of breath. *Of course, you will be there,* he thought. *It's the Kaezzar prime.* He didn't want to waste any more time on the ambitious general, hurrying back to his place by the prime's side.

Julian walked briskly up one of the aisles as delegates slapped him on the back in admiration. Captain Atron, his Chief of Intelligence, turned out of one of the rows of seats, matching his steps toward the exit. There were no words between them as they left the amphitheater before turning left toward the buses that had been arranged for the delegates. They stopped in their tracks, seeing the throng of reporters who were huddled around the tall

Sillian leader next to the transportation hub.

In the commotion, the two men in their black uniforms, trimmed in yellow, disappeared down a deserted side alley in the failing light of the late evening without being noticed. The light breeze was cool, urging their brisk steps.

"I didn't think you were going to tell them," Captain Atron said.

"I wasn't, but events forced my hand. You saw what happened."

"It was clever, if in fact it proves true. The TaaSha region is in a far corner of the Athar. Even though you had pre-warned us to watch the plane of Crann Bith, it was difficult to pinpoint the traveler's end destination. The general region was the best we could do."

The pair made a left turn down another cobblestone alley, and the light from the short lampposts replaced the sun, having finally set over the horizon.

"It is true, Captain," Julian said matter-of-factly.

"How do you know the people we tracked are the leaders of the peace movement?"

"I just know these travelers are important. I only *suspect* they are the leaders of the movement." Julian slapped Atron on the shoulder. "Trust me," he said through a less than convincing chuckle.

The pair came to an intersection with a main road where Julian once again put his hand on the captain's shoulder, pulling him to a stop. "This is where we part for the evening," Julian said. "You are going back to headquarters."

"Why?"

"To relay the orders I'm about to give you for Captain Renier."

"You are sending the assault squad on a mission—tonight?"

"We work for the cause day and night," Julian reminded his subordinate.

The captain nodded.

"Do you have your pocket planner with you?" Julian queried.

"Of course." Atron popped the clip at his belt, then removed the small planner from the pouch.

"Turn on your atlas mode."

The captain moved his fingers over the small keys. "Done."

"Bring up the TaaSha region."

The fingers again moved over the small keys.

Julian had engrained the coordinates in his mind just before he burned the paper message he received from Peron a few days ago. "Zoom in on coordinates 11-0345-1."

Atron's fingers moved again, and then he looked up at Julian. "What's so special about these coordinates within the TaaSha region?"

"That's where you're going to direct Captain Renier. He knows the mission; he was just waiting for a target site."

"Why here?"

The cooler night air was settling in, and Julian blew his warm breath into his partially closed fist. He looked furtively from left to right before lowering his hand. "Because that's where the Soichaint leaders I'm searching for are."

"How do you know that?" the captain blurted.

Julian wasn't about to tell his subordinate about Peron. He wasn't going to tell him his spy was on Crann Bith and had allied himself with a high-ranking Celtae general. He was not going to tell him the general had also tracked his quarry's transposition, but being at the source, they easily locked onto the destination—and he was definitely not going to tell Atron how much money the flow of information was costing.

Julian took a simpler approach. "I know because I'm a god damn general, and you're a captain! One day, if you pull your head out of your ass for a few minutes as my Captain of the Intelligence group, and get the information that is your job requirement, then perhaps, one day, you'll be a pissy, short-tempered general as well!"

Atron clicked his heels together and saluted. "Yes, Sir!" He turned sharply, hastily making his way along the main road toward headquarters.

Once the younger captain was out of earshot, Julian chuckled. *He will make general one day,* he thought. *He's sharp and a good officer. I need to keep a close eye on him,* he concluded. Continuing his walk to the MagTrak station and home, he summarized the day's events in his head. He would awake in the morning with his name buzzing through all the socialite and military circles. However, in his future, there was more to come. The Toltec worlds were left in confusion today with half worrying about the Kre, and their efforts will be focused on diplomatic mending. The remainder will secretly send their military forces on secret missions to the TaaSha region, hoping to find the Soichaint and the accompanying glory.

Julian smiled. He had a head start. The other Toltec will have to pick and choose amongst the 28 planes of the region. *I know where Nolan Harrison is, and I'll find him! The next time I'm called to a meeting with the Kaezzar prime and the senator for war, I will be the senator for war!* He laughed aloud, satisfied with the happenings of the eventful day causing his present daydream.

Captain Atron was well out of range of Julian when he pulled the pocket planner from the pouch at his belt for a second time. As he walked, he pulled up the atlas mode again but went to the index. He had restrained himself until he was out of sight of his superior, but now his curiosity was piqued. He needed to know the name of the plane. He keyed in the coordinates, 32-0345-1. It took a moment for the name to appear. He whispered it to himself— "Iswan."

Chapter 3

Purple sparks exploded off the sidewall of the tunnel as the fireball of energy skipped twice before fading to the angled rock floor. Nolan had just released the energy burst from his fingers as he had done in five-minute intervals for the last two hours. There was an impatient sigh from his lips as the light revealed the same as it had each time he repeated the exercise—just more uninteresting tunnel, curving off into the darkness.

With Nolan close by his side, Garawin led them along the tunnel as it wound slowly downward. Daniel was close on Nolan's other shoulder, keeping pace but remaining quiet. He decided he would let Garawin answer the multitude of questions coming one after the other from the ever-curious Nolan. Ranaa didn't let Nolan too far from her side, walking three paces behind the man who was her savior, while Germaine brought up the rear just out of the circle of lantern light.

"So far I'm not very impressed with your world," Nolan offered.

Garawin held up the lantern as the light created bouncing shadows. "Do not judge too quickly. The small portion you have seen thus far is not representative of the world as a whole."

"How much further do we have to go before I see the accurate representation?"

"It's not really how far, but how long. We have a little over an hour until that time," Garawin answered.

Nolan felt just as he had when he first arrived on Crann Bith, knowing very little. He didn't understand how the answer to his question switched from distance to time, but he put that aside for the time being. "Is an hour here the same as an hour on Earth?"

"It's close," Daniel replied.

"I don't understand that," Nolan replied with a perplexed tone to his voice. "It was the same on Crann Bith. An hour there was also similar to an Earth hour, but all three are in different planes of reality. What are the odds of that?"

Daniel did not look to Nolan as he answered, preferring to keep his eyes on the dirt floor of the tunnel where the occasional irregularity could easily turn an ankle. "It's not unusual. All these planes come from the combined psychic energy of the many purebloods. This is the common thread holding the Athar together and gives it a commonality of at least the base languages, time, and to a degree, measurement."

"So, an hour is an hour everywhere?" Nolan asked as his fingers scratched at his head.

"No, not at all," Daniel explained. "But they are close as long as the planets within the planes are roughly the same size. Now, the fact Crann Bith, Earth and Iswan are approximately the same size is pure coincidence. However, in the universe on this plane, there are larger planets and smaller planets, and consequently, on each, an hour would be relatively shorter or longer just as it would follow a day, month or year would be distinguished by the proportionate amount."

Nolan furrowed his brow, showing his frustration as he glared at his mentor. "I just wanted to know how freaking long until we get out of this tunnel."

Both Daniel and Garawin chuckled.

Looking out from under the brim of his leather hat, Daniel said, "In Earth time, we have a little over an hour of travel left."

Nolan just shook his head, firing another purple fireball from his fingers down the length of the tunnel. He felt a finger tapping him on the shoulder. Turning, he faced Ranaa who had a quizzical look on her face.

She looked up, thinking before posing the question. "I have heard you say this word *freaking* twice. I have not heard it in my village before, so please explain it to me."

Three times, Nolan's lips moved to speak, but he was having difficulty formulating a simple answer. After a minute, he finally said, "A freak is someone who is different or unusual."

The yellow flecks in her eyes sparkled in the light from the lantern. "So, is it the tunnel which is freaking because it's unusual, or is it the length of time which is freaking because it's different from what you would expect?"

Nolan's steps slowed. "Neither really. It's just a saying. It's a slang word I use to express my frustration."

Confusion still clouded her eyes. "So, you are the freak?"

"No, not at all." Nolan shook his head. "How do I explain this," he muttered. "Okay, let me try to explain it this way. When I say *freaking*, it's to replace an even worse slang word we use on Earth—a curse word considered very bad. Some would even say it's vulgar and really shouldn't be said in mixed company."

She put her finger to her chin, thinking for a moment. "It seems odd you want to say a curse to show your frustration, but you say a different word which seems to have a different meaning altogether? Why would you not just say what you mean?"

"It's not that simple," Nolan replied, searching for words as he heard Daniel's chuckle ahead of him. "Words show people's emotions. I suppose I want people to think I'm frustrated enough to say the curse, but honorable enough not to."

"I'm not familiar with your ways, Nolan. Maybe my questions are foolish, but if you wanted to show your frustration, then why would you not just say 'I am frustrated.' Why use one slang word to indicate that you would have used an even worse curse if you wanted to—but didn't want to because of your sense of honor." She shrugged. "I think I have a lot to learn of your ways."

"Oh hell," Nolan muttered.

"Hell—is that slang or a curse?" she asked, her eyes innocently curious.

Nolan was glad it was dark in the tunnel otherwise all could have seen him blush as both Garawin and Daniel burst into laughter. He could even hear laughter from Germaine, who was behind him, just out of visual range of the lantern's flickering light.

Nolan threw another fireball, hoping it would break the line of questions, and thankfully, it did. This time, rather than skidding off into the distance, the fireball thudded into a solid rock obstruction ahead of them. It bounced, falling downward, but it did not break into sparks as it hit the ground. Instead, it continued glowing brightly, indicating there was a pit at the base of the outcropping.

"Chara's Drop," Garawin whispered.

As they carefully walked to the edge of the pit, Nolan asked, "Who is Chara?"

Garawin held the lantern over the hole, looking downward. "Chara was one of the two exploring brothers who found this passage. Chara's drop is within this tunnel called Ren's Rush. Chara was first in line and fell to his death here. I suppose if Ren would have been first, and Chara would have continued to find the exit, then we would be in Chara's Rush looking down Ren's Drop." Garawin chuckled, satisfied with his humorous play on words.

The others were all focused on the pit as Nolan let a fireball fall from his fingers, revealing its depth. This allowed them to see fifty narrow stairs cut into the side of the rock pit, winding around its circumference.

"Follow very carefully," Garawin stressed, "but don't dally. Our time is becoming short."

Nolan was filled with more questions each time Garawin spoke, but with Ranaa's attentive ear close by and the narrow steps ahead, he felt it better to keep his lips shut tight and his focus on the trek down.

He felt Ranaa's hand clasp his as the group, led by Garawin, made their way down the steps. Nolan kept his back angled against the wall with his feet gingerly feeling for each step. Several times small portions of the steps would crumble away, tumbling down into the pit. Each time his heart thudded as if it would rip through his chest, and each time he would use his training to slow his breathing and his tension. He was in control.

It didn't take them long to achieve the bottom of the pit. There were nervous smiles amongst the group as they looked up at the path they had traveled. At this level, the tunnel continued off into the distance, but there was a dim light breaking the darkness, visible around a far corner. Nolan headed toward it, but he had not made more than two steps before he felt Garawin's hand on his shoulder.

Garawin pointed the lantern to a low opening in the side of the rock. "This way," he said as he stooped and led them into a smaller tunnel branching from the main line.

Each traveler followed in turn. The space was confining with barely enough room to turn and look to the person behind, but the discomfort did not last long as this smaller tunnel also showed rays of dim light ahead. Shortly thereafter, there was a slight breeze and the taste of fresh air on their lips. It didn't take long for the group to exit the tunnel and find themselves on a ledge no more than twenty feet wide, hanging from the side of a smooth, almost vertical cliff.

In the dim light identified with morning on this world, Nolan peered over the edge, estimating the drop to be some 300 feet to a small, motionless lake at the base of the sheer drop. As he lifted his gaze to the horizon, all he saw were browns and grays, crisscrossed with the rivers Garawin had promised. From this vantage point, he could see small villages dotting the waterways and, off in the distance, two larger shadows he assumed were cities. There were trees, which appeared to be bleak entanglements of thorny branches, and as he looked closely down the side of the cliff, he saw bushes and spiny flowers, but there was no color. He sighed, turning to Garawin. "This isn't what I expected. It's an improvement over the darkness of the tunnel, but this is as drab a world as I've seen."

Garawin smiled. "Things are not always as they first appear. Just wait." He led the group around the edge of the cliff to an area having a large rock overhang and motioned them to move underneath. He pointed his finger off into the distance as rays from a low hanging sun slid under the outcropping, casting his shadow across the floor of the small plateau.

The increasing sunlight just brought more attention to the less than colorful world, but as Nolan followed the direction of Garawin's finger, he saw gray, billowing clouds in the distance. Underneath, pushed forward by the churning flow, was what had to be a wall of pounding rain so dense no light passed through it.

"We will wait," Garawin said as they all shrank back deeper under the outcropping.

The billowing clouds came closer and closer. With it came a murmur that turned into a rumble. As the wall of heavy rain hit the side of the cliff, the roar turned deafening. They were protected from the deluge by the outcropping, but the water pooled an inch thick, flowing off the side of the plateau.

Nolan was becoming even more disappointed with this world. After ten minutes, the rain stopped and the group moved out from their protection. All of them were more cautious than Garawin, who waved them confidently forward.

What the Earthman saw amazed him. From the far distance a wall of color raced toward the base of the cliff. The gray and brown were magically bursting into a sea of deep-green and bright-red, dotted with vibrant blues. His mouth hung open in amazement as he looked down to the lake, watching the metamorphosis. The thorns on the branches of the trees were

25

in fact not thorns at all, but leaves now unwinding from their tightly coiled positions as the sun awakened them. The dots of brown opened just as quickly, bursting into brilliant flowers. Even the spiny plants below the tree level transformed as each changed before his eyes. In the morning sunlight the bright pattern of color was absolutely beautiful against the now cloudless sky.

Nolan was about to speak, but a finger held up by Garawin stalled his words. "Wait," was all the prince said.

Nolan's eyes grew wide as once again he heard a rumble, but this time from behind him. He took a step back, thinking the wall of rain was returning, but Garawin's hand on his shoulder stayed him. The noise level once again grew, but this time it was different, seeming to come from within the depths of the rock wall itself. Vibration came next as the small plateau shook, but still the prince held firmly onto Nolan's shoulder, keeping him in place.

Suddenly, a torrent of water burst from the face of the cliff just above them and to their left. Nolan realized immediately that the rush of water was coming from the exit of Ren's Rush. He surmised the rains must be cyclic for the runoff from the plateau above them to maintain the smooth walled tunnel he now knew to be a runoff channel. As he looked off into the distance, he could see several more such waterfalls pounding into the valley below.

The waterfall above Nolan slammed into the stillness of the lake far below them just as the early morning song from several colorful birds played across the sound of the rushing water. They floated on the updraft suspended in the timeless moment. The winged creatures mingled into the panorama of color laid out in the valley below. The final touch which left Nolan absolutely speechless was the rainbow formed in the spray swirling up from the waterfall. It was so close he thought to touch it, but he was fearful the magical vision would end.

Garawin's hand slid around the back of Nolan's neck onto his far shoulder as his free hand swept outward across his body. "This, Nolan Harrison, is Iswan."

Chapter 4

Nolan stood in a wide stance with his hands on his hips as he looked back at the cliff they just descended. From this vantage point on the lower plateau, it was difficult to see the stairs hued into the side of the sheer rock face that allowed their descent in a moderate degree of safety. When Garawin first showed him the steps from the upper plateau, he gave the Prince of Rivenloc an *are you crazy* look. However, the prince took the lead himself, and when he had descended 50 feet, Nolan gained enough confidence to follow.

As soon as Nolan began the trek downward, Ranaa stuck close by. The young woman hadn't been far from his side since he saved her in the red haze of the Dead City. She had also made quite a transformation. Now, in the light of day, the warm sun had dried her white-blonde hair to a thick texture holding a subtle curl. Her golden eyes sparkled every time she looked at him, and each time he had difficulty pulling his own gaze away. She was stunning, but he knew this wasn't the time for him to begin the emotional climb again, nor, based on the mission to be completed, was this the time to begin a relationship. He decided, in his own mind, to keep the woman at arm's length until he could find her a quiet, peaceful haven.

Even though the time felt fleeting, the Earthman was thankful they'd slept for two hours before the descent. The short respite, and the thoughts of the adventure ahead had him sharp and refreshed. He needed the frame of mind and the energy as the downward trek turned into a two-hour, arduous task.

Nolan's thoughts were interrupted by a tap on his shoulder. "The barge is here," Daniel said.

Turning, Nolan looked through the opening between the tall, feathery leaves of the silver-green bushes bordering the lake at the base of the cliff. The bushes reminded him of the sword ferns from his native Washington state, and as he walked through them, he could feel the mist on his face from the winds skipping across the surface of the lake. On his left, the lake curled around the rock face, disappearing into the hazy distance. Garawin had told him, even though it was a large elevated plateau, all on Iswan knew it as the Great Rock.

The waterfall ceased long ago, leaving the tree-lined lake at peace. Nolan continued to be amazed at the beauty before him. The lake was the deepest blue, complimenting the flowers abounding both on the ground and in the trees surrounding it.

There was a sharp whistle from the barge. A pot-bellied man with a dark suntan was waving his hand toward Nolan. "Let's go! The barge is leaving now—with or without you!"

Nolan and Daniel, with Ranaa close behind, ran through the short grass until their feet echoed on the wooden dock. They jumped onto the barge just as it was sliding away from the rickety platform and out toward the open water.

Nolan turned to Daniel. "He wasn't kidding. He would've left without us."

Before Daniel could answer, the same voice came from atop the barge's cabin. The man, who Nolan assumed must be the captain, was again yelling through the openings in the large steering wheel. "As right as the sun's in the sky, I would've left you. No dallying on this barge. Just make your way up front with your friends. That's right, way up there under the tarp where you can't get in trouble." He took one calloused hand off the wheel and pointed toward the prow.

Garawin and Germaine looked comfortable in the short deck chairs. Garawin, with a pipe to his mouth, leaned back in the fabric and wood-framed chair. The legs were thick and less than a foot high, resulting in Garawin's relaxed position with his feet crossed and stretched out in front of him.

Nolan pulled a similar chair into position, facing the other two men and the stern of the vessel. The barge, as Daniel had called it, was really what he knew in Earthen terms as a sloop. It was 60 feet long and broader than what he would have considered sea-worthy, but then this was not a sea. In fact, at this time, since the barge needed to move into the wind, it was being pulled out toward the open lake by two rowboats full of well-muscled men. Looking up, just under the edge of the tarp, he viewed the two tall, stout masts where the sails, still tied securely to the spreaders, were not ready for deployment.

"Why don't you just use the engine?" Nolan asked.

"There are no engines on Iswan," Daniel replied. "No engines, no gasoline, no electricity and no refined energy."

Ranaa pulled her chair beside Nolan's, stretching her legs out in front of her. He was irritated with himself, trying to keep her from his thoughts, but he failed continually with her and her scent ever so close. It wasn't perfume. It was just her. She smelled fresh and sweet—sweet as a meadow full of spring flowers, and fresh like the pinecones that dot the trees surrounding it.

Refocusing on the men, Nolan said, "Surely there is energy. There's abundant water here in the lake that could supply thermal energy and the waterfall this morning has boundless amounts of kinetic energy."

Garawin smiled. "We could convert the energy if that was our wish. However, the people of Iswan choose to live a simpler life. No refined energy, no pollution, no—what do you call them—credit cards."

"There must be exceptions," Nolan replied.

"Very few. The Protocols of Iswan are clear. In fact, the First Protocol states - 'We live a simple life free of the evils of energy,'" Garawin offered.

"Think about it," Daniel interjected. "I found you in an isolated cabin in the deep woods. You were running away from the very things this world does not allow."

"I never quite thought of it that way."

"You have a lot to learn about this world, and you will see more when we get to Kaleo," Germaine said.

"What is Kaleo? Where are we going? Lastly, and once again, what are we doing here?" Nolan asked.

Daniel chuckled. "Ever the curious one. That is good."

There was a momentary interruption as the sails furled open. As the barge lurched forward, their chairs slid against the thick wood planks of the deck. Creaks and groans came from all about Nolan as the wind took the vessel on a port tack toward the distant shoreline. The men, who had secured the rowboats, were now scurrying about the barge, securing the lines which led from large rings in the deck to the edge of each sail's spreader. There was a thinner spreader bar at the bottom of each sail, and this was given some slack, allowing the wind to fill the two cloth sails while each burst into color against the bright, blue sky. One sail was dark-green while the other was bright-yellow. The barge was now alive, moving with the growing power of the wind.

One barely clothed man was at the top of each mast, checking the bindings of the numerous ropes holding the sails in place. With only shorts on, they shimmied down each mast while their skin hugged the surface of the weather-aged wood that had been pummeled smooth by seasons of wind and mist. Notwithstanding the creaks and groans, the barge moved steadily forward. Nolan felt more confident, observing the precise actions of the crew monitored by the ever-watchful eye of the grizzled captain who barked orders incessantly.

Garawin pointed up toward the sails. "Yellow and green are the colors of the city of Kaleo. That is our destination."

"How far?" Nolan asked.

Garawin looked out into the open water of the lake. "The wind is against us. If it does not change, the trip will take at least eight hours. When we arrive, it will be well into the late evening."

"Are the Second and Third Keys in Kaleo?" Nolan asked.

"Not as far as we are aware," Daniel interjected. He paused for a moment. "We do not know where the other Keys are."

"What!" Nolan leaned forward, wide-eyed. "How the freaking hell do you expect to find them?"

"We have clues."

"You have clues," Nolan repeated while his eyes were wide with amazement.

He felt Ranaa's fingers on his arm. Oddly, the touch calmed him, and he leaned back once again in his chair. "Okay, I'm listening."

Daniel looked toward Garawin who nodded his reassurance. The older man who was both Nolan's protector and mentor took a deep breath—a sure sign to Nolan that Daniel was going to take his time with his words.

"We are going to Wolar's Fang," Daniel began. "It will take

approximately fifteen days, and it won't take long for the many parties who are interested in your whereabouts to follow us. Consequently, we will need stealth and diversion to help us along the way."

Nolan tapped his fingers on the arm of the chair. "Couldn't we use our powers to accelerate our progress?"

"That would be foolish," Garawin said. "This expansive plateau of Iswan is an alliance of kingdoms. All the kingdoms have signed the Protocols of Iswan, and although there are some Anasazi who live amongst the nine scull kingdoms, most live in our home province of Rivenloc. My point being the general population is not used to seeing unfamiliar powers used as we might need to. Place that on top of the normal anxiety people have over strangers, and we would have a significant risk from the general population, not to speak of the alarms we would send out to the Toltec who will definitely follow. Remember, although this world is sympathetic to the peace movement because of its long history, it has not openly welcomed our group. Even the Council of Kings does not know we are here on this mission to find the Keys."

"Wisely spoken, Garawin," Daniel affirmed, "but speed is of the essence. We would not want the Toltec to find us."

"Agreed," the prince replied. "We have decisions to make." He reached his fingers into an inside pocket of his jacket, pulling out a wrapper of paper. As he leaned forward, he quickly unfurled the parchment, fold by fold, until a wide map of Iswan was on the decking between them.

Nolan leaned forward, his interest piqued.

Hitting his finger onto the map, Garawin said, "We are here." He pulled his finger toward a city labeled Kaleo. "And soon we will be here." His finger lifted and pointed toward the northeast. This would be the safest route, leaving the Kingdom of Roevin and then moving across Allanmore.

Nolan reviewed the map. He saw on the far east coast an island labeled Wolar's Fang. The shape, in the form of a predatory animal's fang, gave obvious reason for the island's name. Just looking at it sent a shiver up his spine. "What is so important about Wolar's Fang?"

As Garawin traced his fingers along the many rivers and canals lacing eastward over the map, Daniel answered, "There is a library of the old world on Wolar's Fang. In it are kept antiquities and writings from the days of old. They lie there long forgotten. Most citizens of Iswan do not choose to remember those days because this area of the Athar has been untouched by the war for some time. Only the very old will remember when the Toltec and Celtae sent squads this far into Anasazi territory. Now, with the Celtae and Toltec more concerned about each other, the risks from the smaller Anasazi nation have left forays to this region on hiatus. Those of us who remember our past know, that in time, death and destruction will once again find this world."

"It sounds like an impossible search, looking for clues amongst the multitude of decaying books." Nolan envisioned the memory of the library he'd slept in within the Dead City on Crann Bith.

"Certainly, we need help," Daniel admitted. "More unknown than the library of old is a shepherd who resides on the largely uninhabited island. This shepherd is long on years, but we have heard research of the secrets from the books have filled them. His knowledge of the books and artifacts is what we seek."

"Why haven't others gone before us to search him out?"

Germaine, who had been silent for most of the trip, spoke. "Because the island is cursed. The one described as a shepherd wields magic, and no one goes to Wolar's Fang for fear of their life."

Garawin looked up from the map and smiled. "That is the folklore. Remember many of the sculls in remote areas of Iswan think of *my* Anasazi people and our powers as being magical. Only one thing is assured." He looked from face to face. "We are going to Wolar's Fang, and truth will rise to the surface. It always does." Garawin's words gave confidence to the group.

Nolan pointed to the map. "Going due east is more direct. Why don't we choose this direction?"

"This path would take us across the heart of Mallee," Garawin said. "Mallee has been an unstable kingdom for some time now. There is constant fighting between rival leaders who hope to bring the kingdom under their control. With such a state comes a level of lawlessness, and as such, river bandits are always a risk.

"Are the river bandits more of a risk than the Toltec who surely will follow us?" Daniel asked.

Garawin rubbed his chin. "Probably not."

"Then we go east," Nolan firmly said.

Suddenly, the bellowing voice of the captain reverberated through the air. "Hard over!"

Instantly, men were scampering about the deck as the pot-bellied captain spun the wheel hard in a counter-clockwise direction. The travelers all grabbed the nearest fixed object as the ship tilted viciously. Spinning on the spot, the barge sent a large wave toward the shore.

Nolan's eyebrows rose as the barge was almost right on top of the shoreline when the wave crashed into the coarse rocks, sending up a thick spray. Through it, Nolan saw a movement. He shook his head, closed his eyes for a moment and peered even closer the second time. He thought, certainly, he had seen a face framed by a leafy bush, but the second look proved only to see the spray washing on the leaves.

Nolan's head snapped back toward the deck as the wind filled the sails, pressing the vessel back on a starboard tack. The sailors had finished rotating the spreaders and tied down the lower, loose ends of the sails. One brave sailor was running along the railing, holding a rope tight in his hands. At the same time, one of the sails billowed, blocking his path.

Ranaa let out a gasp as the man jumped from the railing out into the water. However, before he hit, the rope drew taut, and his momentum carried him in an arc. His bare feet skirted the water before he was whistling back up toward the deck. Having cleared the railing, he let loose the rope. Flying ten feet into the air, he hollered out a triumphant whoop as he spun. As the other men cheered and hollered, he miraculously landed square on his feet.

At that precise moment, the sails caught a gust of wind and the barge lurched. The sailor's momentum, along with the unexpected motion of the ship, threw the man off his feet, careening him, with a thud, against the side of the cabin. The other sailors howled, throwing up their arms in disappointment.

One of them yelled, "Almost perfect, Garon!"

Out of breath, Garon raised an arm in the air, signifying his almost perfect control of the waves.

"That's enough games, you useless excuses for sailors!" the captain hollered. "Back to work!" The men turned instantly to their stations as the captain chuckled under his breath. He threw a skin full of water to the breathless Garon who was lying on the deck, and at the same time the captain gave him a sly wink.

Nolan smiled. Even though it was very hard, the men were genuinely happy at their work. Maybe Garawin was right when he talked of the simpler life and the benefits coming with it.

His thoughts went back to the face in the bushes, or the *supposed* face in the bushes. *Was it really there, or was it a trick played on his eyes, caused by the sunlight dancing through the water's spray?*

The self-deliberation continued until his stomach heaved. "Oh god," he mumbled. "It's been a long time since I've been on a ship." The last words were lost on the group as Nolan jumped to his feet and ran to the railing. He just made it as the contents of his stomach emptied into the ocean.

The door creaked open and the man stepped into the dimly lit room. A second man sat up instantly, pulling a knife from his sheath. Seeing his fellow woodsman, he relaxed and rose to his feet.

Nodding, the first woodsman's face was shrouded in shadow from the large-rimmed hat as his dark eyes peered out from underneath it. "The barge is coming in to the port, and we need to be ready at the docks."

The second man donned his own hat and pulled a gray cloak over his shoulders. Picking up his longbow and quiver of arrows, he slung both over his back with the practiced hand of a killer. Both woodsmen stepped out of the large room as their silent steps down the stairs matched their bland appearance. Neither would attract attention.

There were very few citizens on the streets as they stepped into the cool, night air. The second man was tall, having to bend to clear the top of the arched doorway leading from the back of the inn. Keeping to the shadows, they darted from doorway to doorway, preferring the darkness to shroud them for the mission at hand. The two cloaked woodsmen were invisible in the night, and they hadn't made a sound, nor had they drawn any attention with their quick arrival at the docks.

Squatting with their backs against a wall of wooden crates, the first woodsman whispered, "Wait here at the ready."

The other nodded while sliding his bow off his back. He pulled an arrow from the quiver, cocked it, and in a barely audible whisper, he said, "I'm ready."

There was a dull thump from the other side of the boxes. The first woodsman snapped his head around, peering around the corner of the crates. The barge, lit only at the bow and stern, slid against the long dock jutting out from the main boardwalk. He looked one more time at his associate, then silently slid into the darkness.

The first woodsman was an expert at the art of stealth, camouflaging into the thick, wooden posts situated every 20 feet along the dock. He controlled his footprint—even being aware of the movement of air around him as his covert steps carried him forward. Seeing movement on the barge, this was as close as he dare come, so he flattened himself against the back of another row of crates. Controlling his breaths, he cocked an arrow to the rosin string of his bow. Grimly looking at the sharp, barbed tip, he thought, *this was an arrow for killing.*

"The trip has been much longer than expected," Garawin whispered. "It's late, so we best keep quiet on the streets."

The other members of the group all nodded their understanding in the hooded cloaks they had been given. Garawin led the way, giving a slight wave to the well-paid captain who nodded back. The group, led by Garawin, hastily made their way down the ramp and then moved along the side dock toward the boardwalk.

An instant vision of danger flashed into Nolan's mind, but it left as quickly as it came. The flash was not understandable. All he knew was there was something wrong. He put his hand on the prince's shoulder and whispered in his ear, "There is danger ahead."

"How do you know?"

Nolan's eyes looked directly into Garawin's. "I just know it to be true. Believe me."

Daniel, having overheard the words, moved in front of Nolan, motioning Germaine to do the same. With the three men in the lead, they sidestepped suspiciously down the dock. Their knees were bent and ready to pounce while their hands were on their knives and swords if the need for defense arose.

Nolan heard it first. Off to his right, there was a subtle creak of wood as a bow was drawn taut, and instinctively, a fireball formed at his fingertips. Both Germaine and Daniel crouched with their weapons now drawn, ready to attack.

Garawin's arm flashed out in front of the group. "Wait!" he hissed.

The archer had not moved a muscle. His arrow was aimed at the center of the prince's chest. Garawin carefully took a step forward. Raising his hands, he gradually pulled back the hood from his head, and his face came out of the shadow. "I am Garawin, Prince of Rivenloc."

Moments went by, seeming like an eternity. Nolan's heart felt as if it would burst from his chest. Finally, he saw the archer relax his grip on the string, and the bow lowered.

As the woodsman walked forward, from under the rim of his hat, he said, "Master Garawin, it is I, Rin of Lomond Woods."

Garawin smiled as the two men embraced each other. "I hope you have not been waiting long."

Rin's face creased into a smile. "We would have waited as long as we had to."

"Where is Larm?" Garawin whispered.

Rin pointed to his right, and a slight whistle emitted from his lips. All their eyes turned. There, on the edge of the boardwalk, stood another archer with his arrow cocked and ready for the kill should any of them make an aggressive move. Rin waved, and Larm lowered his bow, settling back into the shadows.

"Follow me quietly," Rin said. "You look like you need some food and rest. Both are close by."

There were no further words. Nolan assumed introductions would come later. They moved up the dock with Germaine falling behind to bring up the rear. Larm had the same thought as he came out of the shadows beside the warrior, and each of them took a side of the street as the travelers made their way back to the inn.

It didn't take long for the group to find themselves in the room the Lomond woodsmen had reserved for the night. Once a lantern was lit, bringing a low-lit, warm ambience to the large room, introductions were made.

"This is Rin," Garawin began. "I do not want to say he works for me as that would not be altogether true. I pay him a salary, but he is my student and hired aide when need be. He has been with me since he was a boy, so he is much like a brother." Garawin proudly described the younger bowman.

Garawin turned, opening his arm to the other man. "This is Rin's half-brother, Larm. They are of the same blood and Rin speaks of him highly. He has saved my life in the past, and I would trust him with it once again if need be."

Nolan looked at Larm, open-mouthed. He was a monster of a man. Standing at least six-feet-six-inches tall, his build reminded Nolan of the thick maple trees rooted in the forests of his home. When introduced to Larm, Nolan's sixth sense was still on high alert. Something was not right. He shook the man's arm, but was wary, and as he stepped away, Nolan saw it and froze.

There were two statues of blue-skinned beasts on the other side of the room. They were clothed, half-human and half-gargoyle as far as Nolan could discern. Four feet high, they had thick muscular arms and legs. Their faces were wide and all their exposed skin was deeply wrinkled, and that was more prevalent on their wide, unshod feet. Both statues had thick, black hair, closely resembling fur, with a thin strip carrying on down their backs underneath the neck of their shirts.

He was not sure he saw it, but then it happened again. One set of yellow eyes blinked. The head turned and looked squarely at Nolan. The creatures were alive!

Chapter 5

Julian looked at his image in the tall mirror. Turning to his left, then to his right, he inspected the clothing he just put on. He ran his hand down the side of his hip along the dark-brown, leather breeches. His fingers turned up, grasping the bottom edge of the dark-blue tunic and tugged it downward. The corners of his mouth drooped in a frown as the small wrinkles in the fabric would not flatten out. Sitting down on the bench in the dressing room, he pulled on the knee-high, leather boots. The black leather was soft and fit snugly along his calf. As he rose to his feet, he took one last look at his just removed, clean-cut uniform while subconsciously letting out a sigh.

He wasn't in a good mood. He had been awakened in the early morning hours by a runner from his assault squad on Iswan. The message from Renier was, "Come right away. They had a good lead."

Stepping back into the corridor lined with numerous dressing rooms, he made his way into the main assembly theatre of the transposition station. He glanced at the runner who was dressed in similar clothing, fitting for the covert work he was trained to perform. His outer layer of clothing consisted of a thigh-length, leather coat, and topping his straggly hair was a beige hat having a rim lined with a dirty line of sweat.

The far wall of the assembly area was covered with tall cupboards, and each was filled with clothing suitable for the different planes the Kaezzar intelligence staff traveled to. Julian walked back to the same one he had previously removed his present wardrobe from. In it, he found a suitable coat made of dark-blue leather, faded from use. The clothes were sterilized after each trip, but he still slapped the coat with his hand, ensuring it to be free of the dust that was more in his mind than on the material.

Julian pulled the coat over his shoulders. Drawing the zipper up, he walked into the circle of ceiling lights in the center of the room. He put his hand on the shoulder of the runner and gave a *thumbs up* to the dispatcher through the window of the control room.

"Let's go," Julian commanded.

The runner nodded, and immediately Julian saw a location marker light up brightly in his mind's eye view of the Athar. He willed himself there and felt the pull. The familiar feeling of his stomach becoming light, followed by the sense of falling forward, came over him. He always had the urge to put one foot forward to balance himself, but years of practice taught him this was a mistake. Just as quickly as the feelings came, they left. As he opened his eyes, he saw he was in a dimly lit room on the plane of Iswan.

Captain Renier saluted right away. "Welcome to Iswan, General."

The only acknowledgment from Julian was a barely perceptible nod of his head. "Let's get right to it. Tell me about this lead."

"It would probably be best if we let our informant tell you himself." His finger came up, pointing to the wooden door at the end of the small room.

The soldier guarding the door turned the knob and swung it open. After a few moments, a large man stepped through the opening with his head tilted forward to avoid hitting the archway of the low room crisscrossed with rough-hewn wood beams.

The man was shaped like a bell with an overhanging belly above hips that were even wider. Seeing an empty chair, he walked toward it with an obvious limp from his shorter right leg. As the man lowered himself into the chair, the lantern on the table reflected off his bald head, but when he lifted his face, highlighted in the light, the view surprised Julian. The man had the face of a child.

Round as a pie, the man had puffy cheeks and thick, rolling, red lips. One tooth on the left side of his mouth sat on the outside of his lip, and it had twisted his upper lip over time. His eyes, close-set and small, vibrated in their sockets. He looked up and smiled at Julian from his boyish face filled with innocence.

"I understand you have some information for me," Julian probed.

The man lifted his hands above the table while his fingers picked nervously at the hangnail on the finger on his opposite hand. "I like your coat," he said in a voice much deeper than his appearance would give one to expect.

With a raised eyebrow, Julian glanced over at Renier as he pulled out the chair situated at the opposite end of the table from the curious man. "What's your name?" Julian asked.

"It's a pretty blue." The man responded. The protruding tooth caused drool to naturally settle on his lips. He brought the sleeve on his shirt up to his mouth, wiping away the moistness.

Julian chuckled. "I get it. You want money."

"Sweets," the man said.

Renier stepped forward, pulling a rod of striped green and red candy from his pocket. He broke off a small piece and put it on the table in front of the man. Even before Renier had leaned back from the table, the man's hand flung forward, grasping the sweet, and just as quickly, he popped it into his mouth. For a moment the man closed his eyes as his lips shifted into a perfect circle. Happy groans came from his mouth as his cheeks pulled in, sucking on the candy.

Julian looked over at Renier. "You woke me up early for this?"

"Be patient," the captain replied.

Satisfied for the moment, the man opened his eyes and said, "I am Bent."

Julian leaned forward toward the man.

"At least that's what people call me. Some people call me Silly Bent and that's okay too." His eyes went a shade darker. "Some call me stupid, but that's not okay. No—no. I don't like that at all. So, you can call me Bent or Silly Bent. My friends who I play with call me Silly, but that's because they're my friends."

Renier stepped forward, placing another section of candy on the table in front of Bent. "Tell him about the men you saw."

Bent fingered the candy, and then popped it into his mouth, causing his words to slur. "Three men came to our town. They were travelers from another world."

"How do you know they were from another world?" Julian interrupted.

"Because they weren't from Iswan." Bent gave his head a slight shake as he twisted his nose while glancing at Renier.

"Well, that's obvious," Julian curtly replied.

"If it was obvious, why did you ask?"

Julian gave Renier another fleeting glance, pointedly showing his frustration.

Renier shrugged.

Julian tried again. "How do you know they weren't from Iswan?"

Bent tapped his finger on the table.

Renier promptly put another piece of candy in front of him.

Bent said, "Some people think I don't do things very well, so they don't ask me to work except sometimes the farmers ask me to help pick fruit." A mischievous grin came to Bent's face. "Don't tell them, but sometimes I eat the fruit—some of it, but not all of it. If I ate all of it, then they would really think I'm stupid." He laughed while spittle slid off his tooth.

"Let's get back to the strangers," Julian coaxed.

"So, the thing I do well is *watch*." Bent just kept on talking. "I watch the village. I watch the canals. I watch the people. I have a spot on a bench across from the village store, and there is also my favorite rock by the Eastern canal. I like to watch from there also." He tapped his finger on the table, and the candy cycle repeated.

"What did the strangers do?"

"They bought supplies—enough for me to see they were traveling far."

"I'm sure many people travel and buy supplies, including residents of this world."

"Their clothes were different."

"How so?" Julian asked.

"Their clothes weren't right just like your clothes aren't right."

"But these are clothes from *your* world."

"For sure they are," Bent said while nodding his head up and down. "Uh huh, they are, but they don't sit right on you. When they walked, it was obvious the clothes didn't belong on them."

"You have to be kidding me," Julian said with a raised voice.

Bent shrunk back into the chair. "I told you I watch people, so I know."

Julian tapped his fingers on the wooden table, showing his impatience.

"What else did you see?"

"I watched them go to the canal where they boarded a flat canoe. When they were far enough that I had to squint to see them, I saw two other canoes come out of the trees to join them."

"I'm told many people on Iswan use the canoes on the rivers."

"Iswan has many, many canals and rivers. Everyone is born with a paddle in their hand." Bent grinned. "These men were not. I could tell by the way they held the paddles."

Julian rose to his feet, and his finger curled, motioning Renier over to him. Once his captain was close by, he whispered in his ear. "I've had just about enough of this shit. The man is an imbecile," he seethed.

Bent continued in the background. "Their stroke was not smooth, and they looked when they put their paddle to the water. No one here looks. We just know."

Renier whispered back. "Bent is slow, but I believe him."

"You believe him!" Julian said through clenched teeth. "I'm glad your hunting and fighting skills are better than your judgment!"

Bent popped the candy from the table into his mouth. "They were going east on the Slither canal. With that many supplies they're going to Mallee—very dangerous—uh huh."

"Don't call me again unless you have something more than the words of an idiot!" Julian said. He turned, taking a step toward the door.

Putting a finger to his chin, Bent looked upward with a wide smile. While focusing on the sweet in his mouth, the words kept flowing. "And then there were the beautiful earrings they had."

Julian stopped in his tracks. He turned and looked back at Silly Bent. "You said earring?"

"Well, yes, but earrings if I think of all three of the strangers. Each man only had one earring, and there was a pretty jewel in each one!" Bent clapped his hands in glee.

Julian snapped his gaze back to Renier. His research into the Celtae on Crann Bith taught him of the two clans and their penchant for wearing their colors to signify their allegiance in the form of jeweled earrings. "Break camp and make your squad ready at once. You will go east after these men—find them and kill them. No questions. No quarter, and for god's sake stop giving Bent candy!"

Chapter 6

It stopped. The morning rain had been pelting off the roof of the shanty just as it had every morning since Nolan had arrived on Iswan. Holding his hand out under the edge of the wooden planks forming the roof of the structure, he let the drops of water fall into his palm. Thoughts rushed through his mind as the pace of the drops slowed. Some would call it a trance, and some would call it daydreaming. It was an ironic state, giving an oddly calm exterior appearance. However, inside, his mind was tense with the thoughts of all that had occurred as well as the foreboding of what was yet to come.

Ranaa's hand slid a few inches under his, catching the same rain drops as they slid off his palm. "Is the rain the same on your Earth?" she asked.

Pulled back to reality, he said, "Not at all. First of all, it depends what area of Earth you're on. In some regions, it doesn't rain at all, and we call these deserts while in other areas it rains each and every day. The environment is a delicate balance there just as it is here, but it's a very different balance."

"You miss your Earth?" Her voice was as soft as the flowers opening in the bright sunlight following the rain.

His shoulders shrugged as his hand dropped, and he put both hands into the side pockets of his pants. "In many ways, yes. I don't have children, and I have very few friends left on Earth, but my father is alive, and I miss him. In my last few years there, I lived outside society and the strife that comes with it. Instead, I lived with myself, worried about myself, and I only had myself to satisfy or disappoint." He chuckled. "It sounds so simple."

"And now that has changed. *You* have changed. The world, or as Daniel calls it, the Athar, is held on your shoulders." She put her fingers through the crook of his elbow and shifted closer.

Involuntarily, he inhaled deeply. He loved her scent, and it drew him to her. Between that and her touch on his arm, both gave him comfort and sent his heart racing in the same moment. Turning, he lifted his hand to the side of her head. His thumb pressed a stray, white curl from her forehead. That's when it happened. He bent his head, looking into her golden eyes and pressed his lips to her forehead. For a few moments he let his lips linger there, allowing her sweet taste to flow into his lips.

She leaned into him, but his fingers tightened in her hair as he pulled away. *No*, he thought. *I can't let this happen. People close to me die, and more will die, but not her.* The thought echoed in his mind as he stepped back and picked up his pack. "We had better head to the canoes. The others are almost ready."

It was only a few strides to the canal and the boats that had been their home for most of the past four days. At first, Nolan's arms ached with the long days of paddling. He knew his first few strokes today would also bring pain, but his muscles were growing, and the sinews were strengthening. Each day the ache went away that much faster.

"We were wondering if you two were coming," Germaine said through a grin.

"Where else would I possibly go?" Nolan replied. "I have the power to travel the Athar, yet I feel compelled to spend my days torturing my arms and spending my nights in run-down, shanty huts. Where else could I have this much fun?"

Daniel, leaning over in the canoe, turned his head and raised an eyebrow. "Just get in. You have learned much since you have been in my charge, but that does not mean this foot cannot still smack into your behind from time to time."

As Nolan stepped carefully into the canoe he said, "You have me at a disadvantage."

"What do you mean?" Daniel replied.

"You are my mentor, full of knowledge and wisdom beyond your years. That's a lot of knowledge." Nolan winked at the older man as he helped Ranaa into the craft.

Daniel took his place halfway down the right side of the canoe and picked up his paddle. He pointed it at Nolan. "If we survive this adventure and make it back to Bailemor, we shall spend some time in the arena to dispel the disadvantage you speak of."

"Agreed," Nolan said jovially while his smile masked his underlying fear. The odds of their survival, with so many chasing them, appeared dismal. He took his seat on the left side of the wide canoe across from Daniel while Ranaa sat back on her heels just behind the two men.

The canoe was similar to the Earthen configuration just much larger. It was 25 feet long and five feet wide while needing at least four men to maneuver it efficiently. Consequently, Larm, the woodsman from the east coast of this land, sat in the stern. The brute strength of his large frame moved the boat forward while his innate knowledge from living his life on a world of water expertly guided the vessel through the canals crisscrossing Iswan.

Tok sat in the bow. He was one of the two blue creatures Nolan had first met at the inn when they arrived at Kaleo. Both he and Stirm were Stors from the Northern Mountains. It took Nolan some time to become accustomed to them—not only to their existence, but to how they interacted with the other humans of Iswan. When Garawin first described them, Nolan had difficulty not thinking of them as slaves, but as time went on, Nolan saw the Stors and the humans lived a mutually beneficial, symbiotic relationship. The humans used the Stors for general labor. Their bodies were thick with untiring strength, and they genuinely enjoyed being busy with the manual tasks they were hired to perform. Their keepers treated them well, understanding their value to the society. Their protection was even documented as a requirement in the Protocols of Iswan. They were not pets, nor slaves. A loving servant, both well cared for and paid, would be a more fitting description.

Stirm was assigned to the general group while Tok had been assigned as Nolan's personal Stor. Initially, Nolan felt uncomfortable with the arrangement, but as he saw the pride in the Stor's eyes as he went about his chores, it lessened his trepidation.

Communication with them was also difficult. The Stors were mutes since their evolution wasn't as advanced as that of humans. At first, Nolan had questioned their intelligence, but quickly realized their occasional pauses were just their methodological mind thinking before acting. *Not a bad trait*, Nolan thought.

"Stop dallying! Let's go!" The words came from Garawin. In the lead canoe, he was already out into the moving water carrying them east along with Rin, Germaine and Stirm.

Larm pushed his thick, wooden paddle off the grass-covered shoreline, and the second canoe slid into the current. Except for the chirping of birds in the trees dotting the shore, it was quiet. The sun shone low in the eastern sky, and the colors in the flowers and leaves had completed their daily bloom.

"Every morning I'm in awe of the change the rain brings," Nolan said.

"It is different but not so unusual," Daniel replied. "I recall on your Earth you have cyclic activities fueled by the energy within your planet. Your tides happen each and every day. If I remember correctly, you also have hot springs and geysers you could set your watch to."

"True enough, but this is a much more monumental change."

"This planet is different. You have noticed the absence of rolling hills. The expansive plain we are on is generally flat until the terrain lurches up to the plateau we began our journey from. You remember it as the Great Rock." Daniel turned, pointing in the sky behind him. "Look closely. You can faintly see the outline of another planet."

Squinting, Nolan turned and peered into the sky. He hadn't noticed it before, but there was a faint discoloration to the blue sky. It was large, and now that he knew where it was, he couldn't understand how he hadn't noticed it before. "I don't understand. It must be very close, yet the image is so faint."

Daniel continued paddling the canoe forward as he spoke. "Nature and the elements are different from plane to plane. What we would call magic is just a different reality. On Iswan, there is a rare element found in the ground called taledion. It is unusual in that it absorbs energy in the form of light. Appropriately, the planet is also called Taledion because it is made almost wholly of that element. What is rare here is abundant there."

"How do you know?" Nolan asked.

"Well, for one, because it absorbs the light, and that is why it is difficult to see. Two, because the Rivenloc have teleported there, verifying the discovery."

"So, the planet Taledion affects the climate here."

"Exactly," Daniel said. "Its position is constant to Iswan. As this planet rotates, the pull of the sun and Taledion work in a careful balance, creating the constant eastern wind. It travels across the far ocean, becoming saturated with moisture. The effect of the warmer land mass, and the blockage from the Great Rock, causes the droplets to fall in droves across the lower plain. Over the ages, the plant life has adapted. When the sun sets over the horizon, the plants close, preparing for the hard, pressing rain that will come. The plants have evolved to survive, only opening once the rains have departed, and the sun takes its place."

"Amaz…" Nolan's words were cut off as his face snapped to look at the left bank. There was only a very light breeze, yet the long, light-green leaves of the bushes were swaying.

"Did you see the face again?" Ranaa asked.

"I thought I did, but it wasn't really a vision. I felt someone was there," Nolan answered.

"You have had the sense at least once a day since we arrived," Ranaa added. "It might be the light and rain playing tricks on you."

"No," Nolan said. "Someone is there. Someone has been following us since we arrived at the lake. We should go ashore and investigate."

Daniel's blue eyes turned to Nolan. "Have patience. If they know we know, it gives them an advantage. Be aware, as we all are, but let this play out, and we shall soon find out who they are and what they want."

"He could just be seeing things," Ranaa pressed.

"That is very unlikely," Daniel responded. "He has the power of the seven pureblood races in him. Everyone, including sculls, has intuition, but he has more, and those powers are still emerging."

"Why is that?" Nolan asked. "I have good control over the shield and the fire, and I have teleported. The other powers the elders had to move objects with their minds or to sense events yet to come—even to read the thoughts of others, are more difficult. I know the powers are there, but right now, only as rough and very fleeting feelings. Why?"

"Right turn upcoming." The words came from Larm in the stern.

Nolan increased the pace of his strokes while Daniel pulled his paddle from the water. Daniel took a skin from the bottom of the boat, bringing it up to his lips, and the cool water within brought relief to his thirst. Corking it, he returned the skin to its place and took a moment to consider his answer. "I suspect some of the pure mind powers you mention are slower in evolving. It makes sense because in the ancient pureblood races not all the powers developed at the same age. In Celtae, Toltec or Anasazi children, our powers begin at adolescence. When the voices of the boys change and hair begins to grow on their bodies, their powers emerge."

Nolan raised the corner of his mouth as he tried to remember. "The Shang pureblood race was clairvoyant, right? When would their powers appear?"

"The difference is subtle. The Shang children's power to move objects came near the end of the adolescent period at the same time maturity set in. It was the same for the Bantu children who had the power to foresee the future, and the Kush who had the power of illusion. No one knows why there was a difference, but I suspect that is why some of your powers are still latent."

Another noise brought Nolan's attention to the right bank. The leaves of the bushes were rustling. He whispered, "There's something there." His knuckles were white as his constricted grip was tight on the paddle.

A wide-mouthed skimmer bird was gliding along the shore. His long wings beat down every few feet while the feathered tips flicked the surface of the water. It skirted the surface underneath the wide, tropical leaves that curled over the shoreline. The shade it created was a favorite place for insects of all sizes to hover. The skimmer bird knew this, and, with its mouth wide, was scooping them from their ill-conceived safety.

The bird suddenly curved upward, but it was too late. The long, pink tongue snapped out from the bushes, slapping into the panicked bird. Just as quickly as it emerged, the tongue curled around the bird and retracted back into the confines of the bushes. A moment later, a wide, leathery face poked out from between the leaves. One wing was still hanging from the jaws as it looked from left to right, and its yellow eyes peered at the two canoes momentarily. Deciding the safest haven was the water, it slithered its four-foot length into the current. The three-inch spines running down the center of its back curled through the water until, with a burst of bubbles from its submerged nostrils, it headed for the bottom of the canal to feed.

In the bow, Tok turned, and he had a wide smile. A chalky rasp came from between his large teeth. It was the sound Nolan had learned represented a Stors laugh.

Daniel joined in. "There you go. We are being followed by tolip lizards!

A small one mind you, but nevertheless a species posing no danger to man."

Nolan smiled and didn't respond further to his friend's jest. He didn't understand the blurred visions that crossed his brain, but his mind was still on high alert. The one thing he did know for a certainty was that someone was out there, and it was not just the lizards.

It was dusk. The canal was wider, having been cut to the width of a channel adequate for the numerous watercrafts traversing back and forth across the city of Thento. Thento was the capital and largest city of Roevin. Stone buildings, knit tight together, fronted each side of the channel above the six-foot-high block wall jutting up out of the water. Every 20 feet stairs came down from the narrow street atop the wall to the water level where docks of various lengths and widths cut into the channel. Being the supper hour, many boats, canoes and even some smaller sloops were securely moored to the steel rings staked into the wood planking of the docks.

Nolan took quick bites of the dried fish, cheese and bread laid out on a cloth in front of him. The traveling group had decided to press on, eating as they went. It would be safer not to draw attention to them in the city. Rather, they would press on into Mallee.

Nolan tried to keep his face lowered as the occasional boat would pass them, but he couldn't help but be in curious awe of the city. In the distance, he could see larger buildings—some as much as four stories high. They were all made from stone cut by hand without the aid of power tools. Colorful tapestries hung from the windows, decorating the otherwise bland, stone buildings. On the right bank he could see an even more impressive building topped with three golden domes.

"That is the home of the King of Roevin. It also serves as the official government house from which he and his group of advisors judicate over the land," Daniel explained.

A group of soldiers in dark-blue uniforms walked across the front of the building with swords hanging across their hips. The outfits were loose fitting, covered with a short coat that certainly gave them a casual appearance. The wide hats, ringed with black ribbons, reminded Nolan of romantic soldiers from Earth's history. Having spent several days on Iswan, he began to understand how people enjoyed life even without the comforts of refined energy.

They paddled several hundred yards further until they saw a sign posted on the side of a bridge arching over a narrower side canal. It read - *This way to Mallee*. Not wide enough for the two vessels to go in side-by-side, Nolan's canoe followed Garawin's under the bridge. Here, closer to the buildings and the sidewalk at the top of the short block walls that bounded the canal, the sounds of city life came to them. The travelers could hear voices and laughter coming from above.

As they paddled around a corner, Nolan heard louder voices and music. Looking up, he saw a tavern, and along the front there was a sidewalk where patrons were seated. He surmised it must be a popular activity, having an evening drink or a meal while watching the world go by.

The canoes traveled under another low bridge, coming out onto a small, almost perfectly round bay. Across from them the canal continued, but a stone archway was over the water with a stone parapet attached to each end. Several soldiers on guard could be seen pacing across the top of the archway between the stone parapets while one guard was down at water level. They wore blue uniforms similar to those Nolan had seen at the king's royal residence.

Garawin's canoe slowed as both vessels crossed the small bay. Once they were side-by-side, Garawin said, "This is the checkpoint where we leave Roevin. It should not be a problem. After we cross, there will be another checkpoint where we enter Mallee. There will be more questions there, but let me do the talking. It will be much simpler, but no matter what happens, stay calm."

The fellow travelers all nodded their agreement just as they came up to the Roevin checkpoint. Garawin's canoe rubbed the side of the stone wall, and he nimbly jumped up onto the narrow walkway. Nolan could not hear their words as Garawin talked to the guard, but it only took Garawin a moment before he hopped down into the canoe. He waved his arm, indicating they should follow as they were already moving underneath the stone archway. Nolan kept his head low as they moved into Mallee territory under the curious eyes of the Roevin guards. He could tell by their watchfulness that not many travelers took this route, and it didn't take him long to understand why.

In their travels through Roevin, the canals had been clean. Workers continuously traveled the canals, pruning bushes and overgrown trees, especially along the waterways close to the towns and cities. Here, as soon as they left the stone archway, the atmosphere was much wilder. The bushes along the shoreline mingled with overgrown, wild grass, and the branches of the trees from the left bank to the right, touched overhead. With the twilight upon them, they had difficulty seeing. Even the holes in the canopy were covered with the long strands of moss growing wild on the branches.

Paddling carefully, the group turned another bend and saw light in the distance. Moving closer, they saw the light came from two torches burning brightly in front of a small house on the left bank. A man sat in a chair with the back on a 45-degree angle against the wall of the shack. As the sounds of paddling came closer, with a blackened finger, he lifted the brim of his hat that was pulled down over his face.

As Garawin's canoe pulled up to the small deck that separated the space between the shack and the canal, he once again jumped up onto the platform.

The man rose from his chair, brushing the dust from his thighs. Slouching as he put all his weight on one leg, he flipped his hat back on his head with the same dirty finger. "Where do you think you're going?" he said.

Nolan's canoe stayed back from the shack, but he was close enough to see the condition of the guard. When he spoke, Nolan saw only a few teeth, and they were black with rot. His clothes were ragged even though on his red shirt was an official looking emblem.

"We have business in Lomond Woods and need to make our way across the Eastern canal," Garawin stated.

"Better that you go around, stranger. Mallee is not a safe place. There are warlords and bandits—lots of them."

"This is the shortest way." Garawin's eyes showed his insistence.

The two men stared each other down for a few moments before the guard shrugged. "Have it your way, but you need to pay the tax."

Garawin's eyes were smoldering. "Is the tax to protect us from the bandits, or does it go *to* the bandits?" His words were slow and steady.

"The guard's mouth turned into a wide smile stinking of rot. "One silver each, and there are nine of you. He counted the fingers on his hands." Looking up, he said, "That would be nine silver in all."

Garawin did not take his eyes off the guard while he pulled out his coin pouch. It was heavily laden for the trip. His fingers counted out the nine silvers and handed them to the man.

The guard kept his eyes on the heavy coin pouch as the prince returned it to an inner pocket. He brought his other hand up to rub his eye. Turning his gaze upon the silvers, a small fortune to many on Iswan, he said, "You didn't hear me correctly. I said nine gold, not silver."

Before Garawin could respond, there was a loud crash from a thick branch that overhung the canal beyond the hut.

Nolan, now on his feet in the canoe, had his hands raised in front of him. His eyes were glazed over as a second large rock was willed from the far bank and flung into the same branch. This time the branch came crashing down into the water. In the same moment, an errant arrow sliced through the air, impacting the water beside Garawin. The rasp of steel cut through the air as the prince drew his sword.

In the tumble of branches crashing into the water, two guards who were hidden in them, splashed into the water. Two other guards popped out from behind a thick tree trunk, but the fireball from Nolan's fingers was speeding toward them even before they had turned to face the traveling group. Their bows fell to the ground as the fireball consumed them, and they staggered their last few steps of life, falling face first into the cold water.

Two arrows from Rin and Larm finished the two guards that came down with the branches. When Nolan returned his gaze to Garawin, it was to find the prince standing ready with his drawn sword, covered with blood, overtop the body of the toothless bandit lying on the dock. There were a few moments of silence as the group waited to see if any other guards would appear, but they did not.

Not addressing anyone in particular, Nolan said, "They had no intention of letting us pass. I'm not sure how I knew that or where they were hiding. I just did. Besides, it's been a long day, and we don't have time for this shit. It's time to move on into Mallee." His last words were not a question but a statement. He lowered himself into a sitting position and picked up his paddle. The others watched Nolan with an unsteady gaze. In a soft voice, Nolan said, "Let's go."

With that, Garawin returned to his canoe, and they all stroked the water with their paddles in unison. However, now Nolan's canoe led them on their path. A cool wind circled over the burning bodies of the two guards floating down the waterway. The breeze turned up in a circle before gliding down the winding canal, following the travelers as they disappeared into the foggy darkness of Mallee.

Chapter 7

Black smoke curled up from the fires atop the grass-covered hill. Each fire rose several feet into the air, fueled by the dry wood taken from the trees dotting the surrounding hillsides. The central hill was different, being bare of trees, and on its center driven into the hard soil, was a high cross.

Nolan coughed as his senses came back to him. He righted his head that had lolled to the side, and he pried his eyes open. Immediately, they stung, attacked by the smoke circling around him. Shaking his head, he spat, but nothing came out of his dry, parched throat. Trying a second time to open his eyes, he squinted through the smoke, gazing out onto the surrounding hills.

A noise came from below, and a moment later he felt a cascade of water thrown over him. Groaning in agony, he now remembered where he was. He looked down to see the soldier walking backward with the empty bucket. He had a smug grin on his face highlighted by black-rimmed, ghoulish eyes.

"It's about time you woke up!" the soldier said.

Nolan flexed the fingers of his left hand and winced in pain. He turned his head to the left, seeing the sturdy rope securing him to the cross. It burned into his wrist, and in the center of his palm, dry blood covered the skin where the metal spike was driven through into the wood. With great effort, he turned his head to the right, seeing his other hand similarly bound and staked. Exhausted, his eyes closed while his chin drooped to his chest.

A few seconds later, he heard voices coming through the smoke. He pried his eyes open once again, gazing down on his naked torso. His trousers were cut to rags, and his caked blood caused the material to stick to his skin. Trying to move his feet, he felt another stab of pain. One atop the other, they were also staked to the thick center post of the wooden cross.

A shadow emerged from the smoke with a yellow jewel sparkling in his earlobe. His clothes were clean except for the large trail of blood coloring the right side of his thigh-length jacket.

"Dragon. Let me down," Nolan said. The whisper was the best he could release from his torrid throat.

Dragon had the same black-rimmed, hollow eyes as the soldier. "Let you down? You're the First Key! Conjure a fireball in your hand, and your bonds will surely burn away."

Nolan willed the fire to his fingers, but there was nothing. He tried again. Not even a tingle came to his fingertips. "I can't. I'm too weak."

Another voice came through the smoke. "Too weak? That might be true right now, but with your numerous powers, how is it you find yourself so helpless that you're now pinned to that cross?"

"I—I don't know," Nolan stammered.

A second shadow stepped forward from the smoke. He wore Earthen clothes and a flying jacket. The side of his body was completely burned.

"John! Oh god, John! Let me down."

"You are the First Key—the savior of all mankind, scull and pureblood alike. You cannot release yourself from the cross even though you have the power of fire. You don't remember how you were put on the cross even though you're clairvoyant. Is there nothing you can do?" John asked.

Nolan's head dangled loosely from his neck. He hadn't thought of John, who was his friend and partner at the forest station on Earth, for a long time. "I don't…"

"Of course, you can!" John interrupted. "You managed to get me killed. Everyone around you gets killed. All those who are close to you die!" He picked up a rock and flung it at Nolan, hitting him in the chest.

"You're weak," Dragon hissed. He rubbed his hand across his wound, turning the blood-covered palm toward Nolan. "You also killed me even though you are proclaimed as the savior of the pureblood races. The legend says you'll stop the killing, but we're still dying by your own hand."

Nolan tasted a tear as it flowed down his cheeks and across his lips. "I didn't ask for this," he groaned. "I wanted a simple life. No one asked me to be the First Key, so I had no choice."

Soft footsteps pattered on the small pebbles surrounding the base of the cross. He turned his head, but the unknown person was out of his view. He felt the soft fingers drag softly down his thigh, and he instantly recognized the touch.

"No!" Nolan yelled. "Deahna!"

Nolan's woman walked out from behind the cross, and then she turned to look up at him from her position at his feet. He could see the trail of blood trickling from the hole in her neck. Her soft lips moved, and the voice reminding him of the scent of flowers across a spring meadow. It didn't match her appearance highlighted by stark white, bloodless skin. "I love you, Nolan. I wanted to tell you, but there was no time."

Nolan's body shook with his sobs while the tears now flowed freely, burning his scratched cheeks. Deahna took slow backward steps, fading into the smoke.

"No!" Nolan said. "Come back. Don't leave!"

But she was gone. The acrid smell of burned wood replaced her sweet scent.

I can't do this, Nolan thought. *People think I can save mankind. Who am I? Nothing but a simple man—it is all I want to be.* "I didn't ask for this," he mumbled through his sobs.

"Look at you." A deep voice came from the smoke. "Are you a warrior or an old woman? Pull yourself together."

"I can't." Nolan tried to see the source of the voice through the blackness.

"You have to," the deep voice continued. "We are relying on you to save humankind."

"I can't do it! I'm not strong enough!" he tried to yell, but the words were barely heard.

A large man stepped from the smoke. His hair was tied back in a long, black tail, and a broken arrow protruded from a bloody wound in his chest. "You can do it. Save us," he said in the same deep voice.

Nolan's eyes went wide. "Germaine! No. You're not dead. No!"

They all turned to Nolan on the cross. The lifeless bodies of Germaine, Dragon, John and Deahna took small steps toward the cross, chanting, "Save us. Save us."

Instead of crying out again, Nolan joined the chant. "Save us. Save us!"

Each time he said the words louder. He threw back his head, and at the pitch of his lungs, he yelled, "Save *me*!"

The blanket fell down to his waist as Nolan bolted upright in the makeshift bed. In a panic, his head snapped from left to right in the darkness. The dream faded, and his being came back from the depths of his mind to the reality of night.

A soft touch crossed his sweat-covered chest. Nolan was surprised to see Ranaa lying close beside him under his blanket. "You were having a bad dream. Lie back," she whispered.

Confused by her being in his bed, he resisted, but her insistent hand on his chest pushed him down. He let out a deep breath as his head hit the pillow of soft leaves. "You shouldn't be here," he said.

She pulled the blanket up over his chest before her fingers slid back to rest on his shoulder. "Why?" she said softly. "This is where I choose to be. Do you not want me here?" Her golden eyes were wide and hopeful.

"No. You being here is fine with me, but the others might not approve. They might not look up to me if they see I am distracted."

"They look up to you because of who you are. They know you lead them. I see the change, little by little, every day. They would not feel so if they thought my lying here beside you would detract from your judgment."

"It's also for your safety. Staying close to me might find you injured—or worse."

She chuckled softly. "You are just finding any excuse you can think of to push me away."

A deep sigh came from his lips. "I don't know what to think anymore."

"You don't have to think—just do. Follow your mind, but don't forget you have a heart that is kind and warm. I've seen you watch me, and I see the look in your eyes. Underneath the fear, confusion and sometimes the fire, I see your warmth. You look at me gently, and more than once I've seen your passion underneath the layers of pain."

"I should've left you back in the safety of Kaleo."

Her finger slid up his cheek, touching his lip. "I wouldn't have allowed that to happen. I will follow you to the end of this world or any other. After all, you own me."

"What!" he stammered, louder than he would have liked. He looked around the wood-covered lean-to serving as their protection for the night. Deep breaths from his sleeping friends were all he heard. Looking out the front of the wall-less shelter, he saw Rin on watch by the small fire, and he was deep in thought as he looked out on the calm water of the canal.

"What do you mean 'I own you?'"

Lying on her side, she shimmied closer, leaning into him. "I mean just as the words say. You own me heart and soul. You saved my life, but I feel in my heart it is much more than just that. It was much more than fate that brought you to the Dead City that day when those hunters were going to kill me." For a moment a light came to her golden eyes. "What began as the worst day of a terrible life, turned into the best day of a new beginning. Everything has a purpose. The same force—call it god—call it an enlightened being, wills me to be here with you. Where you step, I step. Where you lead, I follow. Some would call it love, yet it's a love I have no choice in. It has an involuntary nature, and just like breathing, it is just there."

Nolan turned his face, and his gray eyes looked into hers. "This is not the time or place for this to happen for many reasons."

Her face lit up with a smile. "I know. You will find I'm a patient woman. When the time is right, you'll come to me, and I will be waiting even if that will take forever."

"Death and destruction are coming. Forever can easily turn into never."

She leaned up on her elbow. "Have you not been listening? I think a greater force has a purpose for you and has sent me to be by your side. In time, you'll see this. For now, I live for the occasional unprotected look you give me and these rare but special moments when you don't push me away."

He slid his arm around her and pulled her close, feeling her cheek press against his shoulder. "No more words. We have a short time before the beginning of another dangerous day. It would please me if you stayed and watched the sunrise."

She did not respond, but her body shifted toward him, happier than she had ever been in her short, tumultuous life.

Looking furtively from side to side, Nolan dipped his paddle into the water. His senses needed to be on high alert, so he put the memory of the night before to the back of his mind. The darkness of this night was much different, lit only by the small lantern hanging from a rod at the bow of each canoe. They had traveled at a quick pace, not wanting to spend a moment longer than they had to in Mallee territory.

Garawin shouted over, "A few more bends, and then we cross the Great Border canal. Once on the other side, we will be in Lomond Woods."

"The sooner the better," Nolan mumbled under his breath.

Daniel, sitting on his right, said, "What do you see?"

"Nothing certain," Nolan replied. "But my senses are on edge, and much worse than the last few days, so keep your eyes open." The stress was visible on his face as the lines defining his cheek and brow were drawn tight.

Daniel nodded as they crossed another small canal.

"You've not told me about the canals," Nolan said. Still on high alert, he kept up the conversation more for Ranaa who he continued to worry about as she sat just behind him in the shallow canoe.

"What do you want to know about them?" Daniel responded.

"Why are there so many and why so few lakes? It's an odd arrangement."

"As odd as the fewer canals and the more abundant lakes on Earth would be to someone from Iswan. The worlds and their origins are different."

"These canals aren't man-made, are they?"

Daniel paused for a moment while his eyes inspected the right bank. "No. That would be a monumental task even with modern technology. The origins of this world are much different. When your Earth was in its infancy, the energy bubbled and boiled in the form of hot lava, fire and steam for tens of thousands of years until the momentum eventually slowed. Balance came to your Earth as it does to all things, leaving high mountains and low valleys in its wake. It was not so here on Iswan."

Nolan turned to his mentor. "What happened here?"

"This world also has a molten core as it did millions of years ago. In this planet's early years, when its internal energy tried to reach equilibrium, it took much longer than it did on Earth. Consequently, a hard, thick crust developed with the smoldering lava being contained below. The red-hot internal energy tried to escape, and the planet pulsed. This cycle repeated over and over."

"What kept the energy from breaking through the crust?"

"Taledion. There was a large concentration of it on one side of the planet. It absorbed the energy until it was saturated. At this point, when the planet pulsed, it cracked. Before it could explode into millions of pieces, the concentration of Taledion was thrust into space. It is the planet you see in the sky. Iswan heaved as the molten energy filled the void and a balance was achieved. However, the thousands of cracks in Iswan's crust remained. Now, filled with water, they are the canals we have been traveling on."

"It's amazing…" His words stopped. Abruptly, he flung himself across the canoe, knocking Daniel off the small seat.

As their bodies thudded into the planked bottom, they heard a vibration. Looking up, they saw an arrow embedded in the seat with the shaft still vibrating from the impact.

Nolan yelled out, "We're under attack!"

Chapter 8

"Kill them all!" Julian yelled at the top of his lungs as he stood on the bank from where the volley of arrows had come. Renier's soldiers were well trained. Just as the Celtae energy shields were coming to life, a second volley of arrows pattered into the canoe's occupants. Three Celtae were down from the first volley, and the remainder were dispatched with the second. Julian could not believe it was over so quickly. Nolan Harrison, Daniel Dupuis and their accomplices were dead. In his mind, he could clearly visualize the rank of senator being bestowed on him by the prime of Kaezzar.

The canal was narrow at this point. Consequently, in only a matter of seconds, the canoes drifted into the far shoreline. Julian jumped up from behind the bushes as he saw one of the Celtae, who had been bent over the side of the canoe, rise to his feet. His shield sputtered in and out of semblance as he struggled from the boat before falling into the water at the shore's edge.

Pointing to the armed soldiers beside him, Julian's lips opened to command them, but Renier's hand on Julian's sleeve stayed the order. The Celtae on the far bank crawled out of the canal using his fingers to grasp branches, until he finally managed to pull himself to his feet. There was a tree line in the distance. He ran for it with one leg dragging behind due to an arrow through the thigh. As he passed a large bush, a dark figure sprung from behind it. With one calculated sword stroke, the Celtae was cut down. His shield finally fizzled into darkness as did his life.

Renier leaned toward Julian. "Everything was accounted for, General."

Smiling from ear to ear, Julian said, "Excellent. Just excellent! Now, get the boats. I don't want to get wet."

An hour later, Julian sat on a log in the clearing by the shoreline where the Celtae had been cut down. He nibbled on a piece of dried meat, happy with the thought the disease known as the First Key was dead. Now he could go home to rest and reap the rewards of his efforts.

Renier walked over with a lantern rocking back and forth from his fingers. "As you requested, the dead are ready for your inspection."

"Very good." Julian was not quite sure what to make of Renier. He was a good soldier and leader and one who he should consider promoting. *Promoting a good soldier has its good and bad points*, he thought. *One day he might well aspire to fill my shoes.*

"Are you sure you want to review the bodies?" Renier asked. "It was obvious from their shields these were Celtae scum."

"I am insisting, Captain," Julian curtly responded. He rose to his feet, taking the lantern from Renier, and made his way over to the bodies. They were lined up like wood logs, side by side with their feet facing the river. Each was face down with their hands by their sides. Julian leaned over the first and held the lantern close to his face. His head was on its side and the lifeless eyes stared into the grass. Dark-red, dried blood coated his cheek where Renier's soldiers had cut a hole in his neck to free the arrow that had sliced into it. The jagged hole was the obvious source of the blood.

Turning his face from the light, Julian's cheeks filled with air as he almost vomited. He lifted himself upright and turned to Renier with a nervous smile. "Well, he certainly is dead, isn't he?"

With his face drawn and passive, Renier didn't respond. He held his hand out, inviting the general to continue the inspection. Julian put one hand behind his back while his fingers knotted into a fist in the small of his back. He barely flashed the lantern over the remaining bodies as he slowly made his way by them.

"What is that smell?" Julian asked.

"Death smells differently to different people," Renier offered, his face remaining stoic.

Julian shrugged. "Take anything that looks valuable and dispose of the bodies. I'm going back to Kaezzar." He turned to Renier and nodded, giving a sure indication the inspection was over.

As Julian walked away, Renier said, "Should we leave their golden earrings?"

Stopping in his tracks, Julian turned. "What do you mean 'golden earrings?"'

"The Celtae of Crann Bith wear golden earrings."

"Not all of them," Julian hissed as he stomped back toward Renier. "The ones we're looking for wear *blue* earrings. They're the Akkadians." Julian walked right by Renier back toward the bodies.

The unusual scent confronted his nostrils again, this time stirring a vague memory. "It can't be!" he yelled aloud. He followed his nose to the body at the end. Dropping to his knees, he grabbed an arm and flung the corpse over. On the hand he saw the long scar. Pulling back the coat, the scent intensified. Julian reached into the inside pocket and pulled out the pipe. With a shaky hand, he thrust the lantern into the man's face. Gasping for air, he fell back on his heels. "Peron!"

He reached over to the corpse next to Peron and turned it over. He looked into its lifeless eyes under a bald head. Rising to his feet, he staggered backward, and then turned toward a confused Renier. Julian's face was chalk-white, and his eyes were pulled wide. He could not believe what just happened.

"You fool!" Julian yelled at Renier. "Not only have you been following the wrong group of Celtae, but you've just killed one of the highest-ranking generals of Crann Bith! You tracked and killed the wrong group of Celtae!"

Julian's body was shaking with anger. He pulled the long knife from his belt, looked at Renier but thought better of it. Instead, he strode to the nearest bush and hacked violently at the long leaves. Words were lost to him. Guttural growls reminiscent of a time before the dawn of modern man was all he managed to push from his incensed lips.

Chapter 9

Nolan heard one plunk, then another and a third. The sounds were too heavy for raindrops. He could have mistaken the noises for the sound the sudden movement of a frog in water brings except he hadn't yet seen a frog on Iswan. There was a thud followed by a whir as another arrow hit into one of the short, thin planks making up the bottom of the canoe. There were more plunks as more arrows missed their marks, slicing into the water behind the vessels.

"River bandits! Faster!" Garawin yelled as his arms made firm, long strokes with the paddle, propelling their canoe's bow out of the water.

Daniel was back on the small seat with his own paddle making a quick, steady beat into the water. After pulling Ranaa to a safer position in front of him, Nolan did the same. The Earthman took a quick glance behind him, his brows furrowing as he saw three narrow canoes coming up the canal behind them. There were six men in each canoe, paddling feverishly with a steady, timed stroke which brought a spray of water up behind them. In the front of each canoe, two men knelt while their short crossbows pulsed out arrow after arrow in an arc toward Nolan and his companions. One bow was stronger than the others, making the distance to the canoes twice while the others left their arrows short of the targets. Turning his eyes forward, Nolan put his mind to paddling as fast as his strained arms could muster.

Larm, in the rear of the canoe, growled each time his paddle cut into the water. "Faster!" he yelled. "Follow my beat!"

Nolan, Daniel and Tok in the bow, matched their strokes to the cadence from Larm. White water parted off the sharp bow as they matched the speed of Garawin's craft shooting along the once calm surface.

Garawin yelled over to them. "It isn't much farther, and we will be in Lomond Woods! We can make it! Paddle for your lives!"

Nolan was impressed by the Prince of Rivenloc. He could teleport from this danger if he wished to. *Damn, even I probably could in an uncontrolled fashion,* he thought. *But where would that leave our friends? No, we will have to outrun them together. I won't leave more people behind. Neither will Garawin.*

Another arrow found its mark—this time in the middle of Garawin's canoe. Snapping his head around, Nolan saw the river bandit's canoes had briskly made up one third of the distance to them, and as a result, more and more arrows were falling in the water around them. It was only a matter of time before one of them was hit.

Leaning forward, Nolan moved his lips close to Ranaa's ear. "Take the paddle," he said.

Ranaa did not question him. She moved into the seat and started stroking the paddle through the water.

Nolan moved halfway back between Larm and Daniel. He pointed toward Garawin's canoe, yelling at Larm, "Guide us beside them!"

Larm nodded, pulling his paddle to the left side of the boat. In moments the two boats were side by side, moving as one.

With his legs braced wide apart, Nolan stood with knees bent in the canoe. His hands were held straight out from his body, and his eyes were closed as he focused within himself. He easily conjured his shield as the green aura crackled with energy. He pulled his hands together, and the shield deepened in hue, turning almost black. His eyes burst open as he splayed his arms out wide. The shield erupted outwards, converting to a wide, light-green semi-circle, draping the rear of both canoes.

Nolan's teeth ground together with his exertion. "Now paddle with all your speed," he snarled.

The young Earthman's body lurched with each stroke of the paddles. His body shook with his effort, but still he saw the bandits gaining. The arrows bounced off his shield, but the danger of the numerous bandits boarding them would be next. Nolan took a deep breath and pulled his hands together over his head. Orange tendrils of energy now skipped across his shield, speeding from edge to edge. Above him, the energies melded and a purple ball formed. With a deep-rooted yell, Nolan thrust his arms forward. The purple ball stretched, accelerating down his arms. The long stream of energy snapped from his fingers toward the three canoes filled with river bandits. It blasted into the lead canoe, shooting it 20 feet into the air. The pieces of the men and the vessel not consumed immediately, fell burning back into the water.

His energy shield dissipated as soon as the burst left his fingers, and Nolan slumped to his knees. His chest heaved as his lungs searched for air. At least the other two canoes had slowed their pace, he saw through half closed eyes.

"It's not much further to the border! Paddle!" the prince yelled from the adjacent canoe. Crawling on hands and knees, Nolan turned to face the bow.

"It's just around this bend!" Garawin yelled, urging them on.

However, as the two canoes veered into a sharp, right turn around a collection of boulders topped with a moss-covered tree, their hopes fell. The stone archway, marking the border of Mallee, crossed the river 100 yards ahead of them. At least 20 more bandits stood across the width of the stonework, and their crossbows were cocked with deadly arrows.

Turning his head, Nolan saw the remaining two canoes still following. He knew now their purpose was to shepherd them into this trap. The bandits wanted them alive. It seemed hopeless, but he had to find the energy. Daniel, Germaine and the others had put their own lives aside for him. Now, he had to find the strength to repay them. Almost in a trance, the Earthman looked within his inner self. His strength built, and slowly one fireball formed at each of his hands. His face pointed toward the bottom of the boat, but in his mind's eye he saw the archway ahead of them and the faces of each and every bandit. As his mind went from each dirty, unshaven face, the fireballs grew in size, swirling around his fingertips.

Nolan's gaze snapped up. He knew what would happen. He'd just foreseen it in a fleeting vision. Clapping his hands together over his head, purple sparks showered the canoe. Once again, he flung his hands forward, and the giant fireball accelerated toward the stone archway.

The wide-eyed bandits tried to scurry off the rampart, but the fireball was upon them in an instant. The archway exploded into a shower of flame and bodies with each and every stone being split into pebbles and powder, showering back into the water.

Nolan slumped forward onto his belly in the bottom of the canoe.

"Nolan!" Ranaa yelled out.

"He is unconscious, but still breathing," Daniel said. The words labored through his panting breaths. "Keep paddling."

The bandits behind them who had hesitated, now redoubled their stroke.

The sight of Nolan falling forward renewed their courage. Larm continued to shout out his cadence while the canoes sliced through the bodies littering the canal. Just ahead was a large pond marking the border of Lomond Woods. On the other side, thick, black trees, so tall they appeared to touch the clouds, reached off in each direction as far as the eye could see.

"We are almost there!" Garawin yelled as the canoes shot out into the pond.

However, the remaining bandits were almost upon them. Once again, the crossbows were being cocked, but this time for the kill. Stroking their oars through the dead bodies of their comrades had removed any thought of taking prisoners.

When Nolan and Garawin's canoes were halfway across the pond, there was a high-pitched whistle. The sky darkened as the first wave of arrows from the far tree line curved over their heads into the bandits.

Rin rose to his feet, holding his long bow up over his head. "Bow brothers!" His yell was followed by a loud whoop.

The cry was answered by a chorus of voices in unison from the trees of Lomond Woods. It was followed by another simultaneous volley of arrows curving into the bandits. Their paddles fell into the water along with several bodies, leaving the lifeless vessels to drift harmlessly to a stop.

Rin and Larm navigated the two canoes through a large bed of wide-leafed water lilies and then into a narrow channel on the other side. Ranaa now moved to Nolan, relieved at the warmth she felt when she placed her hand on his forehead.

Daniel glanced up. In the shadows of the woods he saw groups of men behind the wide-trunk trees—each armed with a great supple bow. Most held one point into the ground while the other taut side ended over their heads. The longbows of Lomond Woods had made short work of the bandits and their shorter-range crossbows.

An ear-to-ear smile beamed on Rin's face. "Welcome to Lomond Woods," he said.

Nolan heard a high-pitched screech coming from high above him. He struggled to open his eyes, finally prying them wide enough to be assaulted by rays of bright sunshine—the sunshine that told him he had been asleep for some time. The comfort from the warmth on his face was lost as his foggy vision cleared to see a canopy of leaves high above him. Another ray of bright sunshine broke through a hole in the canopy, highlighting a lanky figure jumping across a wide span from one branch to another. A second red-furred figure followed, stretched out across the same span. The creatures moved quickly across the sky—so quickly one branch, once released by the first creature, sprung back only to be captured by the second set of nimble fingers. It was a beautiful dance, one that, if it was not as exact as it was beautiful, could be even more deadly.

Feeling very weak, Nolan could only muster the strength to point a finger upward, muttering, "Monkeys."

"He's awake." Ranaa's sweet voice floated down to him, and a moment later, her soft fingers were laying on his forehead.

Tight, blond curls fell about her face as it came into his view. Over her shoulder, Tok's blue face blocked what little view remained of the trees above. His yellow eyes showed concern, but the wide grimace Nolan had learnt was a smile showed his genuine, overriding relief.

"They are similar to monkeys, but here on Iswan they are called tree jumpers, or as most call them, simply jumpers." Daniel's voice came from somewhere on his right.

It took a few moments, but Nolan found the strength to prop himself up on his elbows. He saw he was on a wide, flat-bottomed boat. Along either side, several men, each with a long pole, were propelling the barge down a narrow canal. In unison, the men pushed down on the poles, causing the round bases to strain against the murky bed of the canal. Only slightly disturbing the surface water, the poles were shimmied upward only to be pushed downward again.

"We made it?" Nolan asked.

"Of course," Daniel answered. "Thanks to you. That was quite a show."

Nolan looked from one side of the canal to the other. The tall, straight-trunked trees, some easily eight feet across at the base, dotted the landscape as far as he could see. Topped with light-green foliage giving the giant trees the appearance of being covered with shiny emeralds, they rivaled the giant redwoods of Earth in both beauty and size. *Majestic* was the word immediately coming to his mind.

"I only remember bits and pieces of what happened," Nolan said. "Did many people die?"

"It was unavoidable," Ranaa offered.

"Was it?" Nolan replied with a hint of sarcasm carrying through his weak voice. He thought back to his dream and the soldier at the base of the cross. He now recognized the soldier as a river bandit. Although the dream had been broken, and even more so nonsensical, it was clearly a vision with a message.

"Where are we going?" Nolan asked. A large yawn followed his words.

"To see a shaman," Daniel replied.

"A shaman?"

"Yes, a shaman. He is what you would know as a doctor."

Nolan shot up to a seated position. "Where is Germaine?"

"He is in the front cabin." Daniel pointed to a small structure at the front of the barge. "He took a crossbow bolt in the arm. It is not serious, but he does need medical attention."

Exhaling with relief, Nolan fell back to a prone position on the thin mattress he'd been laid out on.

Daniel raised one eyebrow. "What's going through your head, my apprentice?"

"It's nothing." Nolan shook his head. "Just a bad dream."

"Just relax. We are safe now." Daniel's voice was reassuring. "Don't waste your energy."

Ranaa's brow furrowed.

"Don't waste your energy? Isn't it, don't waste your time?"

Nolan couldn't help but laugh. It seemed so long since he'd laughed. They had come a long way and avoided many dangers, but he knew there was more yet to come—much more.

It was less than an hour later when the barge bumped to a stop. Nolan, who had been dozing, saw they were at a small dock in front of a short rise of land. It could easily have gone unnoticed except for the flag waving high up on a pole in front of it. To anyone coming from either direction along the canal, the red flag, adorned with a black cross, could not be missed.

At the base of the pole on a wide, flat boulder sat an old man with a thick, gray beard. He was dressed in a gray robe, and on his chest, a red circle with a black cross indicated he belonged here. As Garawin jumped off the barge onto the narrow dock, the old man picked up his gnarled staff and pushed himself up to his feet. The two men faced each other and put their hands on the other's right shoulder. After the greeting, there was a short discussion. The old man nodded, then turned his eyes to the travelers on the barge.

Two Lomond woodsmen came over to help Nolan to his feet, but Tok cut them off and shoed them away with a quick movement of his hand. Taking Nolan's hand, he put it on his far shoulder. Putting his own arm around Nolan, he helped the Earthman toward the shoreline.

Ranaa gave a pert, "humph," but accepted the fact Tok was better suited to this task. However, the acceptance didn't mean she would not walk close behind—so close the sound of her booted feet on the wood planks had Tok feeling like she was in his skin.

"Are you sure we're in the right place? This doesn't appear to be the place I would want to go for a doctor," Nolan said to Daniel.

"You should have learned by now that things are not always as they appear," Daniel responded.

"I'm glad to see you're well," Germaine said to Nolan. His large frame had just stepped from the small cabin at the front of the barge.

"I'll be fine," Nolan replied with the best smile he could muster. "Are you sure you're okay?" His eyes looked down at the sling cradling Germaine's left arm. Under it, there was a tight, blood-soaked bandage wound around his bicep.

"I will be fine. Daniel is more worried about infection than anything else."

Nolan followed Germaine to the hollow at the base of the short rise of land. Dirt covered the six-foot wall that was crisscrossed with the tips of roots from the surrounding trees. In the center of the short rise was a wooden door with the same black cross centered on a circle of red. The old man opened the door on well-oiled hinges. He ducked to miss the low, arched doorway and disappeared down a narrow flight of stairs.

Garawin pointed toward the doorway, and the travelers descended after the old man. Lanterns on the cut-rock sides of the passageway showed it to be only wide enough for the group to descend one after the other. At the base of the stairs was a small circular chamber where the old man waited. Once they were all there, he put his hand on an imprint in the rock wall and, immediately, there was a drone Nolan recognized.

"That's a generator," Nolan said. "I thought it was a contravention of the Protocols of Iswan to use refined energy."

Garawin turned to Nolan, still supported by the Stor. "If you recall, I said there were exceptions. Medicine, medical care and the hospitals we have on Iswan are comparable to the finest anywhere in the Athar. The shamans, who provide the care and administer the facilities, are all of the Anasazi. As such, the energy is tightly controlled and free from abuse. Everyone on Iswan knows they can come to a shaman's house, free of discrimination, and receive the best medical care."

Nolan could not help but divert his eyes to a section of rock wall as it slid open. Bright, artificial light spread out from the smaller chamber on the other side of the door. As they entered, he saw the walls were made of a combination of smooth metal and a tough acrylic. Once they all entered, the old man put his hand on a small, blue dome on a wall-mounted, silver panel. Nolan hadn't felt this in a long time as there was a sudden rise of his stomach into his throat due to the elevator's acceleration downward.

In a matter of moments, the door slid open once again, and this time revealed a large room with a high counter set in the middle. Behind it, stood a young woman flanked on either side by a uniformed man. Nolan noticed the men were armed with long knives slung in a sheath at their belts. Other men and women scurried across the room from the numerous hallways opening into the processing area. He recognized, other than the armed guards, the scene was not much different from a typical hospital on Earth. The medical workers all wore white coveralls, blending well with the bland walls painted a pale-yellow. Even the black cross on a red circle, highlighting their white attire, was not enough to take away from the sterile appearance of the room.

The elevator door closed behind them, and the old man leaned toward Garawin. "I am going back to the surface."

The prince nodded his acknowledgment. "My thanks, Luther."

The air around the bearded man turned into a haze, and then he was gone.

"I don't understand why he didn't teleport down," Nolan said. "He's older and had difficulty with the stairs."

"He was just being polite," Garawin said through a grin.

The prince moved to the counter, giving the attendant the names of both Germaine and Nolan. He gave a brief description of their injuries after which attendants came to assist the two injured men to an examination room. At first, both Ranaa and Tok showed their objections but eventually acquiesced. They both sat themselves in two of the chairs that filled three rows behind the attendant's counter. Nolan was not yet out of sight, and they were already both fidgeting impatiently.

However, the prince did follow the attendant as he supported Nolan on their way to the examination room. This smaller room was colored a pale-blue. Along one side were a table and two chairs while against the back wall was a narrow mattress on top of a high, steel bench. The attendant pointed toward the two steps in front of the bench and helped Nolan onto the mattress. A shaman entered the room, passing the attendant as he departed. Nolan was surprised to see the healer was a woman. She had short, bristly hair, and her face was highlighted by small brightly-intelligent eyes.

She smiled politely as she looked from Garawin to Nolan. "What can I do for you?"

Nolan's lips moved, but Garawin's words cut him off. "He is lacking sleep and needs some medication for his exhaustion since we must travel again very quickly. It would be immensely helpful if you would give him something to boost his energy levels."

The shaman wrote notes on an electronic clipboard. "Is he a pureblood or a scull?"

"He is a pureblood—a Celtae."

The woman raised a questioning eyebrow.

"Please keep that information to yourself." Garawin's voice was firm, but, at the same time, reassuring.

"Of course, my prince." She bowed her head and scurried out of the room.

"I don't think I need medication. I'm already feeling better after just lying here for a time," Nolan said.

"We are going to rest for a least a day, maybe two, and Lomond Woods is safe," Garawin said. "However, it is better to use prudent judgment here and have you up and about as quickly as possible."

The woman's fingers gripped the doorjamb upon her return and she propelled herself around the corner back into the examining room. In her other hand she held a small needle filled with a small amount of dark fluid. Her eyes looked to the prince. "Are you sure this is all that is required? Are there any injuries?"

Garawin's lips moved, but Nolan's words cut him off. "No, physically I am fine—just tired." He began to roll up the sleeve of his shirt.

A coy chuckle came from the shaman as she winked at Nolan. "Ah, not there."

Nolan rubbed his butt. The point of the needle was not long, but the shaman had insisted it needed to go into a muscle. He was not prepared and had his mouth open to argue when she stuck him like a pig. It left him wondering if the shamans of Iswan needed a license to practice their work, and after the shot, he asked if there was some where he could take a few moments to wash up. He dipped his fingers into the cool water in the small sink. Closing his eyes, he splashed the water up into his face. Filling his palms a second time, he brought the water to his lips and drank. He didn't realize how thirsty he was, repeating the process two more times.

Leaning his hands on the edge of the sink, he looked at himself in the mirror with concern. Deep in the recesses of his mind the beginnings of questions, second-guessing himself, began to form. Why did the use of his energy, albeit a vast amount, drain him to unconsciousness? If he was chosen as the First Key, should he lose his life force so quickly? Most of all, his largest concern was how he felt. It was difficult to describe other than he just didn't feel the same. He felt changed. Tilting his head, he looked closer at his face in the mirror. Other than an added crease of worry here and there, he looked the same as he did when he left Earth almost 18 months ago. His hair was longer with the brown locks sitting over his ears and having a slight curl at the ends.

He squinted, focusing even closer. Peppering his hair were wisps of white. *Perhaps the change he felt was more than just mental,* he thought as he pulled back the hair at his temple. He turned his head and did the same on the other side. What he saw raised his eyebrows in shock. Above each temple, underneath the surface of brown, was a shock of pure, white hair. He sighed, knowing his resolve would have to be even stronger. With Change came fear of the unknown, and this battle was one he must find the strength to win.

Chapter 10

I'm coming—I'm coming," Nolan said.

Tok, just ahead of him, gave a chalky grunt while he waved his hand forward one more time. The blue Stor could make his short, thick legs move quickly when he wanted to. Even though they were traveling through some thick scrub, Tok was barefoot. His gray pants were cut off at the knees, revealing muscles as thick as Nolan's thigh. The branches slapping against him had no effect on the leathery skin covering his stocky arms that were exposed from under the sleeveless, wide-collared, white shirt.

Nolan chuckled as he ducked another low-slung branch while following along the barely discernable path. It was just after breakfast when Tok pulled at his arm, indicating he should follow. The Earthman had picked up much of the sign language the mute Stors used to communicate. Moving his hands, he asked the Stor, who was never far from his side, where they were going.

Nolan never realized impatience could be shown in sign language, but it did as Tok's thick fingers moved in a fluid string of motions, ending with them curling into a fist as he struck his chest hard.

"Okay, okay. I get it," Nolan said to the Stor. "You want to take me somewhere. Just shut up and follow is the message, if I read your fingers correctly."

Tok gave a wide, yellow smile.

Nolan rolled his eyes. "You don't really think you look innocent, do you?" He placed his hands on his hips. "You overgrown excuse for a tree stump."

Tok pulled his elbows in against his ribs, fingers spread wide while he bent his knees into a crouch. Nolan burst out laughing as the Stor did his impression. Tok maintained his stance while his lips parted wide, and the familiar chalky rasp of a laugh came from deep within his barrel chest.

At that moment, Ranaa came from around the corner of the small wooden house they were occupying. She saw the two, rolled her eyes and muttered, "Men," as she retreated back out of sight of the foolishness.

Nolan had spent much of his time with Tok for the last two days—at least whenever Ranaa had let him out of her sight. The two had worked on his signing skills, and he learned much about the life of a Stor, and specifically, Tok's life. He learned the lifespan of a Stor was similar to a human, and Tok was 38 years old. Garawin had been Tok's second lord, and now Nolan was his third. At first, Nolan had vehemently denied the association. However, Tok was adamant. The Stor considered him his lord and master. Tok was relentless and convinced Nolan the relationship was normal on Iswan. It was also a relationship Tok envied since Stors instinctively have a desire to serve, and doing so successfully gave them a great sense of satisfaction. Through sign language, Tok had been clear in expressing his feeling of honor in serving Nolan, the First Key. Subsequently, Nolan had no choice but to relent and accept his position as Tok's lord.

That was two days ago. In the safety of Lomond Woods, the travelers decided they needed a few days rest, so Rin and Larm left to visit their families. However, the visit would be short. Before they returned to Nolan, they would scour the adjoining countryside, villages and cities, searching for information on any who might still follow.

Nolan's mind came back to the present as he watched Tok scramble over a thick log. He followed, sliding his butt across the top and then slinging his legs over. Straightening the bow he carried over his left shoulder, he yelled out, "Where are we freaking going?"

Tok did not hear, having disappeared around a stand of trees. Nolan hustled to keep up, and with his head down, sidestepping rocks in the path, he ran almost headlong into Tok's back. Raising his head, he was surprised to see five other Stors facing them. Tok and one of the other Stors were signing to each other. Nolan thought it odd the others had their heads bowed and their fingers intertwined in front of them.

Even more surprising was the village Nolan saw in the distance behind the group of Stors. It consisted of approximately 20 smaller, wooden houses. Some were single-story buildings while a few towered three stories high. However, this only brought them to just over the height of a single story of a typical human house. The homes were well kept, retaining their natural wood color, but trimmed in bright colors—red and yellow being the most predominant.

Tok, having finished his conversation, turned and flicked his fingers to Nolan. The message to come was clear enough. Nolan followed the group of Stors into a central square in the village. Other Stors came out from the houses, and each bowed to both he and Tok. It must be their way of greeting visitors, Nolan assumed. It was also the first time he had seen female Stors. Their hair was as short as the men's, but there were waves of blue mixed in with the black. Their bodies and faces were thinner, and they carried their cheekbones higher on their faces, complimenting their eyes. They were the same yellow color, but wider than the male's eyes, and they reminded Nolan of the cats of Earth. In an odd way, he found the female Stors attractive.

Nolan sat and rested on a bench in the center square while Tok went into one of the low buildings. Two Stor children, running as they screamed, careened across the square. One was kicking a ball with his small, bare foot while the second was chasing. A Stor woman caught up with them, giving each a slap on their behinds. They scampered out of view while the female Stor turned her yellow eyes apologetically toward Nolan. He smiled back and was surprised to see the woman's face turn a shade darker. *She just blushed,* he thought. She must have realized the same as she quickly scampered off in the same direction as the children.

Tok returned to the square wearing a thin belt at his waist. Hanging in a loop attached to the belt was a large, stone-headed hammer, and in his other hand he carried a small round shield. Painted circles of black and dark-blue alternated from the edge to its center. As he walked toward Nolan, he pushed his hand through the loose leather strap on the inside of the shield, shimmying it up his arm and across his shoulder until the shield sat snugly against his back. He had a wide smile on his face as he signed Nolan.

The Earthman did not need the signs to understand the Stors happiness at finding the conventional weapons of his race. Another quick flick of blue fingers at Nolan, and the Stor was walking toward a path leading from the village.

Nolan had seen the sign quite often this day. "I know, I know. Hurry freaking up." He shook his head as he waved his goodbyes to the Stors of the village. With a few long strides, he was side by side with the Stor. "Where are we going now?" he asked.

Tok looked up as his fingers flicked through several signs.

Nolan read them as best he could. He did not understand a few of the movements, but he got the general message. The Stors in the village had told Tok there was food to be found in this direction. He was not quite sure what that meant, but it suddenly came to him he was following the Stor almost blindly. He felt assurance and trusted the Stor without question. Perhaps it was part of his intuitive sense telling him Tok's convictions were built around truth and honor. His actions told Nolan the stocky, blue creature truly had nothing but good intentions toward him.

They were leaving the lower scrub and smaller trees and were back in the tall, black trees marking Lomond Woods. Small plants and fungi grew through the bed of red, fallen leaves covering the gently rolling ground. Tok looked from left to right. Finding what he sought, he pointed to a ravine on their left. Covering the distance to it, he crouched down behind a fallen branch that was larger than most logs.

"These trees are freaking huge," Nolan whispered as he crouched down beside the Stor.

Tok brought his fingers up to thick, pursed lips. His eyes narrowed, completing the message for Nolan to be quiet. His blue finger hit on the bow on Nolan's back, and then pointed dramatically over the thick branch.

"What?" Nolan said as his eyebrows rose with his confusion.

This time Tok slapped the bow, then pointed to the quiver of arrows on the Earthman's back. His finger pointed out over the branch while his other hand made a quick sign - *Food.*

Nolan removed the bow from his shoulder and cocked an arrow. He hadn't hunted since his days back on Earth. He peered over the branch, down into the ravine. There, the ground at the base of the ravine was trodden into a path, but it was empty.

Tok poked Nolan in the arm. As the Earthman lowered back down behind the cover, Tok signed - *Wait.*

The wait was not long. Within a few minutes, Nolan heard snorts coming from the distance to his left. It became louder as the source came closer toward their trap. Tok poked him in the arm, indicating it was time. Nolan still had the quiet touch of the forest—movement without sound. He rose up on one knee and peered over the decaying branch into the ravine. At the bottom, off to the left, was a short, four-legged creature covered in a coat of thin, brown fur. It stood two feet high and was five feet long. A good two feet of its length was its head, highlighted by sharp teeth under its purple gums. On either side of its powerful jaws shone a long, curled fang.

Nolan took relaxing breaths. *He would wait for the creature to come closer.* It resembled a boar, but it was longer, and its head appeared even more powerful. He wouldn't have more than one shot at the beast. Even though it was presently using its fangs to dig at an upturned section of root, Nolan knew the creature, if angered, could use them to kill just as well as dig.

The creature came closer with its short legs treading carefully as its snout sniffed at the ground and then up in the air. *That's right,* Nolan thought. *You're a careful one, but we're downwind of you. Just take a few more steps.* The creature moved to its left, seeing a short section of fungus-covered bark ahead of it. Oblivious of the trap, it made the fatal mistake of moving toward one of its favorite meals.

Tok, sitting with his legs crossed and his back against the tree branch, ran a tasty twig over his teeth. He tilted his head to the left, seeing Nolan's arm pull smoothly back. The slight flex of ligament at Nolan's elbow told Tok the bowstring was released. There was an abrupt *whir* as the arrow sliced through the air, followed by a high-pitched, life-ending squeal.

Garawin pulled the short bone from his mouth. Chewing the delectable meat, he lifted the bone to his eyes. Seeing it picked clean, he let it drop from his fingers to the plate.

Nolan sat to his left. His mouth was also full of meat from the boar-like creature he shot earlier in the afternoon. Tok had bled and cleaned the creature where it had fallen in the ravine after which he hefted it over a strong shoulder. The pair made their way back through the waning light of the afternoon to Brookhaven. This was the castle where Garawin decided they should stay until the travelers were ready to continue their journey.

The table around which they sat was a huge square of joined wooden timbers. It had been sanded smooth and lacquered to a fine finish. In the light of the three lanterns hung from thin poles at its center, the wide, honey-colored grain had a pronounced beauty. Plates of food lined the center of the table. One had a toppling mound of boar meat while another long platter was covered with baked vegetables resembling potatoes and carrots. In the center was a giant, two-tiered platter of mixed fruits native to Iswan. It was no wonder the conversation was vacant with such an abundant meal.

Ranaa sat on the side of the table next to Nolan. Her fingers held a small piece of meat to her teeth as she took dainty bites. Rin sat next to her, having just returned from his travels. Oddly, Larm was delayed, and Rin made no effort to hide his concern. Opposite Ranaa and Larm sat Germaine and Daniel who had just returned from a brief two-day excursion to Bailemor.

A golden aura surrounded the two men. It was not from any surreal powers. Rather, there was a large fire behind them, and, over it, on a spit turned what remained of the boar. Tok and Stirm were busy cutting the last remnants of meat from the carcass while taking their fill of the savory meat.

Nolan wiped his fingers on the cloth napkin and then brought it up to his lips. His belly was full, and now he was ready to hear what the men had to say. Turning to Daniel, he said, "Tell me of Bailemor. I miss it."

"Bailemor is much the same," Daniel said. "There was a failed aerial attack by a Toltec force which managed to topple two pylons of the Upper city before the covert craft was destroyed. The death and destruction have renewed anger in the city and brought cries of a counter-attack to a pressing level the government of Bailemor will not be able to ignore."

He could no longer hold back the question. "Did you see Lukas?" Nolan asked.

"Unfortunately, no. We are still fugitives on our own world, and as such, we had to remain in the shadows."

Nolan pushed the plate away from him. "Didn't you see anyone you knew?"

Daniel sat upright, holding his hands together on the table. "I did see my bond brother. He was the source of most of the information I have to pass on."

"Is your bond brother well?"

"Yes," Daniel replied. "He flourishes in the Celtae military." He shook his head for a moment before looking up at Nolan with his blue eyes."

Normally, Daniel's eyes were bright with life, but now they appeared lifeless and sad. "Something is wrong with your bond brother." Nolan put forth the words as a statement, not a question.

"He is fine—really. I still try to win him over to the Soichaint. Sometimes

I feel he is so close, but he has so much to lose if the Soichaint movement is not successful. He has a wife and children."

Nolan paused for a minute, hoping the sad words would be lost on the gentle breeze stoking the fire. "What of General Treve? Is he still obsessed with our death?"

Daniel shrugged. "I am sure he is, but not from this world. He has joined his son on the other side of the door marking death in this dimension."

Nolan blinked in disbelief. "How? Where?" was all he could offer.

Garawin's voice continued. "It was here on Iswan. He was not far behind us on the canal. Their party was attacked by a group of bandits, or what we thought were bandits. Rin has learned that the attackers used pureblood powers."

"They had the power to throw energy from their fingers, providing proof they were Toltec," Rin added.

"The whole of Crann Bith is in an uproar," Daniel said. "The war is about to explode to a level not seen before. Celtae and Toltec officials across the Athar are at each other's throats. The Celtae ruling council has demanded the perpetrators be turned over to them for execution. Intelligence officials and the watchers of the Athar from many worlds have deduced the assailants were from Kaezzar."

"You mean…" Nolan said.

"Yes," Daniel continued. "It seems our old Kaezzar friend who attacked us on Earth is the person they are after."

"Unbelievable." Nolan's face was white with shock.

Garawin cut into the silence that followed. "It gets worse. Two legions of Celtae warriors have transpositioned to Iswan. They are in the remote northwest in the wildes of Kaleel. Then three squads of Toltec arrived, and then another legion of Celtae. As suspicion brews, tension elevates. More and more soldiers will come. This is how a battle is born."

Nolan looked from one to the other. His eyes locked on each of them, including Tok who was now seated at the table. With his face set in a stern pose, he said. "Then we must move on and quickly. We've dallied long enough. In the morning we'll begin our journey to Wolar's Fang."

"Agreed," Garawin said. "If we cross Rivenloc, we can make it to Wolar's

Fang by the evening of the second day. We must make haste as I have asked my father, the king of Rivenloc, to call a Council of Kings in six days hence. The arrival of the pureblood forces in Kaleel has the kings of this world ferociously outraged. My hope is the council will withhold rash moves against the invaders."

"Well, since we have an early morning, it's best we get some sleep," Nolan said. "I'm going to take a few minutes to walk, and I hope it'll help me sleep." Rising, he stayed Ranaa's words with a subtle movement of his hand. He gave Tok a similar message, conveying his wish to be alone. With his hands behind his back, he walked through the buildings toward the canal. There was silence in the air except for the wind-stirred rustle of leaves. The cool breeze swept across his neck, and it caressed his brow as it pushed back stray locks of hair. It should have given him reassurance, but it didn't. "Maybe I should have also told you I wanted to be alone," he said with his low voice barely heard above the wind.

Daniel stepped beside him. "I am getting old," he said with a sigh. "My skills are not as sharp as they used to be."

"This is your fault," Nolan whispered. "You found me. Why couldn't you have just passed me by? I would be living a naïve, simple life in the forest."

"We all have a destiny, Nolan Harrison. My destiny was to find you. Your destiny was to be found." Daniel paused before continuing. "Your destiny is to save us all from ourselves."

"Keep your eye on Germaine. I think he is in danger," Nolan said. He hadn't been sure if he should mention it. *Was it a dream? Was it a vision?* He didn't know, but now it just blurted out.

"Why?"

Nolan kept his gaze across the canal away from his mentor. "Call it a strong hunch or intuition—just keep a close eye on him."

"We are safe now. General Treve is dead, and although it has set off a powder keg, it gives us more time, and surely the fool of a captain from Kaezzar will not dare set foot on Iswan again. Germaine can sleep easy tonight, as can you."

"I would like a few minutes by myself," Nolan said. He heard the shuffle of Daniel's feet, and then the footsteps faded into nothing. Looking up at the stars, he considered his plight. He should sleep easy tonight, but he would not. In his mind he still had the itch. It was not General Treve or the captain, but sure as he was from Earth, there was still someone following them.

Chapter 11

The fork pushed the meat in a small circle around the stainless-steel plate. Processed into a patty of exact thickness and diameter, it couldn't move far in any direction before sliding up the inclined separations in the platter. In the adjoining space, white, mulched vegetables were whipped into a spiral. In the last of the three spaces making up the container, fruit, beaten to a pulpy paste, completed the lunchtime meal.

Julian looked up from his fork through the bars of the small, sanitized cell at the guard who sat at the desk on the other side. "This is an unacceptable meal," he said in a berating tone.

The guard, leaning back with his crossed feet propped on the table, didn't look up from the book he was reading. "It's the same food all prisoners get."

Julian threw down the plastic fork. His lips turned down in an irritated frown as the plastic-on-metal sound didn't have the effect he hoped for. He pointed his finger at the guard. "I'm not just a prisoner. I'm a *political* prisoner."

"All the prisoners get the same food. Eat it, and stop talking so much." The guard flipped the page of his book over.

Julian pushed the platter back on the short table in front of him. Rising from the narrow cot, he crossed the three paces to the front of the cell. His face was red with rage, contrasting the white of his knuckles now grasping two of the thick bars. "Additionally, I'm a political prisoner about to be exonerated. When I'm free, you'll pay for your insolence."

"That's not what I hear," the guard said through a chuckle. "Witness after witness has testified that you're both a liar and a traitor."

"That's not true," Julian hissed. "What I did, I did for Kaezzar. I could not do my duty properly with my hands tied behind my back!"

"So, you took matters into your own hands." Goading Julian was bringing pleasure to the guard.

"Of course—one must be decisive!"

The guard slammed the book closed. "And now the tribunal will be just as decisive in finding you guilty. In the city odds are set at two to one favoring your execution here. There's still an attractive long shot at ten to one odds you'll be handed over to the Celtae."

"What is your name, guard?" Julian's eyes narrowed to evil slits.

"Morley, badge number C2701. I hope it comes to your mind when the first wave of electricity rocks your body." The guard threw his head back, laughing at his own wit.

The door at the end of the hallway was pushed open. Two more guards in crisp, gray penal uniforms came to the front of the cell. One of them pulled a thick bracelet from a pouch at the back of his belt. "Push your hand through the bars," he said to Julian.

Julian complied. The guard pulled the bracelet around Julian's thin wrist and locked it shut. He turned the key once, and the bracelet cracked as the low electrical signature traveled around its circumference.

The guard nodded to his comrade behind the desk. "Turn off the displacement field, and unlock the door. The energy bracelet is secure."

Swiveling on the wheels at the bottom of his chair, the first guard spun to a console on the wall behind him. He pressed a flat button identified by a red number three on it. The barely discernable whine dissipated as the displacement field was shut off. A loud click followed, and the door to Julian's cell slid open.

With the two guards behind Julian, it was only a short walk down a corridor, up one flight of stairs and then down a second corridor. The door at the end of the second corridor was blocked by another guard, and Julian came to a stop in front of him. The guard first checked the security of the energy bracelet and then patted down Julian's body for weapons. Once satisfied, he pushed a key into a slot on the wall and the doors behind him opened with a *whoosh*.

The drone of light conversation diminished as Julian moved to his seat in the prisoner's box. This box was on a lower step on the left side of the judicator who hadn't yet returned. Directly in front of the judicator's tall desk was the witness box. Through yesterday and this morning, there had been a long line of witnesses, including Captain Renier and Sub-Commander Rankin.

Julian had dismissed his own advocate at lunchtime yesterday. The young man, fresh out of the Law Academy, continually told Julian his best course of action was to throw himself on the mercy of the court. There was a small chance he could receive leniency and only be incarcerated for the rest of his life instead of being executed. Defending himself from that point on, Julian dug himself into a deeper and deeper hole. Now, with all the witnesses heard, the judge will give his ruling. However, before that occurs, the officials representing the seven members of the Toltec alliance would have their chance to speak and give their recommendations.

The hush that came over the audience of political and military officials turned into complete silence as the door to the judicator's chambers opened. The tall, thin man who entered the Hall of Justice was young for his position. Nevertheless, his face was creased with lines of tension from the difficult decisions he was required to make day in and day out. His decision today would be one of the most difficult of his career, considering it could elevate the ongoing hit-and-run war between the Toltec and Celtae into an all-out blood bath.

As if it was choreographed, as soon as the judicator took his seat, the door to the royal chambers opened. From it, six heads of State forming the greater Toltec nation exited and moved to their seats in the royal box on the left side of the great room. The Sillian king sat next to the Prime of Kaezzar. Next to them, a seat was empty. Once again, the Kre had snubbed the official event. In the Kre's absence, the other world officials had denounced the action since the decision today was critical to the future of all Toltec, including the Kre. The Kre's constant absence from official functions was seen as a weakening of the alliance between the seven worlds. Emergency messages were sent out to the Kre home world, but still the seat was vacant.

The judicator cleared his throat and leaned over the microphone. "I'm ready for closing remarks from the defendant."

Julian rose to his feet. His uniform had been stripped from him and he wore the drab green coveralls of a prisoner. He looked to the heads of State and then to the lower gallery in front of him, filled with officials from both this world and the other Toltec nations.

Julian took a moment before responding with a summary of what he had explained in detail over the last few days. "I understand the political uncertainty of General Treve's death." His voice rose. "However, it was an unfortunate accident. That is all. I was doing my duty, serving my city and confirming my pledge to rid the Athar of dissidents who are members of the Soichaint. In closing, my final thought is General Treve was our sworn enemy and, in fact, a high ranking Celtae. With all due respect, I would suggest this court and the council of Toltec nations is not answerable to the Celtae." He stood straight with his hands clasped behind his back. "That is all."

The judicator leaned over the microphone again. "Royal officials, your final comments and recommendations please."

The Prime of Kaezzar rose to his feet. "Julian Morenz, I will make the comments for this council. You're my fellow Kaezzarite, and as such, it is appropriate I would speak." He turned to the audience as he continued.

Oh god, Julian thought, shaking his head from side to side. *This is going to be a political, self-propelling speech.*

The prime pointed at Julian. "This man has a good heart, and he's a true Kaezzarite. There's ambition in his mind, and it's such that drives growth and progress among all Toltec. However, the question is not Julian Morenz's devotion to his city. This court is to determine if his actions went over and above those accepted by our laws. Clearly, General Treve of Bailemor is dead, and the implications are grave. This one act could very well escalate the war between the Toltec and the Celtae. Now, do not misinterpret my words." He raised his fist and brought it down with a resounding crash on the railing in front of him. "The Toltec nation is strong! However, it's not for individuals to decide when and where we will go to an escalated war with the Celtae. Those decisions come from this council, not from anyone else in this room, and that includes you!" His hand snapped out with his finger pointing at Julian. "You say the death of the general was an accident?" the prime asked.

"Well, yes," Julian replied.

"Was the death done at the hands of one of your assault squads?"

"Yes," Julian blurted without having time to think.

"And it was planned?"

"Yes."

"And was there not a Toltec spy in the general's group, who you had paid three million cort!"

"Yes!" Julian rose to his feet. "But it wasn't like that!"

"Be seated." The judicator's voice came over the speakers, and Julian slumped back in his chair.

The prime continued. "It's clear your accident was actually an assassination. The Supreme Council of Senators *must* approve such political assassinations, and I sit at the head of that council. Such approval was not asked for, nor given." Turning back to the judicator, the prime said, "We are ready to give our decision."

Pushing aside the microphone, the judicator rose to his feet. "As it has been our custom for over two thousand years, I ask the question, is there anyone here, who has not been heard, who wishes to give evidence regarding this case and this defendant? The question is asked once." The judicator's hand picked up a small rubber hammer and hit it against the small bell hanging from a curled rod at the side of his desk. The deep tone echoed around the room. "As it has been done through the ages, the question is asked a second time. Is there anyone here, who has not been heard, who wishes to give evidence regarding this case and this defendant?"

Julian watched the judicator's hand holding the small hammer pull back. *Amazing,* he thought. *With a single stroke, my life will be squashed. I wonder if they will execute me here, or give me to the Celtae.*

"Stay that bell!" The deep voice came from the balcony, shrouded in darkness, and to all in attendance, considered empty until now. A cloaked and hooded figure could be seen rising to his feet from the shadows.

All in attendance were shocked since the request for evidence was purely a procedural formality. It hadn't been invoked in over a hundred years. The figure walked out the back door of the balcony. In the silence, his booted feet could be heard taking firm steps down the stairs. The lower level door at the back of the courtroom was thrust open. People turned, trying to peer into the darkness provided by the hood.

Julian considered the man with curiosity. There was something familiar about his stride, but it went even further than that. It was the confidence with which he carried himself even as an armed guard moved to block his path to the royal box. The man's right hand pulled at the cloak, ripping it from his body. A gasp went through the audience, seeing the metal mesh covering his body and the bright silver breastplate. If any were not sure who he was, the burn on the left side of his face would answer that final question.

"Theron!" The Prime of Kaezzar said as his eyes opened wide in shock.

The Vice-Prime of the Kre worlds pushed the guard aside and strode to a position in front of the royal box. "I speak for the people of Kre. Evidence isn't what I bring, but I do bring an opinion. Take it for what it's worth." He pulled an envelope from his belt and slapped it down on the railing in front of the royal box. Before the small cloud of dust dispersed, he turned and was making long strides toward the exit.

"Wait!" the Prime of Kaezzar shouted.

Theron did not miss a step as he raised his right hand to stay the prime's objections. "All you need is in the envelope!" Then he was gone.

Julian was just as shocked as the others who had witnessed the Kre's actions. *What do the Kre want with me?* he thought.

"Judicator." The prime's voice finally came back to him. "We'll take a short recess."

"Of course, of course. We will take a one-hour recess." He fell back into his seat, and his open mouth indicated his confusion.

"Enter!" The voice came from the other side of the door, and it was pushed open by the guard. Julian entered the small room where he was surprised to see the prime of Kaezzar sitting cross-legged on a plush, leather couch.

"Remove his energy bracelet," the prime said.

"Of course," the guard replied. He pressed the key in the tiny slot. Once turned, the energy signature stopped, and he clicked the ring of metal open.

Julian rubbed his wrist. "I don't understand?"

"Leave us," the prime said to the guard.

Without another word the guard left, pulling the door closed behind him. The prime pointed to the far end of the couch. "Sit."

Julian complied, cautiously walking to the couch before lowering himself into the soft cushion.

"I don't like it when my hand is forced, Julian, but such is the case now.

Our decision was to execute you here on Kaezzar as a traitor. It is not unusual the Kre disapproved, but in the unusual circumstances, not only has your execution been stayed, but you're being promoted."

Julian blinked. "I don't understand any of this."

"Let me lay it out for you then," the prime explained. "As you are aware, the Kre are a smaller faction of the Toltec nation, but they are the fiercest. They drive fear into the hearts of the Celtae. Without them, we wouldn't dare go into an all-out confrontation with the Celtae. With their less than punctual attendance to Toltec affairs of late, our hands have been tied with hesitation more than anything else."

"How does this involve me?"

"Just listen. The letter from Theron basically scolded us on what we were doing. He thought our plan to execute someone who killed a Celtae general without approval was ludicrous. In his opinion, he thought you should be a hero, not a villain. By convicting you, he felt the heart would be ripped out of every Toltec who ever lost a brother or father to their sworn enemy."

So, I'm not going to be executed?"

"If I had my way, I would pull the lever myself, but that will not be possible. The Kre want to use the incident to promote the war, and they've given the council an ultimatum. We go to war against the Celtae on Iswan, or they will pull out of our alliance. We have no choice but to acquiesce. There's going to be a battle on Iswan, but not just any battle. It will be the battle of the ages—one that will hopefully lead to the annihilation of the Celtae race."

"Then, I'm free to go?"

"Not only that, but you're being promoted." The prime flipped a small button over to Julian. Engraved on it was a bursting star.

Julian's eyes went wide. "This is the insignia given to the supreme commander of the Kaezzar military!"

"Correct," the prime said. "The Kre have insisted, since your act was the ultimate act of heroism, you should lead the forces on Iswan. It was the final condition for them to join us."

"I can't believe it. I will serve with the best of my ability," Julian stammered.

"You certainly will, my supreme commander. Do not forget you report directly to me. The Kre appear to like your style, but I don't. Before you act rashly again, it's best you get my approval first since I have my own people who will be watching."

"I will not let you…"

"Captain!" the prime yelled, cutting off Julian's words.

The door swung open instantly. In the doorway, the Captain of the Guard stood at attention. "Captain, meet the new supreme commander of the Kaezzar military."

The surprise on the young captain's face was evident. He brought his hand up in a smart salute. Rising to his feet, Julian returned it.

"Get him a uniform, Captain. Both of you are dismissed." The prime waved his hand toward the door, indicating the meeting was over.

Walking down the hallway, the captain said to Julian, "It's best we get you out of those coveralls. Two rooms ahead, there's a storeroom on the left."

"Excellent, Captain," Julian said. "I can find it myself, but as the new supreme commander of the military, I have an important errand for you."

"Of course, Commander."

"In the basement of this building, at your holding cells, there is a guard by the name of Morley, badge number C2701. In front of his desk there is a cell. Put him in it for a month, and make sure the only meal he gets, three times a day, are those infernal processed meat patties!"

Chapter 12

The wagon ride from Brookhaven to the coastal village of Port Eleron took less than a day. Even though the pebbled road followed the tract of the canal, being off the water for another day was a welcome change for the travelers.

A team of four strong horses pulled each of the two covered wagons— at least Nolan thought of them as horses, considering their resemblance to the fast, four-legged creatures of his home world. The *palusas*, as they were called on Iswan, were taller and thicker than the horses of Earth. Nolan had seen many of them since his arrival at Brookhaven castle, yet none were a singular color. The palusas were a mottling of gray, brown, white and black. Consequently, each beast was very much an individual in appearance, and as Nolan came to learn, also in their behavior.

Since Nolan had always been a lover of animals, he spent time with the palusas and grew an admiration for their trainers. He was in wonderment at the patience and skill of these people who took the animals from a wild state to one where the naturally temperamental creatures suffered human orders and worked as pack animals. Occasionally, a pureblood or scull owned the perseverance to train a palusa for riding, but, as Nolan learned, these people were far and few between since few had the time or dedication to train the animals. Those who did finally break a palusa discovered it was more of a merger than an act of submission. The relationship between the palusa and the trainer became a bond of mind and spirit at that point—one that was never broken until one or the other should die. As such, there were few men of Iswan who rode a palusa, but when one was sighted, they were treated with reverence. A man who bonded with a palusa was considered a hero.

Four palusas pulled the wagon Nolan rode in. He watched their proud heads bob up and down as their thick manes bounced gallantly with their long firm gaits. These palusas, although trained for laborious tasks, hadn't been broken to the rider. It wasn't something Nolan planned for his future. He heard stories of riders being trampled to death by the hardened hoofs of an enraged palusa.

Garawin sat next to Nolan on the wide plank serving as a seat on the front of the wagon. "One more corner and Coral Bay will be in our view where a sloop will be waiting at the dock, and from it, a short trip will take us across the bay to Rivenloc. It will be good to be home, even if for a short time." The prince's words faded to a mumble as his eyes were caught in a daydream of memories.

Ranaa was asleep on a thick blanket just behind the two men in the covered wagon. Tok, with one bare foot hanging out the back opening, looked at the front of the following wagon. It was identical to the one he rode in except for its occupants. Larm and Germaine, with his arm almost fully healed, sat along the front bench while Daniel and Rin rested in the shade of the sun-bleached tarp arching over the wooden frame.

In the dusk of the evening the sun was falling over the horizon, stretching streaks of purple and orange across the sky. The two wagons rolled up to the docks, and with a sturdy pull on the reins, they came to a stop. The travelers climbed down from the wagons, stretching their arms and legs that were stiff from their lack of use over the last seven hours.

"I don't know what's more tiring, pulling the oar all day or sitting in the wagon for the same length of time," Germaine grumbled.

"Let's get the supplies unloaded onto the sloop before we go to the inn across the road," Rin interjected.

"I could use a large tankard of ale. Then I'll sleep like a baby," Larm added through a weary chuckle.

"We're not staying," Nolan stated.

"You can't be serious. We have rooms arranged at the inn," Garawin reminded Nolan.

"Haven't you thought it odd, Garawin?" Nolan asked. "The bandits were waiting for us on the river. General Treve was not far behind us, and the Toltec were right on top of them. If that was not enough, I've seen movements in the shadows ever since we left the Great Rock, and during that time, our every move has been predicted."

"But we have to rest!" Rin added as his weariness was turning into frustration.

Nolan pointed at the woodsman. "That's exactly what those following us expect!"

"Nolan, we can't go across to Rivenloc at night. Our border controls do not allow it. We could be attacked." Garawin warned.

Nolan put his hand on Garawin's shoulder. "I'm sorry," he said solemnly. "We're not going to Rivenloc."

The prince looked at Nolan through blank, less than understanding eyes.

"I've been studying the maps," Nolan said. "We'll forego the stop at Rivenloc. I suspect there could well be a surprise for us as we cross the bay, so we won't wait for the morning. Instead, we'll load the supplies and leave now. Then, we will pass around the eastern tip of Rivenloc, and head straight for Wolar's Fang. It'll be exhausting, but we can rest on the sloop. In three days, we'll be at Wolar's Fang."

For a few moments there was silence. Then Garawin put his hand on Nolan's shoulder. "I pledged myself to follow you," he said with a smile, "even if I do not agree." The prince turned to Tok and Stirm. "Unload the supplies. Larm, Rin, give them a hand."

"Trying to round the point of Rivenloc in the dark can be dangerous," Rin said while obstinately crossing his arms.

"In my opinion, not as dangerous as staying here," Nolan repeated. The Earthman walked to the back of the first wagon and pulled a heavy sack of grain over his shoulder. As he walked by the group, he looked at them. "Let's go," he said. "We can rest on the ship."

Larm chuckled nervously. "Well, at least the sky is clear. The starlight will show us the way. That's if we don't turn into a pile of broken boards on the rocks at the point. That would be unfortunate." His eyes turned back to Garawin. "At least let me get a cask of ale from the inn to improve our spirits," he pleaded.

"Very well," the prince said. "Be quick! We leave with or without you once the supplies are loaded." He walked off toward the 40-foot sloop to wake the captain as he fingered the remaining gold in his money pouch. He knew some of it would be required to placate the captain's protests.

Once upon the sloop, Nolan handed the sack of grain to a ship hand. He paused before stepping down the short ladder to the deck. Seeing Ranaa in the stern gave him cause to hesitate. She was busy spreading a blanket across the bench running the width of the sloop. The sight of her white hair tied back from her face made his heartbeat race. Pulling a shawl around her shoulders to buffer the cool breeze from the sea, her eyes caught his as he strode toward her.

"This is the end of your journey," Nolan said. "I can't put you in any more danger."

Her golden eyes looked up, reflecting the starlight back to him. "Thank you for the advice, but I will stay." Her lips opened into a wide smile.

Squatting in front of her, he brought his hands to her hips, hoping his firm touch would bring some sense to her. "I'm serious Ranaa. This village is in safe territory, much safer than the journey yet to come. I'll come back for you."

"That's not what you just told us."

"What?" Nolan replied as his face creased, showing his confusion.

"You just told us it was safer to leave on this sloop than to stay in Port Eleron," she answered. She crossed her legs, letting her knee rub against his chest.

The touch distracted him. Sometimes he thought she did this intentionally. "That comment was for the sake of the others who are coming with me," he replied.

"I will choose my own path, Nolan Harrison. I have not been a burden so far. In fact, I think I've helped, and I'll continue to do so." She leaned back against the wooden slats making up the back of the bench.

"You don't understand!" he said through clenched teeth. "You are different. You are…"

"I'm what?" She leaned forward bringing her face a breath away from his. Her eyes narrowed, and her smile was wide. Her scent floated to him.

He let his hand slide down her thigh to rest on her knee. She didn't flinch, nor did her eyes blink as she maintained the gaze of the man she loved.

Nolan looked into her eyes and through them. He peered into the depths of her heart as her soul bloomed for him like a flower. In that moment he saw the past and the future, hopes and dreams and the reason men live. He saw his own strength and weaknesses, but also his needs and ambitions reflected in the beauty she held within her. He was amazed that above all, she gave him the strength he needed, yet she made him feel so weak.

"I just want you to be safe," he whispered.

She raised her small fingers to his cheek. "The safest place for me is by your side. This is so whether you are in battle, or on a beach or perhaps even on a sloop going to Wolar's Fang in the dark of night."

The breath attached to each of her words rolled against his lips, and it took all his willpower not to kiss her. One day, he hoped to taste her sweet lips, but not now.

It was as if she knew what was going through his mind. "I told you before, Nolan Harrison, I cannot be away from you. If we meet our end on this journey, then let it be with me by your side. If you leave me here, with a certainty, I will die with my heart broken in two. You own me, and that will never change."

Nolan pressed his hands up to her shoulders as he rose to his full height. He pulled the shawl closer about her shoulders while his eyes avoided her gaze. "The sea breeze can be cold." He turned away to help the others before she could respond—before he could see the tear that floated down from her golden eye, traversing her cheek to caress the corner of her lips.

Spirits improved as the sloop cut through the seawater. The wind drove them along at an excellent pace, putting them well ahead of schedule. The cask of ale Larm brought from the inn was a successful accompaniment to the wonderful meals the cook conjured from the seemingly bland rations. The starlight allowed the captain to navigate the sloop through the rocky shoals at the eastern tip of Rivenloc. Ominously, the rocks were littered with the wreckage of other ships with crews not as experienced or as lucky as they intended to be. The trek across the open sea had been uneventful, but their luck was about to change.

Three days later, as the sloop rounded the eastern cliffs of Wolar's Fang, smoke could be seen spiraling upward in the distance. The tension increased as the sloop turned toward the inlet where the ancient scrolls of Iswan and their caretaker, Corbin the Wise, would be found. Unfortunately, the black smoke was directly ahead of them.

Garawin barked orders. "Captain, best you arm your crew. Trouble brews ahead. When we hit the dock, keep the men ready. We might need to push off at a moment's notice."

The captain nodded. "Aye, Prince!" He turned to his second, relaying the orders.

"Daniel, Garawin and Rin, you're with me when we hit the dock," Nolan ordered.

Germaine's face snapped around to Nolan with a questioning look.

"Germaine and Larm, you'll stay here and help protect the ship. Tok, you'll come with us also," Nolan said.

Tok signed his understanding and reached under the bench for his belt. Deft movements of his thick fingers secured it before dropping the Stor war hammer into the attached loop. Pulling out the shield, he looped it over his shoulder and tested the motion as it slid easily down his arm.

The sloop bounced off the waves as it sped toward the dock. Almost too late, the captain's voice bellowed across the deck. "Sails in!" The cloth sails were loosened in an instant, and the captain turned the wheel hard over. For a few moments the sloop side-slipped through the water until the keel caught. The ship, still moving at a high rate of speed, was now traveling in a path parallel to the dock. Four men, each with a thick length of sea rope in their hands, crouched barefoot on the railing. When the bow of the ship skipped off the dock, all four jumped to the wooden structure below. Each worked fervently to coil the slack rope around a solid bollard set firmly in the dock. It only took a few moments before each was holding the end of the wound rope in their hands with their feet braced firmly against the posts. As the ropes snapped taut, the bow of the sloop lurched up, shooting a spray of cold, black water high into the air. The dock groaned its resistance but held. As the sloop slipped back into the murky water, Nolan and his party jumped down to the deck, weapons drawn.

Garawin took the lead as the group stalked up the dock to the rise of land it was anchored to, and then continued up the long, shallow steps bisecting the grass-covered rise. The stone treads were weathered with time, but the remaining thickness supported their hurried steps up the path. At the top of the rise, the four knelt and surveyed the damage.

"It looks deserted," Nolan said.

Garawin nodded. "The cottage on the right is the home of Corbin. Pray he has somehow avoided the carnage."

The four ran across the short space to the cabin. With their backs pressed to the outside wall, they slid toward the main door which was hanging slack on broken hinges.

Nolan signed to Tok—*Stay here and watch.*

The Stor nodded, and his legs took him down to a squat while his yellow eyes peered back and forth across the veranda. His war hammer was clenched tight in his fingers, ready to strike out at danger if it should arise.

Nolan slid his hand around the doorjamb and nudged the door open. There was no reaction—nothing but silence. Nolan nodded to Daniel, and in unison, they both stepped into the doorway. Nolan squatted with his sword drawn while Daniel, above him, had his bow fully flexed, ready to release the deadly barbed arrow if the need came. However, the room was devoid of life. Nolan sucked in his breath, seeing the two bodies. Daniel released the tension on his bow, and the two men carefully entered the cottage, followed by Prince Garawin.

Each body was tied to a chair, facing the other. Garawin went to the body on the left. He looked closely, wiping the blood from the swollen face, and his shoulders slumped. "This is Corbin, or at least what used to be Corbin. I met him once years ago in Rivenloc. His face has been beaten to a pulp, but I am sure it is he."

"Who is the other man across from him?" Nolan asked.

Garawin turned and looked at the second man. His battered face was even more hideous than Corbin's. One eye had been cut out, and as Garawin looked down his arm, he saw all the fingers of his left hand were removed, leaving only bloody stumps. A wave of nausea came over the prince as he backed away from the bodies. "They have been tortured. Whoever did this must have forced the location of the Second and Third Keys from them!"

Daniel moved forward, continuing the grizzly task of first inspecting one body and then the other. He turned back to Nolan and Garawin. "I think Corbin was stronger than you think. It does not appear he gave the answers the attackers searched for."

"What do you mean?" Garawin said, wide-eyed. "Look at them!"

"Exactly," Daniel replied with a calm voice. "Look at them. They were made to watch each other. Corbin's servant was tortured first, and Corbin was made to watch. At the same time, Corbin was beaten about the head.

There are no other wounds on his body." Daniel moved toward Corbin's side, pointing to his neck. "If you were the interrogator, and you received the information you wanted, what would you do?"

"Kill him quickly," Nolan replied.

"But there isn't evidence of a quick death," Daniel continued. "His throat is not slit, nor is his heart impaled. This man was beaten to death with his lips sealed to the end. The secret of the Keys died with him."

"We must get to the library. That is our only hope," Garawin said as he regained his composure.

The trio departed the cabin of death and ran across the grass to the rock wall some 30 yards in the distance. Over the centuries, the rock face had been chiseled by hand to resemble a building. The solid, wooden door in the middle of the carved surface covered the entrance to the cave housing the scrolls of the Ancients.

Their hopes fell as they smelled the acrid smoke wafting toward them from the top of the chamber atop the rise. Garawin pulled the door open. What was left of the afternoon light bathed the cavern, confirming their worst fears. Scrolls were strewn throughout the chamber along with what had been wooden shelves but were now nothing more than smoldering shards.

The three men walked into the chamber. They did not expect to find anything intact, and after their thorough inspection, they did not. It took some time, but Nolan picked up almost every scroll, finding each burnt beyond recognition. He kicked at the ashes, but nothing came from them except the soot clouding the air.

With his spirit broken, Nolan left what remained of the scrolls and the room behind. He felt the cool air slap his face. The night was now pitch-black with the stars covered by a blanket of cloud and mist. "What now?" Nolan asked.

For a few moments there was silence. Then Garawin spoke. "We must go to the Council of Kings. Someone there must have a clue to the location of the remaining Keys."

"It's hopeless," Nolan uttered.

Daniel looked up from under the brim of his faded leather hat. "No. There is always hope. We have come too far to lose that. If we lose our hope, then we are nothing. I am not ready to admit the ultimate defeat, so as long as Celtae blood runs through my veins, I will search for peace."

"And as long as Anasazi blood flows through my veins, I will stand beside you," Garawin added.

A guttural rasp was heard from below. Tok hit his shield with his hammer and made a quick succession of signs with his fingers.

Nolan smiled and shook his head. "How could I lose spirit with you around me? How could I do anything else but be part of this?" He cleared his throat and a deeper voice arose. "With the blood of all the Ancients flowing through my veins, I'm with you."

"In that case, there is much to do. We need to bury the bodies, rest, and in the morning run for the coast." Garawin was always the quick thinker and the first to move on.

Nolan shook his head. "No. They'll expect that. Rather, we leave right now under the cover of darkness."

Garawin's eyes bored into Nolan. He was giving the young Earthman a chance to change his mind. However, Nolan understood the doubt-filled look. He had convinced the travelers to change their plans at the last moment, yet still the mission ended in failure. Somehow, their enemy was able to foretell their every move. Nolan didn't understand how that was possible, but he was going to find out.

"We are wasting time," Nolan said. "Let's go."

With their hopes shattered, the group of four strode down the steps to the sloop. As Nolan stepped up the short ladder and over the railing, he hailed the captain. "Can you make it to the finger of South Palor in the dark?" The Finger was the name given to the peninsula of land, closest to the north point of Wolar's Fang.

"I could navigate these waters with my eyes closed," the captain barked.

"Very well," Nolan responded. "We'll run without lights since whoever destroyed this place is probably still lurking on the water."

It was obviously not the first time the captain had been asked to use deception and stealth. "Lights out!" he yelled at the crew. The lanterns at the bow and stern of the sloop were snuffed into darkness. "Push off!" he hissed. The words were just barely loud enough for the four men on the dock to hear him. The ropes were uncoiled, and the men jumped nimbly over the railing with their wet feet landing in silence on the wood planking. In unison, four shipmates pushed off the dock with long oars, and the current caught the sloop almost immediately, dragging the vessel north.

The captain let the ship drift for ten minutes while his eyes squinted as he constantly searched from side to side. He, along with every other person on the sloop, was attuned to the silence of the night.

The hair on the back of Nolan's neck stood on end with the combination of tension and the chill breeze. Looking to his left, he could see the shadow of land end, leaving their path to the Finger open.

The observant captain had been waiting for the same sign. "Sails of darkness," he whispered to his first mate. The mate scurried down the steps, repeating the order to the crew waiting on the deck below. Immediately, they launched into action. Some climbed the rigging while others manned the knotted ropes tied to the steel rings anchored in the deck. The first mate looked to the men and raised his hand in an upward sweep. Two black, triangular sails slipped up the mast and billowed into life as the wind caught hold of the canvas. The sloop lurched to the left with an eerie wooden groan as the wind pressed the vessel in a northwest tact. The prow cut through the waves, throwing a spray over Nolan and his fellow travelers.

Nolan overheard the captain whisper, "Let's see who can catch us now."

Nolan leaned toward the captain. "How long till we land?"

The captain turned his face, letting the wind hit it squarely. "The wind is with us tonight, so we will hit landfall in three hours."

The captain knew the sea well. It was almost three hours later when the lookout saw lights from the villages in the distance. The travelers decided to settle onto blankets along the starboard side of the craft, and as the hours of travel had passed, their tension withdrew, but each of them kept their weapons close at hand.

"It looks like good fortunate has given us some luck tonight," Daniel said to the others.

"We are not there yet," Garawin added. His negativity created by the day's events had not yet left him.

"Quiet," Ranaa whispered. Her soft voice had an unsettling resolve to it.

"What is it?" Nolan asked.

"What do you hear?" she asked.

The group remained silent. They focused on their hearing, but still heard nothing unusual. "There is only the bump of the bow against the waves. Otherwise, there is only silence," Rin said.

"Then listen closer!" she said. "I can hear the bow slapping against the waves with a regular rhythm, but listen closer."

Germaine heard it first. "I hear it. In between the slap of our bow against the waves, there is another slap. It's faint, but it holds a steady beat."

"There is another ship close by," Ranaa said.

"Take cover!" Garawin pitched his voice to the captain and crew, but it was too late. The first volley of arrows was already over the crest of their arch and plummeting downward toward the sloop. In the darkness some fell harmlessly in the water, but many prattled into the deck. More than a few found their mark as crewmen screamed out. One fell from his perch on the mast, finding death even before his body hit the cold water below.

There was a growl from the wheel. Nolan turned in time to see the captain, who was clutching an arrow embedded in his leg, take another in his neck. He staggered to the railing before toppling over the side into the darkness.

"Germaine!" Daniel shouted. "Take the tiller!"

There was no response from Germaine, who was leaning against the railing. Daniel reached out and pulled on his shoulder. "Germaine, take the…"

Germaine fell to the deck and rolled to his back. There was a trail of blood from the corner of his mouth. The blood spattered as he coughed while one hand held the shaft of the arrow embedded deep in his chest.

Daniel fell to his knees beside the warrior. "Germaine—no. Not you." He clasped Germaine's hand in his own and brought it up to his cheek where the tears from Daniel's eyes mixed with the blood on his fingers.

Germaine gasped for air. Between them, broken words came from his tortured lips. "My time is done, my brother."

Daniel's lips quivered. "No. A little further and we will be on land where we will find a shaman." Daniel spoke with hope, even though he recognized the death in the warrior's eyes.

"My life is fulfilled. My missions are complete." Germaine's eyes turned up to Nolan who was behind Daniel. "Change is life and life is change. You're now who I was and more. You'll protect Daniel, and he'll protect you. Have faith in each other, and you'll find what you seek."

Nolan thought it ironic. Germaine was a quiet man whose deeds said more than his words. Yet, in the last moments through his pain, he put more thoughtful words together than at any time in past conversations with Nolan. *Simple words*, he thought, yet they proved the wisdom held deep within his soul. "It's not much further, my friend," he said. "I'm not ready to let you leave us."

Germaine managed a painful smile. "Then you'll have to accept my apologies." With his last word, his head lolled to the side, and the hand holding Daniel's went slack. A last sigh of air left his lungs as his chest shrank, never again to fill with the wonder of life. A gust swirled around Germaine's body, taking his last breath, and it spiraled up until caught by the wind pushed in a wild path toward the sails.

Nolan heard the roar as the renewed wind burst the sails into life. Perplexed, his gaze remained locked. He would have sworn he heard voices in the wind.

Daniel's voice broke Nolan's mood. "Garawin! Come with me to the tiller!" More arrows could be heard hitting in the water with a few finding the ship's hull. "Nolan, see if you can do something about the other ship."

The Earthman turned to his right. Rin and Larm were firing into the darkness, using the sound of the enemy's bowstrings to assist their aim. To Nolan's surprise, beside the two men, on one knee was Ranaa. Her shawl was thrown aside revealing the tight muscles of her shoulders and arms flexing as she handled the bow. It was obvious she had been training as arrow after arrow left the small, powerful weapon. Almost before one was released, another was being cocked, ready to fire.

"Let me help," Nolan shouted. His shield had been energized almost from the first arrow, but now a purple fireball formed at his fingertips. He leaned back and then pitched forward on his front foot, releasing the fireball high into the air. As it fell, the sky was lit up, disclosing the dark ship not 40 yards off their starboard side. In that short span of time, Nolan saw three of Ranaa's arrows pierce the chests of the assailants as the remaining attackers scrambled and ducked. "That will not help you now," he yelled. Another larger fireball, fueled by his anger, was pulsing at his fingertips. He clapped his hands over his head before thrusting them forward, accelerating the fireball toward the enemy ship. The task drained him for a moment, and as the fireball was sent on its way, his shield sputtered.

"God!" Nolan cried out as the force of an arrow impaling his right shoulder knocked him five feet back onto the wood deck.

Ranaa's face was above him in an instant. "Please, no!" she said while her eyes looked down in a wild, pleading gaze.

In the background, Nolan saw a great fiery plume explode into the night sky as the fireball found its mark. "I'm fine," he said through slack lips. "We're fine." Those were the last words before he lost consciousness.

"The rocks!" Garawin shouted. "Take hold!"

In front of the shoreline, jagged rocks loomed menacingly out of the dark water. There was no time to change the course of the ship—only time for the warning before the *crack* of breaking wood on rock echoed through the crisp air. Garawin was thrown over the wheel, and the dull thud of his head hitting the railing mingled with the sound of the front mast as it cracked at the base. Both the sail and mast toppled into the water, followed a few moments later by silence where the quiet was broken only by the moans and groans of injured crewmembers in the battered, motionless sloop.

When Nolan came to, it was in the grasp of strong fingers holding both his ankles and wrists. Opening his eyes, he thought he was seeing double, but he was not. Holding his ankles was a huge, black, half-naked savage. Another, who would have been his twin, had a tight grip on his wrists. As they carefully searched for footholds in the knee-high water, a creaky voice could be heard in the distance.

"Carefully now! He's very important!" the voice yelled.

The strong legs of the two men quickly found their way to the sandy beach where they lay Nolan down on his back. His vision was still foggy, but it cleared when the lantern was thrust toward him. Beside the lantern was a face, wrinkled with age. It was black as the night sky, speckled with sporadic whiskers as white as the sand he lay on. The sparse beard merged into the white band of hair framing his bald head. The man was not unfamiliar. Since they arrived at the lake at the base of the Great Rock,

Nolan had seen moving leaves and bushes. He thought he might have been imagining things. Nolan knew better now, considering the face that always disappeared just before he could distinguish it time and again was real, and now, with a wide smile, was staring down at him.

Chapter 13

Nolan stood beside Daniel a few yards in from the line where the forest of trees met the sand. In front of them, lying with his arms crossed and wrapped in the remnants of a sail removed from the sloop, lay Germaine's body. Tok looked up from his position in the three-foot-deep grave with both eyebrows raised in a questioning gaze.

"Deeper," Daniel said.

The Stors returned to their grim task. Clumps of moist dirt flew out of the grave from the shovels handled by both Tok and Stirm.

"Aren't you going to mark the grave?" Nolan asked in a subdued voice.

Daniel shrugged. His eyes were red from the tears he shed, but he knew life goes on, and it was time to put Germaine's body to rest. "No, his body is but a shell of who he was. His essence has moved on."

"I'm sorry for the circumstances. Germaine was a great friend—even more to you than to me," Nolan continued. He pushed the words from his lips, finding them awkward. Germaine was dead, and no matter what his or anyone's words were, death remained the fact they faced.

Looking down at the wrapped body, Daniel put his hand on the Earthman's shoulder. "I have shed my tears and made my peace with his passing. Hopefully, the world his spirit now resides in is a better one, free of war and the death it brings."

"You believe in the afterlife?" Nolan broached a subject they hadn't discussed before.

"It would be foolish not to. Let me explain my views. Perhaps it will give you some comfort with the loss of our friend." Daniel leaned over momentarily. "That's deep enough," he said to the Stors. Straightening, he turned his gaze back to Nolan. "I categorize people's beliefs into three groups. First there are people who have a faith. On every plane I have hopped to there are people who believe in a supreme being or power. Since all humans have some level of vanity, these people believe in a place where they can meet or live with this supreme power. On your world of Earth, you have God, Buddha, and Mohammed, to name a few. You have heaven and hell. Given different names, each plane and faith have such places and gods of their own. The important point is these humans believe there is somewhere their spirit goes after their existence in the Athar ends."

Nolan listened as he watched Tok and Stirm climb out of the grave while dusting the dirt from their clothing.

"Then there are those who consider themselves above a faith yet still have difficulty dealing with their own frailty. Such a group exists on all planes. They believe in what we call *reincarnation*. Again, another less than evidential concept fulfilling people's need to disavow their loss of existence, except it is not so thought out and is more individualistic."

"And the third group?" Nolan probed.

"These are people who do think it out." Daniel managed a smile. "There is the Athar of science. If you really think about it, no matter what words we use on any plane, the basic laws define nothing as just lost. Of course, matter and energy can be transformed, but it cannot be magically gained, nor can it just vanish."

"I'm not sure I understand."

"Then consider some examples." Daniel turned and pointed toward the ocean. The sea waves were barely visible, but the two men could hear them pushing up the shoreline on the other side of the trees. "When water is frozen, it turns into ice. When we heat it, it turns into steam and heat. Nothing is lost. This is the rule of science applying to all things."

"So, you're saying Germaine's energy is not gone, just transformed?"

"I am saying even science tells us his energy, his essence, consciousness or soul—whatever you want to call it, cannot just vanish into nothing. Science defines such as an impossibility."

"Do you think he's in a better existence?" The Earthman looked up to the sky through the narrow gaps in the branches.

"Neither of us knows. All we do know is one day each of us will find out, notwithstanding our faith in science, our faith in ourselves or our faith in faith itself. I have quite a few years on you, and still my values shift from group to group. However, common to each is my belief Germaine is not gone. He has just moved on."

Having seen the Stors finish digging, the remaining travelers, who had been respectfully keeping their distance, now crossed to the gravesite. They were comforted by Daniel, hearing his last words. Nothing else was left or needed to be said.

Daniel squatted, taking a corner of the sail into his grasp. Nolan and the others each did the same. Germaine was a large man, but already his shell felt light, now devoid of the spirit that made him who he was. Each lifted, pulling him over the deep grave. The edges of the sail slipped through their fingers as his body lowered into the bottom of the grave. Bowing their heads for a few moments, they each silently remembered the memories of their friend and companion. Some whispered a prayer, hoping it would speed his soul to a better place.

Reaching down, Daniel's fingers raked through the pile of dirt. His fingers tensed, and when they pulled free, a loose ball of soil was clenched in his grasp. Throwing it on the sail-covered body, his voice cracked with emotion. "It has been a long road. Be at peace my friend."

The tears on the faces of the traveling companions couldn't be helped. Each picked up handful after handful of dirt before throwing it upon Germaine's lifeless body. Daniel looked at the two tall trees providing shade from the warming sun. One was dotted with deep-blue flowers. The other was devoid of flowers, but was just as magnificent with yellow and green-striped leaves. From the direction of the forest, a cluster of dark green bushes bloomed with small lava-red flowers. Their voraciousness for space matched their beauty, and as a result, if he came back next season, the grave would be difficult to find under the colorful bed of green and red. Germaine will be satisfied with his last resting place, and as such, the knowledge balanced Daniel's sense of uncontrolled shame. Germaine had been a man who followed his own path, but Daniel's urging to follow this one led to the warrior's death.

Nolan's thoughts mirrored Daniel's. With great effort, he pushed them to the back of his mind. Germaine had given his life for the cause and even more so for him, yet he knew the time for mourning was past. He nodded to the Stors and they picked up their shovels, accelerating the process of returning Germaine's body back from whence it came. Giving Garawin a look indicating it was time to move on, he tugged on Daniel's shirtsleeve.

He had pushed the strangers who pulled them from the water to the back of his mind, but to all things a time will come, and now it was time to learn more of the mysterious saviors. Wincing, Nolan flexed his fingers. His right arm was cocked at a 90-degree angle, supported by the makeshift sling cut from the same sail wrapping Germaine's body.

"How does it feel?" Garawin asked.

"Remarkably well," Nolan answered. "I'm still amazed. My shoulder feels stiff, but with only a minor amount of pain."

Garawin leaned his head to the side with one eyebrow raised. "You are lucky on two accounts. First, the arrowhead went through your shoulder and did not hit any bone. The wound was clean, without steel or wood slivers. Second, the old man who pulled you from the ocean is a wizen from Kaleel. The tribes of Kaleel are considered wild savages by most on Iswan. Their language is difficult, but what pushes many to this conclusion is their lack of modesty since they are as comfortable naked or clothed."

"Then why did you let him remove the arrow?"

"Because he knew how to do it," Garawin replied. The matter-of-fact answer showed Garawin's impatience. The prince knew they would have to leave soon to arrive at the King's Council on schedule.

Moving closer to Nolan, Daniel continued the prince's explanation. "Garawin knew the old man to be a wizen of Kaleel by the necklace he wears, strung with colorful jewels. Wizens have many purported skills, but there is one we know to be proven. They are skilled healers. For each person they save, the patient's family gives them one colored jewel. If the patient does not recover or dies, the wizen returns a jewel to the family. This wizen has a long necklace with many jewels indicating his level of competence."

"Besides, we did not have much choice," Garawin added. "You were shivering and not only from the cold. I knew enough from the smell of the wound, and your state, to know the point was tipped with pureblood poison. It is used only by the unscrupulous dregs who do not know the word honor. The poison sucks the energy from a pureblood, so if the wizen had not acted quickly, your powers would have been slowly sapped from you until you died."

Nolan's memory of the early morning past was foggy at best. He remembered being lifted into the grass that marked the border between the forest and the sand. He overheard the brief discussion between the wizen and Garawin after which the frail man, barely more than skin and bone, leaned over the Earthman. Although old, the wizen's eyes were bright with an unusual opaque glaze, masking the pitch-black pupils. He put his hand on Nolan's neck where it met his shoulder. "Sleep," he had said. The words came smoothly off his lips, offering a hypnotic tone. The wizen's fingers were old and wrinkled, but they had a surprising strength. Pinching down, his fingers with many years of experience found the delicate nerve center, and Nolan was coaxed into instant unconsciousness.

When Nolan awoke, he felt very little pain in his shoulder. The wizen had expertly removed the arrow shaft, cleaned the wound and packed the bandage with a poultice of moist herbs. Nolan opened his mouth, but he found the dryness made it difficult to speak. The wizen's fingers took the opportunity and pushed a packet of the same mixed herbs into the space between Nolan's gum and cheek.

"Chew slowly on this. It will numb the pain," he had said.

Over half the day was gone, and with Germaine's burial now done, Nolan strode toward the wizen with his mind once again focused on the present. The old wizen was black as the night and difficult to see in the shadows of the lean-to that kept the warm sun off his back. With closed eyes, his foot tapped on the packed dirt while he hummed a tune, appearing quite oblivious to his surroundings. Nolan, Garawin and Daniel stepped up the rise from the sand to the small plateau supporting the structure that was sturdier than it looked. Nolan was curious at the reluctance of the other two men as they stayed just outside the perimeter of the structure and waited while their feet shifted uncomfortably.

The humming stopped as did the old man's naked heel bounce. He opened one eye, looking momentarily at the three men. "It's curious that you are afraid. Is it fear of the unknown or fear of what you do know that keeps you out in the sun?" His eyes closed, and at the same time the heel joined the rhythm of his humming.

The three men looked at each other foolishly before stooping to enter the lean-to. There were several tree stumps tilted on end under the roof of thick branches held together with a mixture of leaves and mud. They lowered themselves on three of them facing the old, white-bearded man.

Nolan cleared his voice before speaking. "It's lucky for us you were here to help last night."

The humming stopped for a moment. "You confuse luck with destiny," the wizen said. His lips clamped shut as he returned to his humming.

"I don't understand," Nolan replied. "I have never met you before last night." Nolan was distracted. He hadn't heard her, but Ranaa's scent wafted on the slight breeze. Quietly, she sat on a stump beside him.

Looking at Ranaa the wizen smiled wide. His eyes appeared to be inspecting every inch of her. Once satisfied, his gaze turned back to Nolan. "Your lack of understanding surprises me. The woman beside you should give you enough clues regarding the concept of destiny. She is in yours as are your friends, and so am I. There are very few things in the Athar that happen by chance." His foot had stopped tapping the ground, and he didn't return to the humming.

"You talk of the Athar as if you were a pureblood," Nolan responded. His words passed quietly off his lips, not wanting to offend the man.

A hearty cackle came from the wizen. "You don't have to be a pureblood to understand you are part of the Athar. My blood goes back many generations, and my memory is strong, so I remember my roots and those of my forefathers."

Garawin put his hand on Nolan's forearm, staying his words. "Ages ago, before the time of the Anasazi on Iswan, even before the time of the Ionians, there was a small band of Bantu who called this plane home."

Nolan's brows furrowed as he thought back. "The Bantu—they were clairvoyant, were they not?" His finger tapped his lips, speaking as much to himself as anyone else.

"My forefathers had dreams. They could dream day and night. Awake or asleep, events came to their minds." He cackled again. "Even today the Kaleel tribes who are descended from the Bantu wonder if the power is a blessing or a curse."

Leaning forward, Nolan's head tilted up. "How would you know?"

The wizen pointed at Daniel accusingly. "Have you taught him nothing?" He rolled his eyes before setting his gaze back to the Earthman. "Descendants of any pureblood race still have rogue children who retain vestiges of the power. On the plains of Kaleel these people are special and raised in the wizen ways."

Blood rushed to Nolan's face, partly due to his anger at being lectured but more so in embarrassment. "Does this wizen have a name?" he said slowly.

"I am Chu—Chu of the foot tribe of Kaleel."

"So, how does Chu, of the foot tribe of Kaleel, find himself on a deserted beach on the other side of Iswan from your home plain, and clothed even?" Garawin interrupted.

Chu kept his dark eyes focused on Nolan. "I'm here because my dream told me to be. Ever since I was a boy, my dreams told me of your coming. My father and grandfather had the same dreams as did their forefathers before them. The power weakens with the ages, so my dreams are jumbled and confused, but the patience of a wizen gives me the faith to see the message."

"What are the words of your message?" Nolan responded almost before the wizen finished his sentence.

"Not words but a vision. It's your face surrounded by flowing white hair blown by the wind, and there are many thousands of faces behind you, following you."

Nolan blushed for a second time. Earlier in the day, while washing in a small pool of water created by rocks along the shoreline, he saw his face. The whiteness at his brows was expanded. Now the leading edge of his hair was solid white, peppering back through the brown as the wind blew the locks back. He knew it was from his use of the power. It was changing him. His hair was the only visible metamorphosis, but what concerned him more deeply were the changes he could not see and the changes yet to come. He said the words, even though his inner sense told him he would be wishing them back. "Why me? I'm an ordinary man."

Chu shot to his feet. He thrust his hands under his armpits and paced back and forth in front of the travelers. Nolan could sense the anger in the small man's frail body. After walking back and forth a few times, Chu returned to his stump, lowering himself onto it. He took a deep breath to relax himself before speaking. "A man such as you should know better than to use lies and deception. You can see my nature easily enough, both outside and in. You know my words to be true. You have come a long way to get here. You have passed as many trials as you have yet to surmount, and, with that, I offer a level of respect. I expect no less in return from one who is the First Key to peace."

The jaws on all four faces looking at the old man dropped simultaneously.

Nolan stammered. "How do you know?"

Chu rolled his eyes again. "I'll explain it again and for the last time. My family has been waiting for you to arrive. I do not know why just as my ancestors did not. All of us knew that, when the time came, we and the secrets we hold in our minds would be needed."

"Secrets?" Four voices said the word almost in unison.

Chu leaned over and picked up a slender young shoot carried under the lean-to by the wind or perhaps even by a small animal. It was still green with moisture, making it pliable. The wizen flexed it over his knee, testing it in a way that reminded Nolan of Daniel's learning twig from what seemed so long ago back on Earth. Chu put the point in the ground and crossed his hands-on top of the other end, while leaning his chin on both. His eyes pierced into one and then to each of the other travelers as he spoke. "The secrets you searched for on Wolar's Fang were not there. They were never there. Rumors of the secrets being on Wolar's Fang were a necessary diversion, and great sacrifices were made by many."

"Why the ruse?" Nolan asked. His words were soft, seeing the pain in the old man's eyes.

"The ruse was necessary to protect the location of the secrets you search for—the location of the Second and Third keys to peace."

"Where are the secrets?" Garawin blurted out. His voice was raised, revealing his renewed emotion.

Chu's dismay at the traveler's lack of understanding was visible in his wide-eyed gaze. "Why, *here* of course." His wrinkled, bent finger came up and tapped his temple. "In my head."

Chapter 14

Nolan lay on his side, covered by the woolen blanket pulled up under his chin. He, along with the other travelers in the group, were lined up underneath the lean-to with their feet facing the fire pit. One of the giants from Kaleel watched the fire, keeping the embers alight while using just the right amount of sand to keep the flames from signaling their position to any who might be watching. The sand in the embers maintained the heat Nolan could feel in his toes protruding from the end of the blanket.

Ranaa lay in front of him just out of reach of his steady breaths. He pushed away the impulse to lift his blanket, wrap his arm about her and pull her form into his body. He needed to focus on the mission at hand and, even more so, the mission he knew would come to bear before the night was over.

In his mind, Nolan recounted the discussion with Chu and the revelation of the secrets of the Second and Third Keys housed in his mind. The old wizen said their path lay toward Shadowrise, a city at the northern tip of the province of Allanmore. Nolan stopped Chu's words at that point. He feigned weariness from his wound and said they would continue the conversation later. However, in actuality, he didn't want any further information regarding their destination divulged. Having time to mull over the events since their arrival on Iswan, Nolan came to the conclusion there was more than just chance keeping their foes seemingly one step ahead of them at every turn. He agreed with Chu's words – "Nothing was left to luck." There must be a spy amongst them. How else could the bandits have known their course of action? Even though he'd changed their plans at the last moment, how could their enemies have known their destination at Wolar's Fang and arrive there before them?

The slight sound was barely audible. Nolan, his ears tuned with anticipation, distinguished the sound. Behind him, a blanket was being pulled back. He closed his eyes tight as his heart struggled with mixed emotions. The sound of quiet steps leaving the lean-to verified his conclusion. However, he couldn't help but think, *if only he had done so days earlier, then perhaps Germaine would still be alive.* He had difficulty not shooting to his feet and killing the spy on the spot, but he knew there would be accomplices. He needed to find out whom the traitor reported to.

Nolan waited a few minutes, making certain the spy had cleared the lean-to. Silently, he pulled back his own blanket while being careful not to wake Ranaa or any of the other travelers. Germaine had died because of him as had Deahna. He didn't even try to put the emotions aside. Tonight—revenge would be his.

In a fluid motion, he pushed himself up with one hand while pushing his feet into his boots that had been strategically positioned earlier in the evening. Rising, but remembering to keep his back stooped to avoid his head hitting the roof of the lean-to, he reached down for his leather coat. There was a slight rustle and Nolan froze. The giant Kaleel savage, who was sitting on a stump in front of the fire's embers, stirred. His chin, resting against his chest, shifted for a moment. Once Nolan heard the steady deep breaths of sleep return, he stepped quietly over each of his sleeping companions. Seeing the one empty blanket, he ground his teeth together. The soft, leafy branches they each used to lay on were pushed into a pile to give the illusion someone was still under the blanket.

As Nolan stepped out the side of the lean-to, he pulled his belt from the small branch and wrapped it around his waist. Again, he held back his tears and put his efforts toward holding back his rage. The belt and the two long knives hanging from them belonged to Germaine. Long ago, the warrior told Nolan if ever something happened to him, he wanted Nolan to proudly wear them.

Nolan stepped out from the starlight into the darkness of the forest. He took a deep breath, smelling the bark, the leaves, the soil and the insects making their lives within it. *It wasn't so different from his past life in the forests of Earth,* he thought. Flexing his shoulder, he winced. The pain was slight, but his shoulder still felt weak as remnants of the poison from the arrow was still in his body. Most had been washed from his wound by Chu, and the poultice drew much of the remaining death from his blood. However, his body fought the small remaining amount trying to infiltrate his nervous system. It kept his arm feeling weak and also kept his psychic abilities limited, but it wasn't enough to deter him. He was the First Key. He was the leader of the group and expected to be the leader bringing peace to mankind. This was something he needed to do alone. In his mind, he laughed, realizing he wasn't sure if he needed to prove his leadership more to his followers or to himself.

Ahead, to his left, he heard a crackle of branches. His head snapped toward the noise, and he shifted silently in that direction. With knees bent, he walked on the balls of his feet. After 30 yards, he pressed his back against a wide tree trunk before sliding down into a squat. Being careful to control his breathing, he listened. After a few moments, he heard the crackle again. As Nolan slid his face around the edge of the tree, he saw a dark figure in the distance moving through the brush. The crackles of the spy's feet against the pieces of leaves and branches covering the ground came regularly. The shadow thought himself far enough from their camp and clear of any risk of being heard.

Nolan slid from behind the tree and moved another 30 yards across the thick forest. This time, he squatted behind a large, jagged rock jutting up through the forest floor. The spy was some 30 yards ahead and still oblivious to the fact he was being followed. Nolan kept to the shadows and darted from tree to tree, keeping his impatience in check. His heart urged him to fire an energy ball toward the spy and be over with it, but first he needed to know where he was going, and, more importantly, who was the man going to meet.

Nolan followed for another 20 minutes. They were now far from their camp. The forest ended and turned into a meadow covered with knee-high grass. The spy pulled his hood close over his head and hastened his steps across the tall grass to the woods continuing once again on the other side. Being wary, Nolan skirted the meadow and kept to the shadow of the trees ringing it. As he came closer to the point where the spy re-entered the forest on the far side, he heard muffled voices.

"Are you sure?"

Nolan was crouched behind a fallen tree. With his eyes just clearing the top, he peered into the darkness. The voice had come from a tall figure facing the spy.

"I'm telling you all I know. They're going to Shadowrise. From there, I don't know," the spy said.

"The last time we talked, you said they were going to the King's Council being held in Sherto."

"That is still the plan," the spy said. "We will go across South Palor to the city of Sherto. From there, we'll continue to Shadowrise, and no, the wizen didn't give any further clues as to the location of the Keys."

"A wizen!" the tall stranger blurted out.

"Yes. I'm not sure what to make of him," the spy whispered. "He says he knows where the Keys are."

The tall stranger paced back and forth under the forest branches before returning to face the spy. "Wizens are bad luck. They're half-crazed savages from the plains who profess to know magic. Surely the others don't believe him?"

The spy shrugged. "They do."

The tall stranger lifted his hand to his bearded chin, contemplating the new information. His face snapped up to the spy's. "Okay. We'll play on for longer since we need to know the location of the Keys. Find out from the wizen where he believes the keys to be. Once that is established, kill him."

The spy nodded his understanding.

With the discussion at an end, the tall stranger turned, and his long cloak whirled with his motion, revealing a long sword strapped to his side. He heard the movement of air, but it was too late. He had only begun to turn when the long, serrated knife blade pierced his spine. With arms and legs limp, his lifeless body fell forward into the moist dirt covering the forest floor.

Instantly, the spy flung himself headlong behind a cluster of boulders. An orange glow came from the other side as the spy's face slid up into view. His eyes looked furtively from side to side for the mysterious assailant.

Nolan stepped out from behind the fallen tree. His face was set in a determined gaze toward the boulders. "Come out. We'll end this now."

Larm's face pushed up over the boulders for a second time. His hand, surrounded by the orange energy afforded him by his Toltec blood, grasped the corner of the rock. "Why—so you can kill me in cold blood?"

"I want to know why you did it!" Nolan's anger boiled over into his words while the purple fireball at his fingertips pulsed.

Larm jumped to his feet. "Why did I do it? Because everything you are is blasphemous! The thought of my Toltec blood mixing with that of the other races in your veins makes me want to vomit!"

"I can't help who I am or refuse the path set before me."

Larm's eyes were wide, and his body was shaking with anger. "Listen to you! Who do you think you are?" His eyes narrowed into dark slits and his voice lowered. "Purebloods and sculls have lived in a balance for more than centuries, and within the pureblood races, destiny has set our path. Who are you to change it?"

"The path you speak of has littered planes with death."

Larm pointed at Nolan. Sparks of energy fell from the fireball at his fingertips. "The strong survive, and the weak are cleansed from the Athar. Is this so unknown to you? Such is the case with all life on every plane. I ask again, who are you to interfere?"

Nolan had enough of the conversation with the zealot. "I'm the same man who is going to kill you where you stand if you don't surrender yourself to me right now."

Larm's hand began to drop, but his eyes, dark with despair, suddenly rekindled with a glimmer of hope. He saw the fireball at Nolan's fingers flickering. Pointing toward Nolan's hand, he said, "The poison still flows through your veins and weakens you. I just might not be the one to die today." His hand rose with the fireball on it providing a menacing message.

Beads of sweat broke out on Nolan's brow. He knew Larm's words to be true. He was having trouble keeping his fireball active. In a few moments it would flicker out altogether. He had to act now. Throwing his arm forward, the purple ball flew toward Larm. The Toltec spy threw his own fireball. The two met in a shower of sparks 20 feet high just in front of Larm.

Nolan felt dizzy for a moment, causing him to almost lose his balance. He heard Larm's laugh across the span, bringing him back to focus. He lifted his hand, trying to will another fireball onto it, but there was nothing. Panicked, he turned and ran. He saw the glow behind him in his peripheral vision and threw himself to the side, rolling in the wet grass. The orange fireball sped by, crashing into a tree and exploded into a thousand sparks just ahead of him.

Nolan was up on his feet and running before the light from the sparks faded. He jumped over rocks and logs in the darkness while ducking low hung branches. In the distance, he could hear Larm crashing through the forest behind him. This time he did not see the orange fireball, but sensed the heat from it just before it hit. At the last moment, he willed his shield.

The green, weakened energy field crackled into life just in time, barely protecting him from the fireball, but the contact threw him ten feet forward into a thicket of brush.

Larm strode forward. With another fireball ready at his fingertips, his other hand pushed through the brush. "You might as well come out and make this simple. I'll be merciful," Larm said through clenched teeth.

There was a flash of light as Germaine's long knife sprang from the brush. From his pounce, the Earthman's momentum followed the stroke toward Larm's heart. However, Larm was quick for a big man, and as he turned his body, the long, serrated edge of the knife missed the killing blow, providing only a painful flesh wound in Larm's shoulder.

The big man howled in pain. He turned to look at Nolan, who was once again on his back, panting in exhaustion and pain. "Maybe I'll not make this so simple for you after all." His hand rubbed the wound, covering his fingers in blood. Wild-eyed, he dragged his blood-covered fingers down his face, giving it a grotesque appearance in the light of the fireball humming at the fingertips of his other hand.

The familiar sound of a sword being pulled from its scabbard turned Nolan cold. Still weak, he began to crawl backward on his elbows. Larm's mouth was open and frothing like a wild animal's as he came in for the kill.

There was a blur of motion behind Larm followed by a loud *thunk* echoing off the surrounding trees. Blood spewed from the big man's mouth as he fell on top of Nolan. After a few moments, Larm's eyes rolled back in their sockets. The man's dead weight had knocked the wind from the Earthman. As Nolan tried to gain his breath, he saw thick, blue fingers grasp Larm's shoulder and pull the body from atop of him.

Nolan looked up and was not sure he saw what his eyes told him. He closed them tight and tried again. When they opened, he saw Tok standing above him, his war hammer tight in his fist with blood dripping from the stone business end of the weapon. His yellow eyes looked at Larm. As they narrowed, his lips pursed together, letting fly a ball of spit on the dead man. The Stor then turned back to Nolan. In a raspy voice, words came from Tok's lips. "I always thought he was a freaking idiot."

Nolan pointed up and tried to speak, but his lungs were devoid of the air required to do so. Nevertheless, with his eyes showing the shock of what he heard, he tried again, but barely a whisper came out. He repeated the indiscernible words a second time. Tok bent to one knee and put his ear close to the Earthman's lips. Nolan tried to take a deep breath and coughed. Finally, with a great effort, the whisper came again. "You can talk."

Tok lifted his face. "Best we keep that our secret for now." He winked at the Earthman as his lips broke into a wide smile. Through his large teeth, Nolan heard the rasp. The Stor was laughing uproariously.

Chapter 15

"Look at my boots!" Julian cried out.

The four military advisors, walking just behind the supreme commander of the Toltec forces, stopped and shifted nervously while their eyes were averted from Julian's.

"They're covered in mud!" Julian continued his tirade. "How am I supposed to maintain the respect of the men and women who are to follow me?" He raised his chin and lifted his arm over his head with his hand making frantic circles. "Come forward, Jelan!"

The big man from Kaezzar strode forward. Since Julian had selected him as his personal bodyguard, the former convict was never far from Julian's side. Once in front of Julian, he clicked his heels together. At the same time, he dropped his chin to his chest and held his head on a slight cant. "Yes, Commander," his deep voice answered.

Julian crossed his arms while leaning back on one straight leg. "Tell me about first impressions."

Jelan looked down at the diminutive man. "They're very important. Many would profess a first impression is the lasting memory one has of a person or an event. It can be so strong as to overshadow subsequent events even if they are, in fact, more telling."

Julian lifted his front foot, then lowered it sharply, digging his heel into the grass. Small splatters of mud shot back onto his other boot. "Look at that. What first impression does it leave?"

"It shows you're a leader who isn't afraid to toil in the midst of those who serve you, and one to work as hard as they do, fighting as hard as they otherwise might not."

Julian shook his head from side to side. "Your answer shows why you'll always be a follower instead of a leader." Julian peeked around him. "Generals, best you listen to this as well." Inhaling deeply, he checked his impatience with the group. "For me to *work*—" his lips had difficulty even forming the word "—in the fields as an ordinary soldier isn't what they want to see. I'm their commander, and they need to have confidence in me." Julian's hands slid forward and out as if to implore his subordinates to understand. "They need to know my focus is on planning the battle yet to come. They need to know the next strategy I develop will be shrewd and successful, for if miscalculated, my decisions could cost many of their lives." His voice turned hard and cold, barely above a whisper. "How can they do so when I appear to not even have the foresight to keep my boots clean?"

Jelan's lips stretched into a wide line. Julian had seen the appearance often enough, and in his mind, assumed it was one of deep thought and contemplation. In reality, the drawn appearance was one Jelan had practiced. The big man found, if he froze in this position, he could keep from breaking out into laughter.

A sharp *crack* broke the cumbersome silence as Julian whacked Jelan in the shoulder with the riding crop he carried with him. "Where is my ride? I've been on Iswan for four days now, and still you haven't found me a suitable mount."

"Our field company has been scouring the countryside for something domestically suitable. There are creatures known as palusas that we are considering."

"Well, get me one!" Julian screamed.

Jelan's eyes narrowed. "The palusas have a volatile temperament since they don't take well to a rider. In fact, from what the locals have told us, taking on a palusa on short notice has been deadly for many experienced riders."

The commander's face went white. His throat moved in a dry swallow. "At least in that you've made a wise decision. However, it doesn't take from the fact I need a mount to properly survey the field of battle."

"We've found another option that will have to do. There are wild creatures roaming the cliffs bordering this great plain. They're known by the savages who live here by the name *sakcaj*. They are primarily beasts of burden, although in times of drought, they've been eaten by the natives to stave off famine. Our scouts found a herd of 40 such beasts and are presently breaking them to saddle. Soon enough you will have your mount."

With his finger pressing on his lower lip, Julian asked, "Is there a white one?"

"Of course, Commander," Jelan replied while his face still held the bemused, wide-lipped countenance. "A large one, white with a pink mane matching the creature's lips, is the first to be broken."

The riding crop came up and slapped Jelan in the chest again. "See to the progress." Julian turned and surveyed the field, mumbling, "Incompetent fools. Muddy boots and a riding crop without a ride—how silly is that?"

Julian's self-centered focus was broken by a large *crackle* on the other side of the field. His eyes followed the rolling swale, first angling down, and then back up the other side of the subtle, grass-covered valley. A good mile away, on the enemy's right flank, a wide section of the field turned opaque. One by one, men became visible, replacing the telltale signs of transposition. Julian also felt it in his mind as so many hopping at once sent a rumble through the Athar. Julian raised his hand over his head to block out the sun and started counting. He gave up at 50 and realized he hadn't been quick enough to keep up with even one hundredth of the marks as they appeared. He raised his arm and snapped his fingers.

Kouros strode forward, handing Julian a pair of binoculars. Kouros, being a native to Kaezzar, was one of the generals he kept close. Raising the binoculars to his eyes, Julian surveyed the group of Celtae just materializing. They wore maroon uniforms with a wide, white, leather collar. Another white band crossed their chests. As he looked closer, Julian saw different types of weapons slung across their backs. A third had bows, another third swords and the remainder had killing balls. Seeing these, Julian sucked in his breath. He had only *heard* of killing balls. The metal, spiked balls, four inches in diameter, were connected to a solid wooden shaft via a short section of stout chain. Even a heavily armored warrior stood little chance against an accurate blow.

"Who are they?" Julian asked.

Kouros had been looking through his own binoculars. "It's not good," he stammered.

"Why?"

"They're from Tenreve. Even worse, the colors they wear reveal them as the Marauders. Our intelligence indicated they were not coming, but we should have known better. If the Kre are here, we should've known the Marauders of Tenreve would follow." Kouros's voice was shaky.

"The Kre can look after them."

"I hope you're right. The two groups have fought many battles over the centuries with each giving as good as they take, but take heed, the Marauders should not be underestimated."

Julian brushed away the comment. "They are just men."

Kouros raised his hand and pointed across the field. "Do you see the leather collar and band across their chests?"

"Yes, why do you ask?"

"The leather comes from a large and ferocious reptile native to their world. Its head is almost as long as its body, and the razor-sharp teeth filling its mouth run almost the entire length of the head. The great lizards are called killers. No, it's not what they do—it's what they are. As such, the name is used interchangeably for both their description and their ferocious acts. These Marauders are the fighting elite, and only the selected few can join them. The selection process is done by the killers. A hopeful candidate fights one to gain the privilege of skinning it, so they can wear the colors. Not surprisingly, the wider the grain in the leather, the larger the creature. Regarding survivors, I understand the fall-out rate to be some 30 percent."

When Kouros turned to Julian, the commander had lowered his binoculars and was staring at him, his mouth hung open.

"What did you expect? This is war. War has warriors on both sides," Kouros said.

Julian cleared his throat and walked back to the other generals with Kouros following close behind. He turned to look at Dragos, the tall Sillian general. "How many Toltec are here?"

Dragos shifted his shoulder, and a small book slid down the length of his arm only to be caught neatly by his long fingers. He flipped open the pages, speaking as he read. "There are 15 thousand Sillians, 18 thousand Kaezzarites and eight thousand Kre."

Julian raised an eyebrow. "Only eight thousand Kre?"

"Theron said eight thousand was all he could raise on short notice. Another ten thousand are expected over the next two days," the Sillian offered.

Julian turned and looked upon his troops. The Kre had taken up a position just left of the army's center. On the slightly angled grade, smaller tents pockmarked the downward slope. Breaking the scene of long, yellow, grass dominating the top of the hill, Theron's large tent broke the breeze that straightened the Kre nation flag set on its peak. The Kre vice-prime spent little time on the field of battle. Julian's invitations for dinner were respectfully declined, leaving him confused. The Kre's single-handed efforts had pushed him into the position of commander, yet the vice-prime remained elusive. At the same time, Julian, remembering the serious wounds of past battles visible on the warrior now statesman, could not muster the courage to question him. For now, from a distance, he would take him at his word.

"How many are there in total?" Julian asked.

Dragos mumbled as he calculated numbers in his head. "Taking the numbers just mentioned and another 13 thousand from the smaller Toltec outlying planes, there are 47 thousand warriors in total. Another 30 thousand are committed, and, we are told, on their way."

"How many Celtae are there?"

The Sillian looked up across the valley. "With the latest arrivals, there are 32 thousand."

The general from Malagar, standing next to Dragos, blurted out, "What are we waiting for? We have the numbers, so we should attack now!"

"Not yet, my anxious comrade." Julian chuckled. "The battle will grow. When we're double the size we are now, then we'll attack. This will be the battle of battles—one that will wipe the Celtae from the face of the Athar. Look at the cliffs to the west." Julian pointed to the distant, jagged cliffs half a mile away. In the rock wall was a deep crevice, cut by the constant erosion from the river springing from its base. In the waning hours of the afternoon, the river was quiet, snaking back and forth across the eastern side of the wide valley only to be lost to view as it was consumed by the high, yellow grasses monopolizing the horizon. "Your faces will be chiseled in the rock face, forever to look over the field where the Celtae were destroyed in the battle to finally leave the Toltec as the supreme power in the Athar. Just above you will be *my* image—the man selected by the people to lead, succeeding where our forefathers could not."

The generals looked at each other. Julian, hypnotized by the far rock wall, had all but forgotten they were even there.

An opaque circle, appearing further up the Toltec hill, broke the awkward moment. Five soldiers quickly drew their swords and surrounded the image beginning to form, but they relaxed once they recognized the figure of Captain Renier. He was wearing a thin, dark cloak spotted with dirt as was his ragged beard. The man was visibly tired.

Seeing his captain, without excusing himself from his generals, Julian strode up the slope to Renier. Putting his hand on the man's shoulder, he coaxed him to walk out of earshot of the others. "You've something to report?" Julian asked.

Renier was tired, blinking his eyes to keep them open. It was far across Iswan, but still, he had to hop back to Kaezzar, wait three hours and then make a second hop to the battlefield. "Unfortunately, the news isn't good. Both our informant and our spy were found dead not far from the point where Nolan Harrison's sloop washed up on shore. It will not be so easy to track them now."

With anger filling his eyes Julian slapped the crop downward. He grimaced as the stinging pain across his thigh was more intense than anticipated. "What now? Where are they going?" he hissed.

Renier ran his fingers back through his dark hair. "I have other informants throughout the provinces of Iswan. There will be a King's Council in Sherto, and it's most likely the group will make their way there."

Julian's face brightened. "Of course they will. These sculls are impetuous. They'll meet and try to decide what to do with us. By now they know there are 70 thousand purebloods on their world with still more to come. I'm sure they are not amused."

Renier looked across the valley. On the far shallow slope, thousands of soldiers waited. They were relaxed, knowing the battle would be some time in coming. The Celtae forces, much as their own, did not mingle. There were five separate blocks of tents with each flying their own flags. At the center were the yellow and blue-clad soldiers of Bailemor. He had never come to face them, but history reported them to be fierce and merciless. He turned back to Julian. "Don't underestimate the Anasazi who live on the far coast."

"They're a small group. They dare not enter this fray."

"Not on their own," Renier responded. "But if they convince the kings of Iswan to unite and join them in repelling our forces, they could be very dangerous."

"Then make sure it doesn't happen, Renier!" Julian yelled. Catching himself, he put his hand on the captain's shoulder and turned him away from the general's whose attention had been caught. "You're in charge of my covert intelligence forces during this campaign. To date you have not been so successful. Make the difference now." He looked into Renier's eyes. "Don't let me down, so don't let the people of Iswan unite."

Straightening his back, Renier saluted. "Of course, Commander."

Julian slapped him lightly on the shoulder with his crop. "Now go rest for a few hours before you hop back to your work." He walked away from the captain. The discussion was over. As he moved to his own tent at the furthest point up on the hill, he motioned with his left hand. The Malagar general caught the movement and hurried up the hill to meet him. By the time the guards in front of the open canopy let General Tyril by, Julian had poured a cool drink. Surveying the soon-to-be battlefield from under the canvas awning, he sipped from the side of the frosted cup.

"Is there something I can do for you, Supreme Commander?" the general asked.

"Your attitude earlier indicated your impatience with our wait."

General Tyril hesitated for a moment, then straightened himself, pushing out his chest. "I'm a warrior and come from a long line of warriors. Fighting is what we live for and one day we will die for. Waiting is something I don't suffer through very well."

"Then I have a mission for you to help take the edge off your boredom."

The general's eyebrows lifted with interest.

"I understand on Malagar there is a dark caste." Julian sipped the cool drink.

"There is a rumor, but it is only a rumor," the general replied.

"Really?" Julian lowered himself into a cushioned chair, crossing one leg over the other. "In the past year and a half there have been four mysterious deaths in royal families near your home plane in the Athar. These reports, or as you suggest rumors, would indicate these Phantoms, or more accurately these assassins, come from the dark caste of Malagar."

General Tyril raised an eyebrow innocently. "I didn't know the rumors were so famous."

Julian chuckled coyly. "Come now, General. There are very few eyewitnesses. There are only tales of seeing shadows and hearing sounds, but when one looks, there is nothing there. Phantoms are a good term for these men. A few who have lived to survive a sighting tell of dark-blue cloaks that move with the night and a streak of white hair they color just before their missions. They say it is their mark—the mark of death."

The general grinned. "The rumors of these Phantoms appear to travel far and wide. I've always considered that if they were real, then they wouldn't be Phantoms hence—not so mysterious. Consequently, they would not be so dark and not so deadly."

One crossed leg was well balanced on the other, and Julian bobbed the top one up and down. "Your point is taken especially after being so wisely explained. If only these Phantoms were real, I would order you to secretly bring ten of them to Iswan, and stagger them north to south across the length of this river world. Nolan Harrison must not get to the battlefield."

The general's grin grew wider. "It's a shame my knowledge leads only to the rumor. However, I'll ask some of my colleagues who frequent darker circles than I. If men are found, I'm sure within eight hours, they would be dispersed between us and this false prophet—the one described as the First Key."

Julian tipped the glass over his lips, emptying it. His gaze remained on the warrior. "Have a good afternoon, General."

Once General Tyril left, Julian slapped his glass down on the wooden arm of the chair. "Word games," he mumbled. *It's a good thing I'm not as impatient as I was in my youth. After all, these little politically correct interludes are necessary.* He tried to convince himself. *I have mellowed my mood with people such as this excuse for a general they send from Malagar—and even with Renier. Failing twice, I should have killed him, but now he is afraid—afraid for his life should he fail again, and his thoughts are correct. If he should fail a third time, the Phantoms will have an additional target on Iswan.* Julian smiled, thinking proudly of how far he'd come and how much he had grown. *Surely, when the battle is won, and I return to Kaezzar with Nolan Harrison's head hanging from the saddle of my white—what did Jelan call it—sakcaj, then I'll be ordained Senator for War and only be one step away from Prime of Kaezzar.*

Chapter 16

"Let's rest for a few minutes," Nolan said.

Tok nodded in acknowledgment. He surveyed the various rocks alongside the path, finally heading toward one he surmised would give his behind the least amount of discomfort. He lowered onto it, followed closely by Stirm who sat next to him. Chu, who seemed remarkably resilient for an older man, remained on his feet, leaning against a larger rock projecting out from the side of the mountain that shot skyward from the blue ocean below.

As Nolan sat on a flat slab of gray shale spattered with freckles of quartz sparkling in the afternoon sun, he sensed Ranaa next to him. She slid across close enough to encroach on his space, but not close enough to appear intimate to those around them. He leaned forward and looked down the 500-foot drop to the hidden lagoon and the small sloop that had been their cramped home for the last two days. As he peered over the steep edge spattered with razor-sharp, volcanic projections, he said, "Do you think Daniel is still angry?"

Ranaa's light chuckle sang on the cool air. "It has only been two days. I'm sure he has settled some, but he'll remember your words for some time to come."

Momentarily, his face twisted into a grimace, remembering Daniel's stinging words the morning following the death of Larm. With his fellow travelers still in shock with the grim news, but nevertheless prepared to depart for Sherto and the King's Council, Nolan announced to his fellow travelers that their plans were being altered.

"You knew Daniel would never accept your proposal to go on to Shadowrise alone with only Chu. Your explanation that a young man traveling with a frail older man would attract less attention, allowing a safer passage, was not convincing. You didn't really expect Daniel to accept such direction, did you?"

Nolan kicked a pebble over the edge. It toppled down, bouncing down the irregular face of the mountain and was lost to sight long before it ever hit the water below. "I knew he would resist, but then it was just a starting position. I also knew, ultimately, the group had to be split. Since we were gaining notoriety and enemies faster than we could travel, I didn't believe such a large group traveling together would be a wise decision."

"I was sincerely worried about Daniel when you offered the explanation. He's not as young as you or I. His face turned so red with rage. I've never seen him like that before."

"I've known him longer than you, and I've never seen him filled with so much frustration. Unfortunately, it was unavoidable." He looked at her and playfully poked her in the shoulder. "You weren't much better. The flaming look to your eyes said it all," he said with a smug grin.

She put both fists on her waist as her eyes narrowed. "This all went exactly as you planned, didn't it?"

"In some ways, it did. I knew a middle ground had to be reached. So here we are with the two of us, Chu, Tok and Stirm. Of course, Garawin had to go to Sherto. After all, he's the Prince of Rivenloc driving the Soichaint. Daniel would have to join him, showing the alliance between the Anasazi and the Celtae. Some evidence indicating the peace movement was all-encompassing was critical. I was quite sure Rin would be returning to Lomond Woods, so he wouldn't go with either group."

"I don't follow you. How did you know?" she said in a tone reflecting her curiosity.

"Traveling back across Iswan would be even more dangerous than our original eastward trip. Even though the group was smaller, it would be easy for our enemies to surmise our next destination would be the King's Council. Purebloods could easily make the trip safely by hopping in and out of this plane. Rin, being a scull, could not do the same. Besides, someone had to go back to Lomond Woods to prepare the woodsmen for the battle to come."

Even though she had difficulty being angry with the man she loved, a brief frown crossed her face. "So, you had it all figured out?"

"Yes, except for Tok. That was a big surprise."

Two days ago, the group had been arguing vehemently in the shallows in front of what was left of the sloop. Sub-arguments broke out within the general argument with some questioning their direction. Rin wanted to go with one group or the other. Ranaa and Daniel would not hear of leaving Nolan even for a moment. Garawin was frustrated and at that point didn't much care what the direction was. He just wanted to move on to Sherto, one way or the other. The words melded together into an irritating drone, signifying the deterioration of the conversation.

Tok's raspy voice attempted to cut through the banter. "Excuse me." There was no response. The verbal combatants were too engrossed in the discussion. "Excuse me!" Tok's raspy voice, coated with a slight slur, cut through the air.

Garawin turned his head for a moment. His eyebrows, initially lowered in irritation, shot up so high they almost hit his hairline. His jaw lowered, hanging slack as his fingers fumbled. Once they found Daniel's shoulder, they clenched in his coat and shook the worn leather. "The Stor talked," he muttered.

Daniel, his finger raised threateningly, was occupied as he chided the Earthman. He didn't respond other than shifting his shoulder just as he would if an insect landed on it.

The prince's fingers tightened on the leather. He shook it violently, almost pulling Daniel from his feet. "Tok just spoke!" he yelled at the top of his lungs.

The other companions all stopped what they were doing. In unison, they turned and looked at the Stor.

"Yes, the Stor can talk," Tok said. He turned to Stirm and pointed nonchalantly. "And so can he. Say something, Stirm."

Stirm raised a thick, wrinkled finger in the air, and in a voice even deeper than Tok's, said, "'Something.'" His yellow eyes brightened as his raspy laugh was heard over the ocean surf. "I've been waiting a lifetime to be able to do that!" He held his stomach, bending forward as he continued to laugh.

Tok just shook his head and turned back to the travelers who all had a shocked look of disbelief on their faces—all except Nolan who had settled with the concept in the hours since Larm's death.

"I have an idea," Tok said.

Some of the travelers moved as if to listen. Garawin still had his white knuckles clenched in the shoulder of Daniel's coat.

"As purebloods, Garawin and Daniel can easily hop to Sherto and make the Council on time. Rin needs to go back to Lomond Woods and prepare the finest bowman on Iswan for battle. What remains as a question is, what happens to the rest of us?" He looked from face to face. Slowly, he saw the blood returning to the drawn flesh of his audience. "There are more secrets to the Stors than just speech. There's a passage through the Northern Barrens known only to the Stors. We can be at Shadowrise in four days."

"That's impossible," Rin blurted.

"Our enemies will not expect us to return to the ocean and travel north to the Barrens," Tok offered in a deep voice ringing with confidence.

Garawin shook his head from side to side. "I agree with Rin. It will take two days to reach the Northern Barrens and weeks to go over the Craggs." That was the name given to the ominous, cold chain of mountains dominating the northeastern edge of Iswan.

Tok took a deep breath. "I'm 38 years old. In all those years, I've not spoken to a scull or pureblood. I wouldn't do so now if I was not confident in my words. If we go north and then through the passage I speak of, we'll meet you in Shadowrise in four days."

Nolan clapped his hands together. "Agreed!"

"We need to move on." It was Tok's now familiar voice, but it was not in his mind. A cool gust of air spiraling up the side of the mountain hit him squarely in the face, bringing his focus back to the present. Turning on the slab of shale, he turned to Tok and asked, "How much further do we have to go?"

Tok stood up stiff-legged, letting the strap supporting the pack settle comfortably on his broad shoulder. "We'll travel another two thousand feet up. It'll take another five hours."

Nolan took one last look down the precipice. Far below, he could barely discern the bobble of the small sloop they had commandeered in South Palor. Seeing the flash of gold, the fisherman had been more than happy to part with the sturdy vessel.

Two days on the cramped boat slashing through the waves, pushed along by the northern winds, put their nerves on edge. Thankfully, Tok navigated the craft into the hidden cove. From the ocean the peninsula of rock visually blended into the mountain in the background. Even the winding path hewn into the volcanic rock was impossible to see from ocean level. Both the lagoon and the trail zigzagging up the steep incline were invisible to any unsuspecting travelers below.

Nolan wrapped his arm around Ranaa with his fingers rubbing her far shoulder as the pair followed Tok, Stirm and Chu upward. The touch only lasted a moment. It was all Nolan would allow. Turning her face up to him, she smiled. There were no walls or barriers, only reaffirmation of the feelings so strong, words were not worthy to describe them. These moments passing between them were played out on a higher level, one where layers of mortal existence were peeled away, leaving only one's bare and unconditional soul for the other to see.

As quickly as the moment came, it left. In silence the travelers trudged up the stone trail. It wasn't long before their thighs ached, and their lungs were laboring with the thinner air.

They stopped briefly several more times before Nolan asked, "Why would anyone come up this path?

Tok, his blue-black hair speckled with snow, replied, "Not many people at all would come this way. It dissuades many from continuing on, and that would be the point."

It was after the next sharp bend in the trail when Tok said, "We're here."

"But the path continues on," Ranaa said. Careful not to dislodge the bow and quiver of arrows from her shoulder, she pointed off into the distance.

"There's an excellent observation point still thousands of feet in the distance, if you were really interested. It's another deception to keep curious eyes from the back door to Storlock," Tok said.

"Storlock?" Chu questioned. It was the first words through his lips since he complained about the cold when they left the sloop several hours ago.

"Storlock is our home. You'll understand soon enough," Tok replied as he looked down at the snow-covered trail.

At this point along the edge of the mountain, the path widened into a small plateau. Tok shuffled his feet through the snow, keeping the leathery soles on the stone surface underneath. He moved in a path back and forth in line with the mountainside, making small drifts of the light snow covering the ground. He stopped suddenly when a light thud indicated his toe contacted something solid. Nolan was curious about Storlock, but Tok's attention to the ground brought his there also.

Bent over, Tok was pushing aside the layer of snow. He took a moment to wave to Stirm. "Come help me. It is here," Tok said.

The travelers walked to Tok, looking down at the uncovered area. A door comprised of thick wooden planks held together with ornate steel bands lay on the ground. There was a large steel ring threaded securely into the top. Connected to it was a chain, frozen to the ground on either side of the door. The rust on the large hinges at the bottom was a sign indicating the door's lack of use.

Pulling the Stor war hammer from his belt, Tok gave two solid blows to the chain. Freed from the layer of ice, he lifted one end, motioning Stirm to do the same with the other. The two Stors pulled, but their feet slid along the icy stone surface. Nolan, Ranaa and even Chu took hold of a link of the thick chain. Together, they pulled a second time. The ice seal cracked and the door pulled up an inch. The rusty hinges creaked and the door slammed shut.

"Again!" Tok yelled.

As the words left his lips, the group heaved in unison. The door pulled open, creaked, but this time left a foot-wide opening.

"Again!" Tok repeated the command.

The door creaked and slowly moved another foot. The group took small steps backward. With each one, the great door opened further. Once over its center, it teetered, and each traveler scrambled to safety. Tok gave one final pull on the chains, and then followed their lead by scurrying to a safe distance. The great door careened back, thudding into the snow, and a great cloud of white snow billowed into the air. When it cleared, a series of chiseled steps were revealed, angling downward into the now uncovered, shadowed opening.

With Tok in the lead, the group carefully descended the steps until they arrived at a small landing. The Stor fumbled his fingers in the darkness until finally the light from the lantern, removed from the small shelf cut in the stone wall, flickered on Tok's blue face. He reached into the shelf again and pulled a barely visible lever. The sound of pulleys and winches could be heard in the stone wall, and slowly, the light from the opening above began to fade. The door above them was being shut. The loud thud was followed immediately by silence. Only the dripping of water from the melted snow broke the eerie ambience.

"Follow me closely," Tok whispered.

Nolan could not help but smile. "Did you hear that thud?"

Tok didn't answer. He just gave him a look that questioned why he would ask a question with an obvious answer.

Nolan gave Tok a quick back-handed slap in the shoulder. "Then why are you whispering?"

Tok's face drew into a somber look, one appearing to question Nolan's intelligence. He left the glare there long enough for Nolan to understand the message before holding the lantern out.

In the flickering light, a doorway could be seen on the far side of the internal landing, and with careful steps the group moved toward it. Nolan was the last through. Being taller, he had to duck to clear the low archway. When he raised his head, it was to see a glint of steel. The point of a short, stubby sword was at his throat, and the others all had swords drawn on them as well. Each sharp sword was held by a uniformed Stor.

Nolan watched the blue creature confronting Tok. The assailant's yellow eyes glistened with curiosity, and then narrowed with rage as he glanced at the humans. Finally, as the eyes turned back to Tok, they opened wide with dismay. "Master Tok! You have returned," he said with confused enthusiasm.

Tok raised a finger and put it to the side of the sword point, pushing it slowly to the Stor's side. "Yes. I've returned."

The other guards slowly lowered their weapons. The leader looked at the humans for a second time, then turned back to Tok with the shock still evident on his face. "You have brought humans," he stammered. "The first humans to ever come to Storlock. The rumors must be true then?" His eyebrows rose questioningly. "The time for the Stors has finally come," he said barely above a mumble.

Tok gave a thick-lipped, wide smile. "It certainly has. Soon, we'll reveal our true selves to Iswan." Tok raised his voice to break the guard from his trance. "Lead us to the city!"

The group was guided through a series of short tunnels, led by the guard and followed by the remainder of the Stors. Making a final turn, the guard abruptly stopped. His fingers turned a small knob set into the wall, and the wide hallway was suddenly bathed in fluorescent light.

"Okay!" Nolan said in a tone louder than intended. "I've held my tongue long enough." The comment was directed at Tok. "First, there are mute Stors who are not so mute. Then I'm told of a city apparently hidden in a mountain range. Now, to top it off, I see the not-so-mute Stors have electricity in the city no one knows of on a world where refined energy isn't allowed."

Tok rubbed his chin as he looked at the Earthman. Dipping his chin, one finger flicked out and pointed up at Nolan's reddening face. "You're frustrated," he said.

"Well, of course! Some answers would be timely. Start with the ability to speak or the lack thereof, whichever you prefer."

Tok pulled on Nolan's arm, keeping the group moving down the lit hallway. "Not speaking has its advantages."

"How so?"

"One listens better when one's mouth is closed. We have Stors serving both sculls and purebloods throughout Iswan. We serve keepers of inn's, fishermen, farmers and also every royal and influential house across the land. There isn't much the Stors do not know."

"Why the elaborate hoax? Just for that?"

Tok grinned. "We're a simple and honest folk. Because of our past that you will learn of soon enough, we have a mission to fulfill. In any case, appearing mute keeps the sculls and purebloods out of our business. They don't see us as a threat."

Nolan tilted his head back and laughed. "I see the electricity, Tok. That's against the Protocols of Iswan. How's that honest?"

They came upon a corner, turning right down an even wider hallway. This one looked sterile with smooth, white floors and walls devoid of seams except at the corners.

Tok kept his smile. Nothing would spoil his mood. It had been over a year since he had been home. "We never signed the Protocols. No one asked us. As such, any deception they might see is their own. We receive a level of respect from those we serve. They don't consider us stupid. Simple would be a better word. They don't bother us, and as a result, they've never found our city."

Having reached the end of the hallway, the guard pushed a button on the wall next to the double doors. The doors slid open once and when they opened a second time, Nolan could do nothing but shake his head in dismay. It was the second elevator ride he'd taken in a week on a world supposedly free of the sins of energy. His dismay grew as the doors slid to a stop.

Nothing could have prepared him for what he was seeing. His stomach lurched up into his throat as he side-stepped forward to grasp the handrail on the other side of the twenty-foot aisle. His stomach felt as if it moved even higher as he peered over the railing. The drop was at least 500 feet deep. Looking across the circular chasm, the far side was half a mile away. Taking a moment to inspect more carefully, he could see the chasm was actually a carefully constructed series of short terraces. Each terrace was ten to twenty feet wide, so the walls of the pit spiraled forever in on itself. Squinting, Nolan could see a small circular courtyard at the very bottom, covered in lush, green vegetation.

"It's amazing." The voice was Ranaa's and came from beside him. She pointed across the chasm to their left. A waterfall fell over the terraces in a fifty-foot-width. It began at the upper level, and toppled end over end smoothly without a ripple in the blue river. Five levels from the bottom, the waterfall slid into a massive basin of circular stone protruding out into the pit. From the large contained pond, a thin blue streak of water spilled out a spout carved at the point furthest out into the pit. The line of blue spilled into a small colorful fountain in the center of the courtyard at the base of the chasm, sending a misty spray, tens of feet into the air.

"This is unimaginable," Nolan whispered under his breath. Dots of blue colored every terrace. As he looked at those closer to his position, he realized they were Stors. Distinguished by their modern attire, they were different from those he had met on the surface of Iswan. Workers wore coveralls and sturdy boots. Business-Stors wore smart, casual suits while the females, being females, had a wide variety of hairstyles. All bustled along the circular terraces. On every fifth level, a track, sizzling with electricity, hung off a sturdier railing ringing the precipice. Short trains hummed along the track, moving at high speed around the continuous curve. The vehicles took the Stors to the shops, homes and factories cut into the back face of the terraces.

Finally, Nolan turned to face Tok. "I see it, but I keep thinking I'll wake up from this dream."

Tok's head bounced on his shoulders as his lips opened with a raspy laugh. The familiarity of the sound lowered Nolan's nervous tension. His clenched fingers relaxed, relieving the pain from his nails that were digging into his palms. The Stor, who was much more than he appeared, waved his hand across the chasm. "The city is very real. Welcome to Storlock."

Chapter 17

The two men trudged through the light, early-morning rain. Their feet moved in unison at a steady pace along the edge of the crushed-stone road. They both wore wide-brimmed hats and long leather coats, not unusual for the season of rain on Crann Bith.

The road, which was really no more than a wide path, made a straight line through a far-reaching field of cane in the Agricultural District of Bailemor. The six-foot-high cane, rich in sugar content, carried pink seedpods at the tips of their thick stalks. In a day or two the field would be a frenzy of man and machine as the pods turned red. This would be the perfect time for the cane to be harvested before the pods exploded and spread their seed, after which the stalks would almost immediately begin to wilt.

Swords would have drawn attention, so both men were armed with long knives hidden under their coats. Their furtive eyes looked up from time to time, but the road remained empty. Only one other wanderer passed them, and he hadn't given them a second glance.

A small, bungalow-style building abruptly broke the sea of cane. The white-washed cement walls were topped with a roof of dried cane stalks stitched together in a tight waterproof weave, and light-brown, wooden shutters were clamped shut over the four windows. The misty rain lingered on the metal latch, drawing a thin red line of rusty water down from it, indicating the shutters hadn't been opened in some time.

Daniel stopped for a moment. "This is the place," he said.

Garawin looked up from under his hat. He gave a slight nod as his eyes glanced up and down the road.

The two men turned toward the structure as their steps caused a small spray of water to spit into the air each time they skirted across a puddle. Daniel wrapped his fingers around the doorknob and paused, looking back one last time. Satisfied they were not being followed, he pushed the door in and entered the single, low-lit room, followed by the Anasazi prince.

The building was nothing more than a rest stop for travelers, or workers during a break from the harvesting in the fields. Simple, wooden benches lined each sidewall, and in the middle of the room were four small tables devoid of color. At the back of the room, bathed in shadows, were two booths with high-backed bench seats.

"Wait for me here," Daniel whispered.

The morning's pensive mood left Garawin in a demeanor void of words. Again he nodded, moving over to rest on one of the benches near the door.

Daniel shuffled toward the booths, first tilting his eyes toward one, then the other. The second booth was occupied by a thin man slouched so far back in the corner of the seat, he seemed part of it. The man had curly, black hair matching the stylish, black beard and moustache surrounding his mouth. His eyes were dark, but brightened as he looked up at Daniel. His arm nonchalantly waved outward, indicating Daniel should sit on the worn cushion opposite him. Once Daniel complied, the man pivoted, pulling his legs, that had been propped up on the bench seat, down onto the floor. He leaned forward, giving Daniel a bright smile. "It's good to see you, brother," he said, holding his arm out.

Daniel's face cracked a smile. He removed his hat and grasped his bond brother's hand. "It's good to see you also," Daniel replied.

A moment of darkness came across Kato Corrowin's face. "You look tired. What have you been up to?" he said with a voice shrouded with concern.

As their arm clasp relaxed, Daniel slouched back in the bench. "Nothing really," he replied sarcastically. "I have been traveling some and trying to help save humanity in my spare time."

Kato clenched his fingers tight into a ball. "Do we really have to talk about this? We've not talked for months and after only a few minutes, here we are on the same sensitive topic."

Daniel's blue eyes were sympathetic. "It is not only my topic these days. It is on the lips of many Celtae, Toltec and scull as well. A large battle is brewing on Iswan. I can't ignore that."

Kato's arm slid up until his elbow rested on the table. His fingers opened imploringly. "For a few minutes, can't we leave it behind?" His eyebrows lifted and his face brightened. "Remember the days when we were young, when we hunted and the sports we played. You always bested me in wrestling, and remember the women." He rolled his eyes as he chuckled.

Daniel rapped his knuckles on the wooden table. Immediately, an older man with an apron tied around his waist slid from a back room toward them. Before the man was half way to the table, Daniel lifted two fingers in the air. The seedy establishment only served one drink, so the message was clear enough. The man turned on his heel and disappeared into the back room.

"I can't help the thoughts filling my mind, Kato," Daniel said. "I remember all those things. I remember our friends who we did those things with. Most of them are dead," he whispered.

The waiter returned from the back room. He placed two shot glasses on the table and left without saying a word. The liquid running through the cane provides a sweet, palatable refreshment. Once fermented and aged, it transformed into cane shot, one of the most potent alcoholic drinks available on Crann Bith.

Kato slid his hand across the table and lifted the small glass to his lips, emptying the contents straight down his throat. Leaning back, he brought up a thumb and forefinger, wiping the corners of his moustache. "So how is this wonder boy of yours—this First Key? Is he still alive?"

Daniel paused, waiting for the fire in his throat from the cane shot to subside. "He is doing remarkably well considering the position he has been put in. *Thrown in* would be an even better term."

"I can see the guilt eats at you. I'll never understand why you so adamantly follow this course of action. If the Athar needs to be saved, or if we need to save us from ourselves, let someone else do it."

Daniel shrugged. "I cannot help who I am. For some, their destiny seems clear early in life. For others, perhaps their path will come in a split moment when the crisis hits."

Kato lifted a finger, waggling it back and forth. "No. I know exactly where that is going. I'm staying out of the business of war and peace."

Daniel's voice was low, but had a bite to it. "You kill people. How can you say you are staying out of it?"

"I kill the enemy," Kato corrected. "War is part of our history. It's the history of every race on every plane."

"Of course, but not to the scale we have as purebloods. On most worlds, war interrupts lives. Here, our lives seem to interrupt the war. It's mad, and even more so, it's sad."

"I'll give you that," Kato said. "But who are we to stop it? It's been going on for centuries. Look what the peace movement has done for you. You're a wanted man here on Bailemor, and you've been proclaimed a traitor to the people. The best you could do for yourself now is to forget about the infernal Soichaint." His voice slipped to a higher, imploring tone. "Walk away from it! Find an obscure world to live on. Find a young woman and live out your life the best you can."

"My path is set," Daniel quickly replied. "Hopefully, one day when the time is right, you will see the way of the Soichaint."

Kato was about to respond, but he was interrupted by the door opening. Three Bailemorians walked in and sat down at one of the tables.

Daniel slid his hat back on his head. "I have been here too long as it is." He began to slide out of the booth.

Kato's hand grasped Daniel's wrist. "Be careful, brother, and stay alive. I wish there was more I could do to help you."

Daniel smiled at his bond brother. "One day hopefully you will. Be well." As he walked to the door, he slid the brim of his hat low over his forehead while his determined, blue eyes once again stared out seeing the world in a different light from most. Garawin was already waiting there. The two men promptly slid out without drawing any undue attention.

Garawin looked at his watch. "We need to hop now," he said as he looked furtively from side to side. Slapping Garawin lightly in the chest, Daniel strode toward the cane field. Followed by the Anasazi prince who put a hand on his shoulder, they entered the canes, pushing aside the thick stalks. The opaque circle began to form around Daniel and quickly stretched to encompass Garawin. Their figures became fuzzy, and before Garawin's trailing foot disappeared into the cane field, Daniel's front foot was stepping on solid ground at the arrival platform on Iswan.

The 20-foot by 20-foot raised, stone platform was in the center of the Rivenloc consulate in the city of Sherto. Being the landing pad for Anasazi transpositions, the platform was in the center of a bright courtyard surrounded by a three-story-high, red-brick fortification. The red brick enclosure was topped with an ornate, wrought-iron parapet running along the entire length of the structure, filling the space between the four high corner towers. Anasazi guards in casual looking rust shirts and light-brown trousers, walked back and forth along the wide ledge at the top of the wall, peering out between the sharp metal spikes.

Sherto was the political hub of Iswan and for many years was the location of general meetings of State as well as the location of the High Court ruling in cross border matters. Each of the nine provinces of Iswan had a consulate of some sort in Sherto. The only unrepresented people were the savages of Kaleel. This seemed to be a mutually acceptable relationship in the eyes of both the men of the provinces and the savages.

Having hopped so often, Daniel easily steadied himself and quickly put the churning of his stomach aside. Once Garawin fully materialized, a captain, carrying a short spear, put the flat, wide blade against his chest and said in a loud voice, "Welcome to Sherto, Prince Garawin!" With those words, a troop of six Outriders snapped to attention with their spears tip up and held tight against their bodies. The Outriders were the specialized, elite soldiers of Rivenloc who were as mysterious as they were ferocious. Although they were trained in every weapon imaginable, the short killing spear was their weapon of choice.

As the pair walked down the three-foot-wide, stone steps leading from the platform, Garawin gave a wave. "Greetings," he said with a wide smile. He turned to face the captain. "How long do we have until the conference begins?"

The captain's face, under long, shiny, black hair, was grim. "The kings were impatient and began early. Your father ordered me to remain waiting by the platform. His orders were clear. As soon as you came, I was to accompany you to the Arena of Kings directly and without excuse." The captain looked away as he said the last words.

Garawin maintained the crisp smile and slapped the captain on the shoulder, relieving his embarrassment. "It's best we hurry along then." The prince turned toward the stone archway cut into the brick wall on the north side of the enclosure. In an instant, on either side, three Outriders with their spears now held out at the ready, lined the prince, Daniel and the captain. They were quickly out on the wide, main road running the length of the political district.

The road was cobblestoned with a wide sidewalk on each side. The soft-soled boots of the Outriders didn't make a sound as the group increased their pace to an easy gait. Since the days of their earliest forefathers, the Rivenloc people had been comfortable running. As children, games of speed and competition to test endurance of foot prepared them for their legacy. Every Rivenloc man, woman and child, over the age of six, could run for miles without much effort. The practiced step, being so inherent in their upbringing, gave those chosen to the Outriders the added caption of *silent killer.*

They passed the gold and silver consulate of North Palor, then the building held by the Mallee, easily distinguished by the globes of stained glass topping the towers with one more colorful than the next. Finally, after passing the Volkar consulate dotted with purple and black stone blocks, they came out onto the wide central square of Sherto. At its center stood the Arena of Kings. The group didn't pause, taking the steps leading up to the primary stratum of the complex, two at a time.

This primary level was decorated with numerous, small courtyards, combining the most beautiful trees and flowers found on Iswan. Garawin and Daniel, with their minds focused on the matter of kings and worlds, didn't take notice as they passed under the block archway in front of the great arena. The Peace Archway, made of perfectly fitting blocks of quartz brought from the far-off mines of Volkar, sparkled in the bright, late morning sun. Additional 20-foot-wide archways ran end over end, circling around the perimeter of the arena. Appropriately, since the archway marked the line of truce for all peoples, it was topped with calming yellow and orange flowers spilling over from delicate vines.

Royal guards in dark-blue livery stood on guard in front of each buttress ringing the oval arena. The stone supports disappeared overhead to meet at one of the three supporting posts that were the core of the arena. The main entry was wide, with numerous thin columns, three-deep, supporting the semi-circular dome of lacquered wood that capped the ornate arena. Around the edge of the dome were the colorful royal shields of each of the nine provinces of Iswan.

The royal guards recognized the Outriders and moved aside, giving the notorious fighters a wide berth. Once inside, they stopped on the entry platform for a moment. This was Daniel's first visit inside the Arena of Kings. The buttresses were visible from the inside, supporting the alternating lengths of wood and glass closing off the roof, creating 30 large ceiling panes. There were three main pylons of stone 20 feet in diameter and equally spaced between their position and the far wall, beyond which were the royal chambers and the council room where, no doubt, the kings were arguing at this very moment. A raised walkway ran from their position to the far wall. At each supporting pylon it smoothly widened, caressing the stone upright, as a snake would hug its prey.

As they resumed their gait along the raised walkway, Daniel looked down into the lower gallery on either side. Stairs intermittently interrupted the walkway's railing, allowing access to the lower level where soldiers from each province relaxed. They wore their colors proudly, and flew their flags and banners. Some sang in deep voices more familiar with war cries than song, and when the Rivenloc mass saw their prince, a great roar shook the arena, vibrating the very foundation of the age-old structure.

At the tall, arched doorway to the royal chambers, Garawin turned and thanked the captain and his Outriders. He gave a last wave to his soldiers and slid into the royal chambers with Daniel close at his heels. Garawin knew the way, but it was mandatory for a royal guard to escort them. They moved down a long hallway and arrived at a wide stairway leading up to another set of closed doors. The royal guard raised a white-gloved hand, indicating they should go on alone.

Garawin nodded and turned to Daniel. "Watch this," he said with a juvenile smile.

Daniel could barely keep up as Garawin took the steps two at a time. As they moved closer, the buzz became more discernable. The kings were indeed arguing. The doors, pushed open by Garawin, crashed into the walls with a thunderous impact, and the room went immediately silent.

"Greetings," Garawin said with the wide smile still on his lips.

Rolan, the King of Mallee and sometimes leader of bandits, was on his feet, leaning over the large, square table. Propped on one hand, the other hand was frozen in mid-air, having just completed a menacing wave at the King of North Palor. His mouth hung open as his dark eyes turned to the Prince of Rivenloc. Finally, his voice came to him as the finger turned and pointed at Garawin. "You! You're the cause of all our problems!"

Garawin, with each hand outstretched, catching the edge of either door as it rebounded off the wall, replied, "Not really. Your people do not have enough to eat because you take too much food and money in taxes. Your people are sick because you continually interfere with the shamans, and lawlessness abounds since you have more bandits than soldiers in your employ." He glared at the Mallee king. "Those issues are no fault of mine."

Rolan's eyes went wide, and spittle came from his lips as words eluded him.

Colinor, King of Rivenloc and Garawin's father, cut in. "Stop that even before it starts, son. This council needs your calming voice and some explanations."

"Agreed." As he walked to his seat next to his father, Garawin said, "My apologies to this revered council." He wondered if any of the kings recognized his deception. The arguing had stopped as he anticipated, and now he had their undivided attention. Pointing to the seat behind him, he motioned Daniel toward it.

Daniel sat back in the cushioned chair. There were two or three advisors in such chairs behind each of the kings. Some were experts at litigation while others were politicians with years of experience. From time to time during the proceedings, they passed notes to the kings providing their opinions.

This was a critical time for Garawin. He was a fine man although there were moments when his emotions would push through his wisdom. There were a few more years to refine his skills before he would be king of his people. During that time, he would assist his father in affairs of State. This was one of those crucial times where a man's character is defined—where a man can prove himself worthy to be a king.

Knowing better than to stand above the kings, Garawin pulled out his chair and lowered himself into it. Controlling his voice to a melodic rhythm, he said, "Please be seated, King Rolan."

It was the closest words to an apology the king would receive from the upstart prince. Rolan crisply straightened the lapels of his robe as he looked triumphantly at the other kings before he took his seat.

Garawin surveyed the room. It was bright with three large windows monopolizing one lengthy wall. Each of these consisted of 30 individual panes of glass etched with small flowers. As the light shone through, it bought the tapestry on the opposite wall to life. The battle scene was skillfully woven into the material with texture such that lithe shadows played over the warrior's faces. The pain, sorrow and exultation bursting from the heroes portrayed in the artwork was breathtakingly accurate.

The prince leaned forward, placing his forearms on the table. He needed to be calm, showing he was in control, and the issue of foreigners about to do battle on this world was also in his control. More than at any other time in his life, he needed to be convincing, but even more so, Garawin needed someone *else* to be convincing.

He glanced from one king to the next, considering each. *That's it,* he thought. King Lothar of Savantee was the one. He was intelligent, brave and lived with a passion for Iswan. He was also one Garawin knew he could turn. *He* was the one Garawin would focus on, playing to his passion so the ideas in the prince's mind would be put forth from King Lothar's lips. To accomplish this, Garawin would need all his silver-tongued ability. With one king pressing the point, only then might the Council of Kings support the Soichaint movement.

"I think you're correct, King Rolan," Garawin began. "I brought Toltec warriors to Iswan." The prince turned and pointed at Daniel. "This man is a Celtae warrior. His deeds are noble and would fill a scroll longer than this great table. He also brought the Toltec here. Yesterday, we buried another Celtae warrior in South Palor. He was a great man who died for the people of this world. The Toltec also followed *him* here. In fact, there are many men and women across this world and many planes of the Athar who would have reason to be killed by the Toltec." He looked each king in the eye. "It has been so through the ages and on many worlds. There is always a reason for a skirmish or a battle, and there is always someone to blame. We always look for a name we can say brought death to our world. One day we will see it is not individual souls who bring this to our world. Rather, it is the system we live in and the norms we accept. Perhaps, this day, we will realize we are leaders and kings with the vision to rise above those following the expectation of finding *someone to blame,* and move on to solving the problem. Are there any in this room who will meet the challenge?" Once again, his gaze pierced into each of the kings, lingering for a moment longer upon King Lothar.

King Molokai of Volkar leaned forward. The light from the window bathed his face with a bright glow, disguising his usually dark countenance. "With all due respect, Garawin, we've all but decided to wait. We'll let the foreigners have their battle on the plains. If a victor can even be proclaimed, their forces will be decimated. They'll leave and not bother us again for many years."

"Or, jubilant on the heels of victory, they might turn their forces west and attack the provinces," King Colinor of Rivenloc added.

"Exactly!" Garawin followed his father's words. "Such has happened before, and it is likely to happen again. The purebloods who have stepped foot on our world have come here for death and destruction. There are already 40 thousand purebloods who have come here uninvited to our world! Are we just to put our tails between our legs and turn the other way? What would our forefathers think? What would our kin, who gave their lives to keep this world free and pure, think?"

Again, Garawin glanced at King Lothar. In the fleeting moment, he looked into his eyes and touched his inner being. In that look, he reminded the Savantee king of his own twin brother whom a Celtae assault squad killed when they were no more than boys. The rumor that Lothar had been frozen in place and unable to act, while his brother attempted to defend himself with a sword heavier than his own weight, had never left the depths of the now great king's mind. The discussion pulled those painful memories to the surface.

King Rolan of Mallee shot to his feet. "We have already decided! We will not foolishly go to a battle we cannot win!"

"Sit down, Rolan!" King Lothar's deep voice echoed in the room. "Grow a backbone. I am not a fool to go to battle just to have my people slaughtered, but this is our land the foreigners have tread on. The act lacks respect." His voice was a low simmer, like a storm about to break over the mountains.

King Rolan waited a moment. Seeing none to challenge Lothar's words, he slunk into his chair.

There was a light chuckle. "You talk of respect over death," the Volkar king said.

"Always," Lothar replied. "If it's the last thing we have, it's our respect from others and more importantly, from within ourselves. What is life when we cower huddled under a blanket or under a canoe in Mallee? This is our land the purebloods have invaded. As such, I want to hear details."

Leaning back, Garawin smiled. His work was done. The seed was planted and the flower was in bloom.

King Colinor of Rivenloc answered. "In small steps, over many years, the Anasazi have embraced peace with the group known as the Soichaint promoting it. We have ten thousand warriors of Rivenloc ready to move at a moment's notice. Another fifteen thousand Anasazi from six allied worlds are ready to hop to Kaleel as soon as we give word."

"That's not enough," the Volkar king stated. "Amongst all the provinces we can muster another forty thousand troops at short notice. My spies tell me that every day scores of Celtae and Toltec troops hop in. There are 40 thousand now, and they are all purebloods with deadly pureblood powers."

"There is a difference," King Colinor offered. "The purebloods fight for the sake of fighting. The Soichaint have a purpose, and we also fight for our land. Our motivation will drive us to victory especially now that the First Key is here on Iswan to lead us."

"You are speaking of the man who slinks across Iswan—the man who killed many of my loyal soldiers," King Rolan seethed.

King Lothar was old with a white beard and wrinkled skin, but his eyes were strong, matching his strength of character. The glare he directed at Rolan cut into him like a razor-sharp knife into butter. The Mallee king shrunk back into his chair.

"Garawin, I understand your friend knows this First Key well. Let him tell us of him," King Lothar said.

With Garawin's nod of approval, Daniel rose to his feet and stepped forward until his thighs pressed into the edge of the thick table. "I will try not to be long-winded, but it is difficult to even know where to begin."

"Take your time," King Colinor prompted.

"In many ways he is an ordinary man with simple beliefs rooted in honor and truth." Daniel pushed his fingers through his hair. "He is also a man who, unfortunately, was given a curse and a burden, carrying the genetic code of all the pureblood races in his blood."

"The fairytale embellishes the mixed blood to be a gift, not a curse," King Molokai of Volkar interrupted with a cajoling smile on his lips.

Daniel's eyes were filled with the depth of truth. The kings, having ruled over their lands and judged many people for many years, could easily recognize it. "It is no fairytale. Both Garawin and I have seen his mixed powers. Even the King of Mallee from his own accounting here has given evidence to corroborate the facts. However, I will repeat, it *is* a curse. His life has changed, and because of whom he is, people around him have died. He cannot go back to his family for fear the death will follow him there. Most people would turn and run from the task, but this simple man has taken the burden and dealt with it. He understands it is his task, although it is not one he has chosen, but nevertheless one thrust unto him.

"So, where is he? The fact he isn't here addressing us personally is insulting," the Mallee king blurted.

"With all due respect to all the kings, his place is on Iswan recovering the Second and Third keys. With all three keys, there is a stronger likelihood bloodshed will be averted. Many pureblood soldiers with such a sign put before them would embrace peace."

"Even though people would call me King, wise choices will easily explain what some perceive as an insult," King Lothar announced. The nod toward Daniel told the Celtae his description was complete, and he could return to his seat.

"The time for words is over," King Lothar said. "It is time to vote in the manner our ancestors have voted over many generations." He pulled a short knife, simple except for the bright-red jewel that decorated the tip of the hilt. With strength one would not expect from the frail arm, he lifted the knife, point down, and thrust it into the table. "The Savantee people are going to the plains of Kaleel to rid our world of the invaders. Who is with me?"

Almost immediately, two more knives were thrust into the table next to the many pockmarks having being put there over many such deliberations throughout the years. King Colinor of Rivenloc and King Ferik of North Palor both had knives vibrating in front of them. Their votes were cast. Seeing his brother Ferik press his knife into the table, the King of South Palor removed his knife from his belt and thrust its tip into the thick table. The motion was duplicated by the Kings of Roevin, Allanmore and Lomond Woods.

King Rolan of Mallee pulled his knife and slid it across the table. "My people are going nowhere." He crossed his arms obstinately. His decision was made long ago.

All the king's eyes turned toward King Molokai. His brow was wrinkled with concern. The decision was more difficult than it should have been. The Volkar king rolled his royal knife over in his fingers. He raised it in front of him, staring at the intricate metalwork as if the answer was there. Finally, he lowered the knife flat on the table with barely a sound. "The province of Volkar will abstain," he whispered.

King Lothar rose to his feet. "So be it! Seven of the nine provinces will unite, and we will drive the invaders from our land. In five days we shall converge on the wildes of Kaleel!" The six other kings who drove their knives into the table rose to their feet and gave a united yell as their fervor was already growing. By the time they reached Kaleel, the united army would be in a nationalistic frenzy not seen for centuries.

One by one the kings left the room with their advisors. King Molokai, his chin hanging lower than it should for one of royal descent, hastened to his antechamber, followed by two aides. Once the thick, wooden door closed behind them, King Molokai, with beads of sweat forming on his brow, turned to the black-bearded man. "I've done as you said. You will make certain your superior knows, and I will be repaid."

Captain Renier smiled at the taller king. "Of course, all will be as I've said. Once the Toltec smash the Celtae army, we'll turn on the Iswan provinces. After all, what is war without loot and plunder? However, when it's all over, we shall leave, and our last task will be to appoint you as High King of Iswan."

"Volkar will be spared the bloodshed?"

"Of course. You have the word of Julian Morenz, supreme commander of the Toltec military forces. After all, a man doesn't succeed to such a position without showing great wisdom, courage and, of most importance, honor in his word."

The shutters on the window at the end of the chamber slammed shut. The wind howled its urgency, but even through the muffling shutter, anyone caring to listen would not help but think, more so than force, the howl was filled with laughter.

Chapter 18

Nolan closed his eyes and lifted his cupped hands to his face. The splash of cool water sent a shiver through his body. The excess fluid fell back into the black, polished-stone sink. As the small rivulets subsided, turning to an occasional drip from his chin, he looked at his reflection in the mirror where his gaze was drawn immediately to his hair. There was more white than brown, and to him, it looked odd. His face was young and strong but still a contradictory trait compared to the white hair stereotypical of old age. The powers he held within were changing him. His mind felt the same, just stronger. His powers grew, little by little, with some at a more accelerated pace than others. More often than not, in a time of crisis, one of the powers would burst forth, frustrating him since it was difficult to tame or control these powers on his terms.

His face was clean-shaven for the first time in two weeks. Without his shirt on, he could see his body changed again since he left Bailemor. It was well muscled, yet thin. *Taut* would be a good word to describe his strong, yet efficient stature.

Turning, he concentrated on the towel hanging from the hook on the wall, willing it closer. First a corner lifted and fell. His brows creased, and again the corner lifted—high enough this time, so the thick towel pulled off the hook. It began to fall and Nolan instinctively flashed his hand out toward it. The towel stopped instantly as if it was held by an invisible string. A line of sweat broke out on his brow as his fingers curled inward, coaxing the towel to hover slowly toward him. Each time the towel began to shake, Nolan would urge it nearer.

"We're going to be late." Ranaa's voice came from outside the corner of the bathroom, and the towel slumped to the floor as Nolan's focus was broken.

Lowering an eyebrow, Nolan took two steps forward and scooped up the towel. As he dried the remaining drops of water from his face, he considered the effort a success. It was the furthest he'd moved an object. He threw the towel back at the hook. Missing by a foot, it slid to the floor. He couldn't help but laugh at the irony of it.

Ranaa's bright smile peered around the corner of the arched doorway. "What's so funny?"

"Just me," he offered.

As Ranaa's questioning lips parted, he pressed his own to them in a quick kiss. He held it long enough to quell her curiosity but not long enough to swell his passion. Before she could blink, he walked past her and pulled his shirt on.

She crossed her arms as she spun on her toes, gazing at his back. Her focus was interrupted by a light knock. Ever helpful, she scurried to the door that was molded from some type of synthetic plastic unknown to her. She bent over to reach the knob, once again proving Tok's holdings were not made for humans.

As the door opened, Tok's bright, yellow smile greeted them. Just behind him was Chu, refreshed from a good night's sleep. As they entered and Ranaa tried to close the door, it bumped into something. Another blue face peeked around the corner.

"My apologies," the worker said. He slid past the half open door carrying a tray of food. Spying the wide table surrounded by short Stor chairs, he hurried over and set the tray down on it and then turned, scurrying out the door as quickly as he came.

"We have a few things to do before we head for Shadowrise," Tok said as he lowered into a chair at the head of the table. As much as Tok played the servant when need be, he had a regal aura about him and knew how to be the perfect host. "Please sit and eat."

It was an odd grouping sitting at the table enjoying the simple meal of fruit, bread and cheese. Ranaa was a scull with no past. Then there was Nolan who had the powers of all the pureblood races within him, yet he kept them pent up inside while much preferring to be considered a very ordinary human who could easily be lost in a crowd. Chu sat next to Tok. The Kaleel savage was obviously not so much of a savage and held the clues to the Keys for survival within his mind. This was the first time the group had an opportunity to sit and talk without the fear of being followed, or the possibility of the powers of the ocean consuming them.

Just finishing a mouthful of bread and cheese, Nolan turned to Chu. "Where in Shadowrise are the Second and Third Keys?"

"I never said they were in Shadowrise," Chu responded nonchalantly with his eyes focused on the platter and which morsel of food to select next.

"Of course you did. You said we needed to travel to Shadowrise," Nolan continued.

Chu raised a finger in the air. "You need to listen better. I indeed said we needed to travel to Shadowrise. I never said the Keys were *in* Shadowrise."

"Then where are they?"

"Not far from the city. It's best to wait until we arrive there to divulge the information. One thing at a time." Chu popped a small piece of cheese into his mouth.

Nolan mumbled under his breath and then looked up at Tok. "How are we to make it to Shadowrise on time? We need to be there by this evening and we're still on the east coast of Iswan."

"There are many things you still have to learn about the Stors." Tok chuckled. "We have a shuttle traveling through underground caverns, and there's a network of such caverns through the northern edge of Iswan. Consequently, it'll take us a little under three hours to arrive at our destination."

"That's amazing!" Nolan offered.

Tok shrugged. "This is a modern city. Perhaps it's still the surprise of those who own the technology on this world that amazes you."

"You might be right my friend," Nolan answered. Suddenly, he lifted his head as he realized something. "Where's Stirm?"

"Stirm is busy this morning. He's in consul with the king of the Stor people. Now, the First Key has arrived as our history foretold, but still, people need to be convinced—especially the kings of the lands."

Nolan shook his head. "You sound like Daniel, talking in riddles."

Tok smiled and pointed at Chu. "He knows what I speak of."

Chu took a moment while he thought. When his lips moved, his eyes were glazed as if in a trance.

"The blood of our father's ancestors will unite in one, and we will follow.

Wisdom, courage and vision will bind us to him, and we will follow.

When the call sounds, brother and son alike will arise, and we will follow."

Chu's eyes looked at Nolan and his shoulders shrugged. "It's a saying we have in the wildes, but then we're but savages."

"One riddle after another," Nolan muttered. "Do you, Tok and Daniel plan out these pieces of less than definite passages which appear on the surface to be filled with wisdom, yet say absolutely nothing?"

The sound of the legs of Tok's chair scratching against the floor tiles as it pushed back gathered Nolan's attention. He wiped the corners of his mouth with a napkin, and then placed it lightly back beside his empty plate. "There's something I need to show you. It's on the way and it'll answer some of your questions."

With Nolan's nod the group arose. Nolan wrapped the belt containing the two long knives, once belonging to Germaine, around his waist. Ranaa slung her bow and the quiver of arrows over her shoulder, and they were quickly out the door. They entered the central chamber of Tok's home where the vaulted room was two stories high, with several doors and hallways exiting from it. A polished, brass railing rimmed the walkway running the perimeter of the second level where several sturdy doors exited from the walkway. In the center of the main chamber of the room was a fireplace open on all four sides. Facing each opening was a comfortable seating area comprising of couches and plush chairs.

As they walked through the main hall, several of Tok's servants passed them. They bowed to Tok, but they bowed even lower to Nolan with wide-eyed looks on their faces.

The entrance to Tok's home was a small antechamber defined by the double doors that came together in a point, ten feet from the floor. Another of Tok's servants pulled the thick steel ring hung from the door, and it swung open on well-oiled hinges. Again, the servant bowed low to Nolan while his eyes remained glued to the Earthman's face.

Once out in the hallway, Tok said, "Mind them not. Most of them have never seen a human. Word has traveled quickly that you're the First Key, and you're here in the city. For them, it's like the culmination of an ages-old fairytale. They were told it by their parents, and their parents in turn told them. The story goes back many generations, and now, it's coming to an end."

They walked around the curved walkway of the fifth level to four sets of double doors. The fourth door had a call button like the rest, but there was also a keypad. Tok pushed the red button and pressed an access code into the keypad. Immediately, a *whir* was heard, indicating the elevator was on the way to them.

"I don't understand, Tok. What fairytale?" Nolan asked with his brow lowered in confusion.

The doors slid open without a sound, and they stepped into the pastel-blue compartment. "It'll become clear in a few moments," the Stor replied.

It was difficult for Nolan to become accustomed to the elevator. All elevators he had traveled on were straight up and down vehicles. This one moved on an incline, accounting for the terraced effect of each level where each was slightly closer to the center of the chasm than the one above. Nolan held the hand railing in the elevator to keep from losing his footing during the rapid descent. Thankfully, the elevator came to a stop, and the doors opened to the colorful atrium of the lower level.

They exited the elevator, and Nolan spun around slowly. The view from the bottom of the city was even more impressive. He strode over to the curved half-wall holding back the water where the mist felt good on his freshly shaven face. The perfect line of water from the pond, several levels above, fell into the fountain held in by the wall. *Amazing,* he thought.

Tok pulled on Nolan's sleeve and motioned him to follow. They walked through an assortment of flowerbeds and short, wide-leafed, tropical trees to a semi-circle of stone cut into the side of the mountain. The stone floor gleamed with polish, resulting in a mirror finish allowing the group to see themselves. It was ever as odd a group to save mankind as one could imagine.

However, when Nolan raised his eyes, he gasped. On the far wall was a huge statue. In it were the intertwined figures of five Stors. Each of the three males carried an object. One held a vial of liquid. The next held a lantern while the third had his hand on the tip of a great war hammer with the stone head balanced on the ground. The fourth and fifth figures were female. One held a book under her arm while another book was open under her gaze. The last woman held a baby to her breast.

Nolan's eyes lifted even higher, and that was when his jaw dropped. Above the statue was a huge ring of brass. Crossed over it were a hammer and a sword. "That's the symbol of the Soichaint!" he blurted.

Tok stood with his hands clasped together behind his back. "Yes, indeed it is. It's also the symbol of our ancestors. Long before this symbol was used by the Soichaint, it was the symbol of our forefathers, the Ionians."

Nolan looked curiously at Tok. "*Our* forefathers?"

"Let me explain," Tok said. "Centuries ago, on the western edge of this world, the Ionians were here along with the Anasazi and a small group of Bantu. As you know, the Ionians developed the complex DNA residing in your blood. However, there were many failures before they achieved this success. Experiment after experiment was conducted with less than acceptable results. Some were horrific. First the experiments were conducted with animals, but eventually human volunteers were needed."

"Human volunteers?"

"Yes," Tok recounted. "The Ionians were zealous in their pursuit of a mixed pureblood. Remember, all this was being done in the shadow of war, and there were many who wanted them dead. Assassins were not uncommon, but still Ionians volunteered for the tests." Tok lowered his eyes. "Many died. Many also survived but were hideously changed and mercifully euphemized. Different DNA strands resulted in different changes to the Ionians who went under these radical tests. Just before the Ionian forefathers developed the blood coursing through *your* veins, the five Ionians who are immortalized in this statue were conceived. However, when the mix of birthing fluid and blood was wiped away, revealing dark shades of blue and black, it was obvious they were changed and disfigured. This was the beginning of the Stor race. The Ionians moved us to this home in the mountain away from prying eyes. Over the centuries we've evolved, and our nation has grown. With tears in their eyes as they left this world, our Ionian forefathers told us to wait for the one who would come and save us all."

Tok, with tears in his eyes, looked up at Nolan. "You're that one, brother."

"Brother?" Nolan whispered.

Chu's low voice carried to them as he recounted the words put into his ancestor's minds centuries ago.

"When the call sounds, brother and son alike will arise, and we will follow."

Tok smiled through the tears. "We're the results of the same experiments. We carry almost the same DNA in our blood, you and I. It would appear very small differences were crucial. We're as much your brothers as are your fellow Celtae, Anasazi or Toltec." He briskly wiped the tears from his blue, leathery face, and his eyes were fired with passion. "The Stor people will serve the First Key!" His voice echoed off the statue across from them.

As Nolan turned to face the statue, he thought of the sacrifices having been made. People had died, not only in his history, but the history of the very distant past. He could not let them down. The weight on his shoulders grew, but he steadied himself and put his hand on Tok's shoulder. "Your assistance is accepted and much needed. You'll always be by my side."

They were interrupted by another Stor in a military uniform who scurried up to them. He handed Tok a folded paper. He nodded to Tok and then to Nolan. There was the same look of disbelief Nolan was quickly becoming accustomed to.

Tok opened the paper, read quickly and then looked to the group. He chuckled. "That would be news of the children. The sculls have finished the King's Council, and seven of nine nations are ready to serve you on the plains of Kaleel. They're raising the great army now. Some 40 thousand sculls are expected.

Chu broke into his chant once again.

"When the call sounds, brother and son alike will arise, and we will follow."

"Yes, I get it by now, Chu." Nolan lowered an eyebrow at the old man and then turned back to Tok. "How do you know this information?"

Tok looked at Nolan for a moment as he would look at a child. "I told you. We're Stors, and we know everything occurring on Iswan."

Without waiting for a reply, Tok led them back through the atrium, but at the central fountain they turned left through a low-lit passage. The moving sidewalk allowed the next few minutes travel through the cut rock to pass quickly. Another long escalator down led them to a last escalator at right angles to the first. What awaited Nolan looked every bit like a train station in New York or London. Stors hurried about their business while small shops occupied the space on the far side of the boarding area. This underground world even had hawkers selling books and papers to read. There were even drinks and sandwiches available for purchase. The only difference to New York, Nolan recollected with an amused look on his face, was the short, blue creatures in place of the New Yorkers.

He chuckled as a train pulled into the station. *This is no New York train,* he thought as he admired the bullet-shaped appearance. It had ten round, aerodynamic cars where each was joined with a universal hitch. There was no smoke, only a low hum from the powerful, electric engine in the first car. Approximately 30 Stors entered the train after which the four travelers moved to the second car that had apparently been reserved for them.

Nolan was the last to enter the car. He took one look back at the Stor city and turned to enter the car. Before he did so, his forehead thumped loudly off the metal jamb running along the top of the doorway. Nolan cursed it. "Freaking Stor-size trains." He rubbed the bump already forming as he ducked and entered the cabin. Still muttering incoherently under his breath, he looked at the faces of his companions.

Chu had a silly grin on his lips. Tok looked the same except his yellow eyes were held even wider. An unusual sound came from his throat as his lips vibrated slightly. Ranaa had her fingers clenched tight into the firm cushion of the inclined seat she was in. Finally, she burst out laughing uncontrollably. Tok spit out his own fit of laughter, followed closely by Chu. Ranaa poked Tok in the seat opposite him and imitated Nolan. "Hello, I'm the First Key." Then she slapped her palm into her forehead. "Thwack!" she said, sending both Tok and Chu into further fits of laughter.

Hunched over, Nolan strode over to them and roughly placed his hand under Ranna's chin. At the same time, he placed a long kiss to her lips. She opened her eyes wide, only to see Nolan's own mocking eyes laughing at her. She tried to push him away, but he held the kiss. When the laughing from the two males behind him finally subsided, he released Ranaa from her bondage. There were no words as she brought her fingertips up to touch her lips. He slid into the chair next to her and felt the seatbelt handle under him as well as the shoulder belts. Nolan figured them out quickly, and with three clicks, he was strapped in.

"I can see this is going to be a fun trip!" Nolan said. He knew he looked somewhat silly with a wide smile on his lips, and the pressure telling him the lump on his head was growing.

The train ride was smooth and enjoyable with banked turns and shallow gradients traversing through several hundred feet of caverns at different elevations. There was very little to see since the caverns at these depths were pitch-black except for the lights from the train, and they were not bright enough to liberally illuminate the darkness. Only once, when another train going in the opposite direction passed them on a curve, did the other train's forward lights shatter the darkness.

The cavern revealed was huge with several ledges on either side. Creatures resembling snakes with short legs scurried back into holes burrowed into the rock. One snake-like creature was not fast enough as another rotund, short-furred animal, on paws appearing to have no legs, rolled off the ledge. Just as the animal's teeth closed on the snake coiling in objection, the darkness overtook the cavern. *Amazing,* Nolan thought. Animals, just like people, adapt. How long has the struggle for life and death between the two species been going on? How long since the one species discovered the light would come at regular intervals, and in that interval, a meal could be waiting? *Creatures change, people change and life changes,* he thought. *The purebloods will accept the change I've been asked to lead.* He closed his eyes, convincing himself—at least for the moment. At least he could take some solace in the fact that it appeared no matter the race, all became drowsy on a good train ride. He smiled just before his deep, restful breaths joined the rhythmic snoring of Tok and Chu.

Nolan felt Ranaa's soft fingers caress his cheek, and his eyes fluttered open. "Awaken. We're here," she whispered.

He rubbed his eyes and tried to lean forward, but there was a weight on his chest.

"Wait," she said while shaking her head from side to side. Her fingers released the two clasps at the shoulder and the one at his waist. She dragged her nails up his torso and across his chest before she slid away and out the open door of the car. Nolan grumbled another curse. The woman held his emotions in many ways. He allowed her to play so with him, but one day he knew he would take her as only a man can take a woman—just not *this* day.

Once out of the vehicle, Nolan saw Chu and Tok were already outside the train, stretching their muscles. With a wide yawn and hands stretched over his head, Nolan asked, "So, where are we?"

"We're at the base of the Mines of Kreath. Run by Stors, the mine provides trebalt—a porous, light stone used for various building applications across Iswan, but primarily for roadways."

As they walked toward stairs cut into the far wall, Tok reached down and picked up a handful of crushed stone near the wall. "Trebalt is interesting. It seems simple enough in this state, but when you add water and compress it, the resulting bonded stratum is as hard as steel. As such, it has many applications in the building industry. As well as bringing income to the Stors, the mine provides an excellent cover for the train station we're just leaving."

They traversed several sets of stairs in silence. Hallways extended from each landing and voices from the offices and simple lodgings indicated to them that numerous Stors worked at this facility. At the upper landing a uniformed Stor came from a glass-walled room containing several other guards. The first guard looked at Nolan with curiosity and then fascination as he read the papers Tok passed him. The guard nodded to his comrade within the room and a lever was pulled. A section of the stone face in front of them swung open, and the four travelers scurried through. On the other side, four more Stors turned to Tok in the lantern light now replacing the fluorescent lighting behind them. These Stors didn't have uniforms, but Nolan noticed the war hammers and shields leaning in the shadow of the wall. This was the border between the modern technology of the world they just left and the simple life of Iswan before them.

The travelers were escorted down several low passages to a large platform. There were metal guides in each corner extending out of sight up the shaft above the platform. A cable, thicker than Nolan had ever seen, supported the platform and every 20 feet along its length was a large basin. Near where the cable wound around a monstrous pulley next to the platform, Nolan could see the heavy basins were filled with water.

Tok motioned the group to follow him onto the platform before he nodded to one of the guards. He pulled a thin cord that disappeared into the blackness of a hole in the rock wall. High above them moving water could suddenly be heard, and several drops rattled off the crude but waterproof angled roof of the platform. The pulley creaked and the platform inched upward. For the first minute, the platform moved slowly, but the speed increased at a slow rate until a moderate pace was reached and maintained. Nolan peered over the side and looked at the full basins of water moving downward on the cable next to them. As each one reached the pulley, a lever tipped the basin. The contents emptied into a channel cut into the rock, and the water ran off into the darkness.

Soon, only darkness could be seen below them as the lanterns on the platform maintained barely enough light for the travelers to see each other. A breeze came down the shaft, causing the lanterns to flicker and play foreboding shadows against the rough-hewn walls of the shaft. Nolan felt Ranaa's fingers slide under his arm, and her warmth pressed against his back. Instinctively, he leaned back into her. *This is another moment to take my breath away,* he thought. The kiss on the train had been playful, but here there was so much more emotion in this simple embrace.

The perfect moment was interrupted as the light from above grew, and the platform pulled out of the shaft. It slowed just as the flow of water into the basins slowed. As the platform came in line with the stone floor of this level, two large, well-muscled Stors pushed over a long lever set in the floor. Metal forks on either side of the platform shot out and locked the platform in place.

Safely secured, the travelers left the platform, and Nolan turned to watch the device work in reverse. One Stor pulled a hinged, metal bar into place, allowing three thick, metal fingers to line up under the lip of the basin. At the same time, two well-muscled Stors made several trips, carrying block weights of stone onto the platform. Once the forks were released and the fingers tripped, the basins tipped as well, allowing the water to fall down a side sluice, and the platform slowly moved downward into the recesses of the mine.

"Amazing," Nolan whispered. He saw they were actually in a long shaft on a slight angle upward to the surface. On either side, Stors worked the rock. Some used shovels while others used large hammers to break apart the stone. *Wait a minute,* Nolan thought. The hammers were actually war hammers, and the shovels gleamed with a sharp edge. These were weapons, and the workers were actually warriors. It was all a façade since they were really here to guard the entrance to their world and the secret it held.

Having been underground and enclosed for a day and a half, the traveler's pace naturally quickened as they moved up the incline. As they exited from the shaft and the warmth of the setting sun hit them, Nolan took a deep breath of fresh air. He looked about the surface of the mine where large mounds of crushed stone dotted the area, and pack animals pulled carts of stone. They were back in the simple life Iswan offered.

On the small barge pushed along by ten Stors manning poles, it took another hour for the travelers to reach the stone wall marking the city of Shadowrise at the northern most tip of Allanmore. Hundreds of miles had been traversed in a single, long day that was far from over.

Tok, who as he professed seemed to know everything, led them up the stairs from the short, stone dock. "The Inn of the Seven Flames is only a short distance from this location. Another 30 minutes, and we should be there."

The sun had now set, leaving the city in shadows lit only by the light from the windows of the dwellings and the lanterns that had not blown out from the rising wind. They took their time as Tok led them up one wide street and then down a narrower side street. For a time, their pace was moderate and uneventful.

"Did you see that?" Ranaa whispered as she walked beside Nolan.

"Yes. It's the third time a shadow has played against the buildings ahead from the light behind us."

Tok increased his small strides until he was next to them. "One thing our forefathers gave me, which you have not received, is exceptional hearing. "There are three people following us."

Nolan nodded and pulled back his long coat, allowing the two long knives to be easily accessible. "Let's hurry, but without drawing any attention. We're better off eluding them than fighting."

Tok loosened the leather strap holding the shield over his shoulder. "This way," he said. They hurried up the narrow street before turning down another side street. "They're closer," Tok whispered.

"I can hear them also. They know we're onto them, and they have put deception behind them. Hurry along!" Nolan cried as he motioned Chu to move ahead of him.

"This way," Tok said as he pointed down a dark side alley.

Without questioning the Stor, the travelers plunged into the dark alley at a full run. They bound over boxes and ducked under tightly wound rope lines holding pots and pans out to dry. They turned a corner and stopped in their tracks. Thirty yards ahead a dark figure, covered in shadow, blocked their path. His arms were crossed, and his feet were firmly set. He had been waiting.

164

Nolan sidestepped forward slowly while pulling one knife out in front of him. He heard Tok draw the mighty hammer, and the gleam of light from the arrowhead, cocked on the bowstring, told him Ranaa was ready. Nolan turned his head for a moment and saw the three dark figures blocking the back of the alley. They were boxed in.

"We don't want trouble, so let us pass. There's no need for a fight," Nolan said.

There was no response from the dark figure ahead of them.

"You don't know who you're dealing with." Nolan's voice smoldered on the edge of exploding.

A voice came from the dark figure. "No, *you* don't know who you're dealing with, or at least, your memory is lacking."

Still some 20 yards distant, the figure moved forward a step. Light from an open window, two floors above, gave his face a light glow. His clothes were commonplace on Iswan, yet the way the sword hung from his hip told Nolan the man knew how to use it. He wore a black bandana tied around his head. Although it was not rare on Iswan, it was unusual.

The light showing the man's face was dim, but still, there was something vaguely familiar about him. Nolan's brow furrowed as he struggled with memories playing over his mind. The steps behind them stopped, and the man in front finally pulled his arms from their crossed position. Nolan cocked his knife menacingly, but the man didn't reach for his sword. Instead, his fingers curled into the bandana and pulled it free. He shook his head and his hair, a shocking, bright blue, shook back and forth across the flickering light.

Nolan's eyes were wide in shock, but his lips turned into a wide smile. He jumped up in the air, giving out a whoop. With all the excitement of their travels and the perils therein, thoughts of his blue-haired bond brother had been pushed back to the deepest recesses of his mind. It was the last person he expected to see and perhaps a person he never expected to see again, yet here he was. It was Lukas.

Chapter 19

"Lukas!" Nolan blurted out.

Quick, long strides took Nolan to his bond brother. Without hesitation, he wrapped his arms around Lukas's shoulders, and one hand clapped him on the back. At first Lukas held his arms uncomfortably out from his sides, but as a wry smile formed on his lips, his arms came around, returning the warm hug.

Nolan pulled back, the palm of his hand slapping into his close friend's chest, resulting in a small cloud of dust puffing into the chill night air. "What are you doing here?" Nolan asked through the shocked look that hadn't yet left his face.

As he tied the bandana back onto his head, hiding the telling blue locks, Lukas replied, "As always, I'm looking after your ass." There was a smug grin on his face.

By this time, Chu, Tok and Ranaa were just behind Nolan. The Earthman turned and quick introductions were made. Lukas looked curiously at Tok, and as his eyes came across the radiant Ranaa with the short bow across her back, the curiosity evident in his eyes grew even as it mingled with sudden warmth.

Lukas lifted his head, looking over Nolan's shoulder. His lower lip turned under his upper row of teeth, and a light, high-pitched whistle was emitted. Raising a pointed finger over his head, he made a tight circle. In response, two light whistles carried back to them from the dark shadows cascading against the not-too-distant buildings. This was followed by barely audible footsteps receding into the star-lit night.

With this task done, Lukas grasped Nolan's shoulder with his fingers and pulled him toward the dark shadow of the alley. "The inn is this way," he said as his eyes looked furtively from side to side.

The group, with Nolan and Lukas in the lead, continued up the quiet alley and back into a larger laneway lit by wrought-iron-encased lanterns hanging from the stone buildings. The grade was slightly uphill, and even though the apprehension of being followed was over, they stayed close to the dark safety near the buildings.

"What are you doing here?" Nolan asked again. "I would've thought you were on some far-off plane fighting for the Celtae cause."

Lukas didn't look at Nolan as he responded. His eyes stayed focused on the path ahead of them. "The Celtae cause is here on Iswan. Both our forces and the Toltec mass on the plains to the west. Fighters from many different planes prepare for a battle the likes of which has not been seen for centuries. It could turn the stagnant stalemate between the equally matched Celtae and Toltec nations."

"Based on that, I understand why you would be on Iswan, but why here in this alley?"

"You find me in the alley because Daniel said you would be coming from this side of the city. He told me to watch out for you."

Nolan heard a light chuckle escape Ranaa's lips. Although it was not visible in the dark night, Nolan could feel his face turning red. Even though he thought it was his last word that had decided their direction just before the travelers parted on the shores of South Palor, it appears Daniel had usurped him. Obviously, his mentor still had connections on Crann Bith, and through those, he was now face to face with Lukas.

Just ahead from the traveler's location there was a wide circular courtyard. An artificial pond took up the central third of the courtyard, highlighted by a life-size figure of a warrior saddled on a wild-eyed palusa. Stone blocks, three-high and neatly packed with a straw and mud mix, held back the pond water that was topped with wide-leafed plants. White flowers, half closed in the chill air, dotted the still, serene surface.

On the far side of the pond was a sign hanging from a three-story building. Lit by one lantern at each side, it read - *Inn of the Seven Flames*. The building was simple enough, but the red, carved shutters on each of the many windows spotting the structure, and the covered porch along the entire length of the building, gave it an elegant aura. The traveler's hurried steps took them across the cobblestone courtyard, and they slid inconspicuously through the wide, wooden, double-hung doors. It took only a few moments for Lukas to sign for the keys to the two pre-arranged rooms. By this time their shoulders slumped from the weariness of the long day, and their feet dragged along the steps as they traveled up the two flights of stairs.

Nolan hesitated when Lukas did not stop. He looked at the key in his hand and reaffirmed the number stamped into the brass was indeed a 23. "You missed the room." Nolan's words carried after Lukas.

Lukas turned and spoke with a low hush on his words. "The rooms are a ruse. So close to our goal, we need to be very careful." A slight motion of his hand waved the group forward. "Follow me."

Lukas continued to the end of the long hallway and opened a door almost too narrow for him to fit through. The rickety stairs on the other side were just as constricting. As they walked back down to ground level, they broke through the occasional cobweb of the rarely used back stairwell where the small door at the bottom led them out into the alley behind the inn.

Lukas held his arms out from his sides, keeping each of the travelers glued against the wall. More with his ears than his eyes, he ensured there were no unseen eyes or unwanted attention. Just as a cloud crossed in front of the stars, darkening the short distance to the stables, Lukas whispered, "Now."

In a moment they were again glued to a wall, but this time it was to the stable with their eyes peering onto the back of the inn. Most of the windows were dark, with only two lit by night candles within. The creak sounded deafening, but in actuality, it was barely audible as Lukas pulled back the latch of the wide stable door. Opening it just wide enough for him to slide through, he led the way, followed by each of the travelers in turn. Inside, the musty smell of animals assaulted their nostrils. Soft neighing could be heard from several occupied stalls set against the walls. Nolan peered through the dim light, seeing the heads of six regal palusas. A sense of security came over Nolan as he felt the strength of both body and spirit the animals exuded.

The group walked around the cloth-covered wagon in the center of the stable to a set of stairs secured to the pockmarked, vertical planks comprising the back wall of the building. The stairs, so steep they could be considered a ladder, led to a trap door in the ceiling. Nolan squinted as his head tilted up with curiosity, seeing light coming from between the ceiling planks. The hinges groaned as Lukas opened the trap door. Once through it, he leaned back down and offered his hand to each of the travelers in turn, helping them into the hidden attic of the stable. This level was short in height such that Nolan could only stand straight if he was in the center of the room running the length of the stable. The thatched roof, supported by thick, square-hewn timbers, angled down from the center to cross the sidewalls at a three-foot height.

There was a movement from the far side of the attic catching Nolan's attention. To his relief, he saw the familiar faces of Daniel and Garawin as the lanterns cast a glow across their faces.

"It's good to see you both!" Nolan said with genuine, heartfelt emotion. He held both hands out, grasping the offered arm of each of his friends.

"And you also, young Nolan," Daniel replied as his thick blonde moustache curled up with a wide smile. "Come and sit. You must be hungry." He turned and motioned them to a low table against the far wall.

Visible in the light of the lantern at the center of the table, fruits, cheese, bread and a few pieces of salted meat were piled on simple wooden platters. As they walked forward, they passed narrow cots where each offered a straw mattress and a wool blanket. Nolan removed his coat and threw it on one as he passed. He noticed Ranaa was quick to place her bow on the cot right next to his before they both lowered themselves into the cushioned chairs next to the table.

There was so much to say, Nolan thought. *Lukas was here. Daniel and Garawin were back after a three-day absence, and now that they were safely in Shadowrise, Chu needs to explain where they were going next.*

But all that was put to the back of Nolan's mind as Ranaa brought a plate of food to him. He took it and began to eat, not having considered how hungry he really was. As he ate, he realized everything on his plate was perfect. Ranaa selected the dark, flour roll he much preferred, and there were a liberal number of red berries. The light-green, pear-like fruits were too sour for his liking, and she had left them off his menu. He smiled. She was observant and knew him much better than he had considered. He looked up, catching her gaze, and smiled even wider. Seeing her eyes brighten, he sensed she knew how thankful he was for the food, but even more so, he hoped she understood how much he needed her by his side.

Once the meal was finished, they sat back in their chairs with their bellies satisfied. Nolan's eyelids were heavy, but before he went to sleep everyone needed to know the plan to come. He didn't know the exact framework himself, but all the people were here with the answers to formulate it right now.

Nolan looked from one to the other of the group before he spoke. "I sense we're close to the end goal, yet there are many questions in my mind as there must be in yours. Each of you holds a piece of the puzzle, and now we must pull it together, so we can all move forward together without confusion or hesitation." With his face framed in hair now more white than brown, he turned toward Daniel. "The battle hasn't started, has it?"

"Not yet," Daniel replied. "There are some skirmishes put forth to test the other's defenses, but both armies are waiting a few more days for more soldiers to bolster the ranks. On each side of the field of battle are some 50 thousand soldiers.

"How many more days exactly?" Nolan asked.

"Three."

Nolan sighed, then looked at the unlikely members of the group before him. He thought, *how can we possibly stop the wave of death to come?* Momentarily, doubt crept over his mind. He considered the old wizen, spry for his age, but nevertheless the years gave him few advantages in the upcoming battle. Ranaa was a surprise in her ability to learn and her yearning to belong. After spending most of her life in captivity, her new-found freedom fueling her drive was impressive, but that wouldn't be enough to stand up to purebloods in a killing frenzy. The rest were capable fighters, but what chance did they have against the many thousand pureblood warriors who at this moment were, in all likelihood, singing self-motivating songs of death and mayhem in prelude to the battle to come.

The corners of Nolan's eyes drooped slightly as his perception of his fellow travelers changed. Yes, they were purported fighters or a hope thereof, but more so, they were people who wanted to end the centuries of death continuing to fill the Athar. In addition, they were no different than the billions of people who inhabited the endless planes of existence. On the surface, they vocalized their support for the war, but deep within many, even though not officially coupled with the Soichaint, detested the death following them at every step. Surely, even the warriors poised for battle on the plains of Kaleel would embrace the deeper moral path of peace when motivated by all three keys and the many fighters already firmly behind the Soichaint who, for the first time, would reveal themselves on mass. He needed the strength to lead them. If he showed it, they would follow.

"In that case, we don't have much time," Nolan stated. He turned toward Chu. The wizen was comfortably settled back in a soft, cushioned chair with his eyelids half closed. "It's time, Chu. If we are to stop the carnage on the field of battle, we have three days to recover the Second and Third Keys. Where do we go from here?"

Chu hadn't spoken much at all since they left the beach of South Palor. With all eyes turned to him, he took his time. His lips went through a ritualistic set of movements, first stretching out and then being drawn back. Then his tongue lightly licked across both top and bottom lip in final preparation for the words, held sacred for centuries, now to be verbalized for the first time. Leaning forward, his dark face came out of the shadow while the dancing flame from the candle on the table reflected in his eyes, giving him a supernatural appearance. "Just north of Kilean marsh, half a day's travel west of Shadowrise, is a high-peaked outcropping of crooked rock. Within the bowels of the rock formation is a hidden chamber, and in it are the Keys we search for." He paused for a moment with his lips set in a tight line. "We're going to Shadow's Crag."

There was an audible hiss as Garawin sharply drew in his breath. "That's not good. That's not good at all," he repeated, and the cut features of his face were instantly drawn with tension. "It's an evil place inhabited by none but spirits. Those who go to the Crag do not return. Nothing but death awaits us there."

"Death awaits those who don't know where the deadly snares and traps are," Chu replied.

"And do you know where they are?" Garawin quickly responded.

"Of course," the wizen quipped.

"How?"

"I have a map."

"Where?"

"In my head." Chu tapped a crooked finger to his temple, and a bright-eyed grin formed on his face.

The prince rolled his eyes. "We should go right to the field of battle. We don't have time to waste. We can still win the battle for peace without the Keys. I will not put my life in the hands of centuries old folklore passed down in the fallible memories of any man, be he young or old."

"But *I* would," Nolan said. From watching Daniel he'd learned the subtle art of persuasion. His voice was calm, soothing and highlighted with confidence. "To convince the people purebloods of the different races can live together, we need the Keys. Alone, it would be difficult, and even if we succeed, much avoidable bloodshed would be spilt." His face turned toward Garawin. "I believe in Chu and will let him lead me to the secret chambers he speaks of. I would ask you to be with me on this." There was a silent pause. "I need the Prince of Rivenloc by my side."

Prince Garawin leaned forward with his elbows on his knees. His hair covered his face as he looked at his boots. With a loud sigh he lifted his head and made eye contact with Nolan. "I made my commitment long ago. Of course, I will be there with you."

Daniel's voice followed. "As will I."

"And I," Tok added in a raspy voice.

Each of the other travelers reaffirmed their fealty to Nolan. The bond brought a smile to all their faces. Then more than one wide yawn followed. Nolan brought his palms down and slapped both his knees. "It's late. Since we have a clear direction, it's best we get to sleep."

Further convincing was not needed, and the travelers each made for one of the cots angling toward one sidewall or the other—all except Lukas who rose and moved toward one of three small windows equally spaced on either long wall of the attic. Kneeling down, he pulled back the thick piece of hide covering and peeked outside.

Squatting behind him, Nolan asked, "Do you see anything?"

Lukas's finger let the hide go as he turned to face his friend. "All is quiet. Hopefully, my three fellow Dreadmen on watch outside will keep it that way."

The Earthman put his hand on Lukas's shoulder. Suddenly he felt silly as he sensed the tears forming in his eyes. The moisture sat there, filling his eyes but not dropping. "You don't know how glad I am you're here with us. I need your strength beside me."

"I pledged to you long ago over that drink in the restaurant in Bailemor, and I would not miss this for the world—or any world. Man makes his destiny and destiny will make the man, and as the sun settles over him, a hero just might be born."

Nolan chuckled and slapped his hand onto Lukas's shoulder just as the blue-haired man jutted his chin over Nolan's shoulder. Nolan turned. Against the far plank wall, he saw Ranaa pulling her cot closer to his.

"I see how she looks at you. Do you have an interest in her?" Lukas asked.

Confusion crossed Nolan's mind for a moment, but he drove it away with a quick wave of his hand. "No, not at all. Daniel and I saved her from a sure death on Crann Bith, and she has stuck with us since then."

"That's good. She is very attractive and has piqued my interest. I might just pursue her. You don't mind, do you?"

Nolan wondered if his fragile chuckle was convincing enough. "No. You go right ahead."

Lukas raised both eyebrows. "You're sure?"

Nolan responded with a nod of his head up and down. "Very sure."

Both men rose to their feet and made their way to their cots. Nolan kicked off his boots and slid under the blanket as the candles were put out— all except the one on the table. Ranaa, already half asleep, snuggled to the edge of her cot and laid her chin on Nolan's shoulder as he lay on his back with both hands under his head. Almost immediately, her breaths became heavy as she fell into a deep sleep. He looked up as the flames, licked by drafts squeezing through the plank walls, played dancing shadows across the wood and thatch roof. He lay like that for some time, and as every minute went by, his eyebrows drew lower and lower.

Suddenly he exhaled deeply, pulling one hand out from behind his head. With the frown still on his face, he poked Ranaa in the shoulder. She stirred but did not awake. He poked her again, but harder.

Her eyes fluttered open and she whispered. "What is it?"

Nolan kept his voice low. "I want to make sure I have been clear. There is much on my mind right now, but deep within you are there. When this other business is over with, and if we are fortunate enough to survive, you'll move to the front of my attention. As you have told me, I own you, and in time, I'll take what I own."

Ranaa looked through her tired eyelids for a moment, wondering what brought the words forward at this late hour. She chose not to ask. Rather, she put the unusual words to the increasing knowledge she was gaining of men and their erratic behaviors. She snuggled her chin into Nolan's shoulder and purred as she fell into an even deeper, contented sleep.

Chapter 20

Nolan's eyes shot open as a firm hand clamped over his mouth. Hovering just above him, he saw Lukas with a finger pressed against his lips in a manner demanding silence. Lukas's hand slid down, and the fingers grasped the front of Nolan's shirt, drawing him upward. Ranaa stirred but didn't awake as Nolan dipped a shoulder and let the woman's chin slide onto the coat curled into a makeshift pillow.

As Nolan lifted his weight from the cot, a slight creak emitted from the wooden legs as they flexed. The candle on the table had burned out long ago, leaving the attic dark except for the scant light squeezing in around the hide-covered, tiny windows facing the inn. Lukas released his grasp and continued toward the same window they had looked out earlier in the evening. As he lowered to one knee, he pushed his hand back toward Nolan, curling a finger to urge him forward. The Earthman complied and moved to a squat on the other side of the window from Lukas.

A finger carefully pulled back the hide as Lukas said, "Be careful they don't see you."

Sliding his face against the wall until one eye could see out the window, Nolan surveyed the alley between the two buildings. At first he saw nothing, but then a movement caught his eye. A figure in an ankle-length dark cloak stood with his back pasted to the corner of the inn. Highlighted by the lantern over the back door, it was the movement of his face under a crop of long, dark hair that gave the stranger away.

"Who is he?" Nolan asked as the curtain was released back into place, covering the thin pane of glass.

"Not who, but they." Lukas whispered his response.

"There are more?"

Lukas nodded. "I believe there are three."

Sleep's haziness left him, and Nolan was now fully alert. "Who are they?"

"Phantoms trained in the art of quiet death." Lukas spit out the words as he pulled a leather pouch from his shirt pocket. Unfolding it revealed a cluster of raven-black hair two inches long, tied with a thin twine at one end. "The white band around the middle of the bundle of hair is the mark of the Guild of Assassins of Malagar, a Toltec world."

"You've already killed one?" Nolan stammered.

Lukas's hand opened further and one leaf of the leather pouch opened to reveal three more identical tufts of hair. "We have dispatched four, and the number is about to grow to seven."

"There must be another…"

"Quietly rouse the others. We must leave immediately." Lukas's words cut off Nolan's. Without waiting for acknowledgment, the blue-haired Dreadman silently moved to the trap door.

As he left and the door was closed, Nolan was left in the quiet darkness. He pulled back the hide from the window to glance down one more time to the dark figure in the alley, but his eyes were drawn across to the second floor of the inn. Dim light came from the two windows of the rooms they were supposed to be occupying. The movement against the far wall told a story as shadows of stealth were cast, followed by a struggle. Lukas's fellow Dreadmen had been waiting in the rooms for the Phantoms. It was over in an instant, and then there was only the calm of the night. Nolan jumped in surprise as a dark figure bounced against the window frame across the alley with a thud. The man, face covered in blood, knew he was about to die. His last thoughts came across the short distant between them and filled Nolan's mind. Nolan almost felt the knife entering the back of the man's neck, and then the psychic connection was lost along with the man's soul. A hand pulled the Phantom away from the window, and another face leaned out from the shadow, giving a light, shrill whistle from his lips. Nolan was surprised when, from below, a responding whistle came from Lukas as he held the collar of a long coat. The Phantom within was lifeless and his boots were dragging along the cobblestones as he was pulled toward the door to the stables.

Nolan's face was drawn and grim. These Phantoms might be considered elite, but on this night the Dreadman prevailed. The Earthman turned his attention to his fellow travelers, giving each a quick shake. The finger pressed to his lips indicated to each that their silence was needed. As the message for their hasty departure was given, each took only a moment to prepare for travel. The trap door was pulled open, and they made their way down the steep stairs just in time to see Lukas covering the dead body with straw in the corner of the stable.

"Hitch the wagon. We need to leave right away," Lukas curtly said.

Garawin turned to Nolan with a questioning look.

"Hitch the palusa," Nolan confirmed. "There could be more assassins about, and I don't get a good feeling from this place. The sooner we leave, the better."

The hinges almost broke as the weight of the six palusas crashed into the stable doors. The two wide panels burst open, and the six finest palusas from the royal stables of Rivenloc easily pulled the wagon down the alley onto the main road leading to the western market area. Garawin held the reins with the pride of the beasts mirrored in his own eyes. He put stealth to the back of his mind as he flicked the reins, urging even more speed from the beast's muscular legs and shoulders. A few curious city-folks, roused from their sleep, glanced bleary-eyed from their windows. If any cared, it would not matter as the travelers would soon be out of reach.

Thankfully, the cobblestones were not the typical rounded shape but had a flat upper surface made even smoother with use over time. Consequently, the travelers in the wagon only had to hang on to keep themselves from being hurled out when Garawin took a corner at full speed with the rear wheels skidding against the road's surface.

Shadowrise was a city at peace, and for the most part, free from bandits or rebels. As such, most of the many gates had a token guard who were there more for record keeping than security. The marketplace gate was left completely unguarded, probably because it wasn't really a gate at all. Several city roads converged onto the large square, and the western side was completely open to the countryside, so the many farmers could bring their goods easily into the market every morning. At this hour, before the rains, the palusa-propelled wagon shot into the empty market square, and the long strides of the beasts easily took the travelers across it.

It was only when Garawin felt the wheels move from the cobblestones of the city to the pea gravel of the country roads, that he pulled back on the reigns. The palusas, enjoying the wild speed, shook their heads and snorted in disappointment, but discipline from their expert training slowed them to a quick walk. As Nolan and Daniel pushed themselves through the canvas covering and sat on the bench either side of Garawin, the sun was just cresting the horizon.

Nolan looked at the lightened sky in the distance. "How long do we have till the rains come?"

"A little less than an hour," Garawin replied. "We will need to find some shelter by that time."

The morning rains would not kill someone, but they could be very uncomfortable. If they were caught out in the open, the canvas would quickly become waterlogged, followed assuredly by unwanted leaks. The palusas born to this environment had a thick hide and could withstand the uncomfortable ordeal if need be.

The rays of light began to brighten the farm land they traveled through as they turned north from Shadowrise. This was still a world of crisscrossed canals, making roads difficult and, as a result, infrequent. Almost always they followed along the shore of a canal until it reached another intersecting canal. Here, if the water was shallow, the travelers were expected to pass as best they could. If it was a wider and deeper canal, a bridge allowed the road to continue. If the canal was deep and there was no bridge, then it was a sharp reminder that on a world of canals, a wiser man would have chosen a canoe for his method of travel.

The sun was rising higher in the eastern sky, and under it the billowing clouds could now be seen. Even lower was the darkness of the pounding rain less than 30 minutes away. Fortunately, as the road veered with the canal around a sharp curve, in the distance they could see a bridge, and it was covered. Garawin clicked the reins against the hindquarters of the palusas and they were instantly at a quick gait.

When the rains finally hit, the sound of the heavy drops pelting into the angled, wooden roof of the bridge was deafening. The palusas brought them to it in sufficient time, and now they rested. Garawin knew the value of the beasts, and even though he was a prince, he walked to each himself, putting feedbags on their long faces. The lantern he carried cut through the darkness as the pounding rain did not allow any light to penetrate.

Ten minutes after it began, the noise stopped as the rains marched westward. In its absence sunlight found the inside of the covered bridge through the many cracks and seams in and between the planks, signaling, like the burst of a thousand stars, that they could move on.

The next two hours were a peaceful reprieve as the wagon kept to the road mimicking the path of the Smaller Allanmore canal. Veering slightly west to utilize the road tracking the Great Allanmore canal would have been quicker, but that route had greater traffic both on the road and in the river. Now stealth was a greater factor than speed, so they stayed to the more obscure route, seeing no other travelers by road and having passed only three canoes on the winding canal.

Nolan moved to the back of the wagon and sat next to Ranaa, enjoying the beauty of mixed patterns as they looked out the rear opening. For the most part this portion of Allanmore was decorated with the heavily flowered trees adorning much of the world. However, intermingled in the forest were farms as the rich soil was just as suitable for nourishing the many fruits and vegetables sustaining the people of Iswan. Just as the landscape to the west became more barren, dominated with tall, mixed yellow and green grasses, they heard the yell.

"Halt!" Chu yelled a second time before the wagon lurched to a stop.

Nolan turned to Chu. "What is it, Wizen?"

"From this point we need to go west and then come to Shadow's Crag from the south," Chu replied.

"That's not correct," Garawin interjected as he turned to look into the covered wagon. "Entry to Shadow's Crag is from the eastern face through the Pass of Trimbalson."

"Nevertheless, our path is not in that direction. We need to go west, then north," Chu said with determination.

Garawin turned about completely and put his fists against his thighs. "Everyone who has attempted to enter the Crag has gone through Trimbalson pass. It is the only safe entry." Irritation accented almost every word from the prince's lips.

Chu's patience broke. His eyes went wild as he cursed over and over in a language unknown to any of the others listening while his arms waved frantically to the sky as if he was beseeching divine intervention. After a time, he returned to the language all could understand. "Garawin, you might be a prince of your people, an excellent breeder of palusa and an excellent fighter, but your listening skills are crap—pure crap!"

"What do you mean?"

"Last night, did I not tell you there was a chamber within Shadow's Crag we needed to travel to?" Chu questioned.

"Well, yes," Garawin managed.

"No! That's not what I said at all. I said there was a *secret* chamber, not just a chamber. If, as you put it, 'everyone' knew the way to the chamber, then it wouldn't be so secret, would it?"

Garawin's eyes narrowed as he glared at Chu. Knowing the discussion with the old wizen was going nowhere, he turned his attention to Nolan. "Kilean marsh is not a safe place. There is sink stone that will suck you in. Once it has its hold on you, there is no hope, only a horrible death as inch by inch it pulls you down. If we are fortunate enough to avoid this peril, there is always the sulfur springs. The poisonous gas is invisible, and if you happen upon a saturated pocket, it can kill you before you know it. However, death is not that easy. The short-legged marrays wait for that precious moment between unconsciousness and death. The large lizards have adapted over the centuries with two things: immunity to the poisonous gas and the patience of a death stalker. They follow any who would be foolish enough to enter the marsh, knowing there is a high likelihood the elements will provide them a meal." Garawin raised a finger, shaking with foreboding as it pointed to the marsh. "That is what awaits you there."

Turning to Chu, Nolan asked, "Are you sure this is the only way?"

"Unfortunately, it's the only way to the chamber we seek. The Ionians not only hid the chamber, but placed it so the natural elements would protect it over the ages."

"What of the dangers Garawin speaks of?"

Chu shrugged. "They are real enough, but I know the way through them. Don't trust only in me, Nolan. Trust in yourself. The First Key would know what I speak is the truth."

The Earthman had already decided to go through the marsh. Sometimes it was a blessing and sometimes a curse, but the sense he got from the old wizen was nothing but truth and confidence. Chu's conviction was rooted in many years of having the secrets of the Second and Third Keys held in the recesses of his mind as it had been with his forefathers. Somehow, now that the time finally arrived, it was like a key had been turned, opening a door in the old wizen's brain, releasing his purpose in being. The strength of character coming from Chu's mind assaulted Nolan's attuned senses, giving him no choice but to take his advice.

"The road to a goal is not always an easy one. Victory doesn't always come without peril, and courage most certainly doesn't come without fear," Nolan said, looking from one friend to the other. "However, I can control my fear knowing the comrades I have beside me, and I have confidence in achieving our goal with your friendship and trust. Together, we go west through Kilean marsh."

No further words were needed. The bond between the seven had grown stronger day by day. Even with the passing of Germaine, whose place was now filled by Lukas, the travelers were tight knit. Even though, from time to time, discussion with different views and opinions occurred, the trust amongst the group held true and kept their course clear.

As such, each of the group took tasks from the direction now set before them. The wagon would be a hindrance in the marsh, so Garawin and Daniel unhitched the palusas. Chu recovered the blankets and light saddles from the back of the wagon just before Tok and Lukas pushed it toward the dank marsh. The wheels clattered off the small rocks as the wagon careened down the slight slope. With a large, gurgling splash, it settled in the water behind a tangle of tall grasses before slowly sinking out of sight. By the time the canvas wagon covering disappeared underneath the murky surface of the water, the six palusas were saddled. Their nostrils snorted, and their heads danced with excitement as they sensed the adventure to come.

Nolan stood at the foot of the tall, white palusa marked only with the fairest of gray splotches. He looked at Garawin, who was already saddled on another of the great beasts. "I thought these creatures did not take to unfamiliar riders," Nolan said.

"Most do not," Garawin replied. "But these are the finest stock with the best training available. Of most importance is their selection. The keepers of Rivenloc test every palusa as soon as it is born. Their temperament is determined then before any training and before the hand of man, pureblood or scull, has influenced their minds. Only one in 50 has the strength of logical choice. These very special beasts have the ability to set aside their wild abandon and determine if the person who would harness them has the character to share the escape they offer." Garawin's gloved hand softly patted the side of his mounts neck. "These six are the finest of those duly chosen."

As Garawin spoke, Nolan shifted to face the palusa's long face. He held the reins in gentle hands as his eyes met the pink eyes of the beast. At first, the creature snorted and pulled his head away, but Nolan's grip on the reins firmed up. The great palusa took a step back, but Nolan confidently stepped forward, bringing his free hand above the beast's nose. At the same time, he pressed his cheek to the side of the long face and whispered his encouragement toward the upright ears. Nolan pulled back his face and once again looked into the pink eyes. The Earthman sensed the bond and could tell the beast sensed it as well.

He slapped it on the neck as he stepped to the side of the beast. Without a further thought, he put one foot in the high stirrup and pulled himself into the saddle. That was when he saw all the others were mounted except for Ranaa. Nolan reached down, offering his arm. Her long fingers, strengthened from her practice with the bow, grasped his wrist, and she was pulled up behind him.

Turning to Chu, Nolan stated, "We're in your hands, wizen. Garawin and you will take the lead." His face turned to his blue-haired friend. "Lukas, cover the rear, but stay close."

As they were led into the tall grasses to the west of the road, there were very few words except for Chu. He barked orders one after the other. "The palusas are to be no more than two-wide, and keep them tight together!" His shrill bark continued for several minutes. "Make sure the nose of your palusa follows directly on the tail of the beast ahead. If you stray from the course, you could fall into the sink stone. That would be a shame as very few are saved if the effort is made, and for me, I wouldn't make such an effort. You've been duly warned, so if you're stupid enough to fall prey to the perils of the marsh, well, one less stupid person on the face of the Athar wouldn't be such a great loss."

It didn't take long for Nolan to shut out Chu's continual barrage of words. The grasses, at first taller than the palusas, shortened the further they moved into the marsh. For the most part there were wandering strips of solid land comprising of stone more than soil. These strips wound through the many bodies of water comprising the marsh. Some were ponds of murky, thick water while others were wet bogs of congealed water grass, appearing solid, but one wrong step would find the palusa up to its neck in the entangling roots choking the water.

As they traveled further into Kilean marsh a deep clicking sound could be heard. At first there was only one, and it was distant, but soon there was a second, then a third and finally enough clicks from all directions such that Nolan could not keep count.

Chu turned toward Nolan. As if he knew the question was coming, he gave the answer. "The clicks are the marrays way of communication. Fear not, they will not attack unless one of you should fall in the water and become entangled. I don't know if we would be quick enough to save you before they went into such a frenzy."

Nolan scanned from side to side. "I don't see them," he mumbled.

Pointing to the left, the old wizen pointed into the grass-covered pond. "Do you see the two logs?"

"Yes," Nolan answered.

Chu turned and gave a white-toothed grin. "Odd to see logs in a marsh where there are no trees," he quipped.

Nolan took solace in the fact he came to an understanding with himself long ago. Every day was a day to learn something new. Consequently, as he saw two yellow orbs open on one of the logs, he didn't feel the embarrassment some would have. The two eyes blinked slowly. They were on the front of the rounded, slime-covered head, indicating the lizards to be predatory. Six feet behind the eyes, the water popped with a swish of its tail. Ranaa also saw the movement, and from it, she shuddered at the size of the lizard. She remembered Chu's words indicating they wouldn't attack, but it didn't stop her grip from tightening around Nolan's waist.

Another hour went by, and the grasses were now almost nonexistent. Shadow's Crag was visible in the distance to the north. It wasn't very tall, but it was still an imposing sight. The small mountain of jagged, red rocks followed no natural pattern as if someone had taken fragile shards of glass and turned them upside down on themselves. Points and edges moved in every direction as the awkward pile of rocks glinted in the late afternoon sunlight. Some of this same red rock now pushed through along their path, and Nolan could see they were laced with a silver material reflecting the sun's rays like a mirror.

It was just as Nolan was admiring the pattern in one of the rocks when the palusas came to an abrupt stop. The narrow path they were traveling along had come to a fork. One path turned north while the other continued west.

Chu's palusa was pointed down the western leg, but Garawin had a hold of the beast's reins. "Should we not go north?" the prince asked. "It would appear this path would take us directly to the Crag."

"That it would," Chu responded. "It would also take us through the sulphur springs. Clouds of gas hover in that direction. The marrays might agree with your choice, but I cannot."

As the palusas continued down the western path, Garawin asked. "How do you know this is the right way, Chu?"

"It's not a simple answer, Prince, but let me try to explain. Have you ever had a dream come true, or to put it more accurately, have you ever had a vision that came from your dreams?"

"I don't think I understand."

"I've never been here before," Chu elaborated, "at least not in the awakened world. However, when I looked out the wagon and saw the marsh on our left and Shadow's Crag in the far-off distance, I knew this was a very familiar place. Once I saw it, it was like a switch turned in my head, and at that moment, I knew through the marsh was this stone path—a path I've traveled in my dreams each and every night since I was a boy."

"There is a lot at stake. I hope your vision is correct," Garawin whispered.

A soft chuckle crossed Chu's lips. "For an Athar rooted in psychic powers, belief in a vision should not be insurmountable, especially for one who can teleport from place to place at the snap of a finger."

Throwing back his head, a loud guffaw left Garawin's lips. His hand slapped the old wizen's back. "True enough, Chu. Even as a prince, it's good to be reminded of humility from time to time."

The next two hours seemed like an eternity. The westward path made a wide arc and was now turned north. Shadow's Crag was very close, but they couldn't afford to lose their concentration. The stone path grew narrower, now only wide enough for the palusas to follow in single file. Occasionally, a hoof would slip, and as rocks plunked into the pond on one side or the other, several slimy marrays would bolt toward the spot amidst a frenzy of deep clicks. Fortunately, by the time they arrived, the palusas had scampered ahead, leaving the large lizards disappointed.

The group came to a gradual rise across their path, comprised of solid rock going in each direction as far as the eye could see. As they crested it, they found themselves on a twenty-foot-wide stone plateau. On the other side of the stone plateau was another twenty-foot-wide expanse of crushed stone stretching out before them. It was also lost to sight in each direction. The crushed stone bed reminded Nolan of the gravel beds known to him on Earth.

Just beyond the gravel bed was the base of the Crag. Nolan's eyes lit up as he saw their goal so close and he spurred his palusa forward. He almost pitched over top of the beast as Garawin grasped the reins, bringing the beast to an immediate stop.

The prince dismounted and picked up a heavy stone. "It's sink stone," he said as he heaved the rock into the middle of the gravel field.

Nolan's eyes went wide as he saw a rippling wave move through the stone bed in every direction. The gravel was fluid, and the thrown rock began to slowly sink. It took a few minutes, but the rock disappeared as did the waves over the surface and any other sign indicating the danger Nolan almost flung himself headlong into.

"How do we get across?" Daniel asked. He looked from side to side, but the field of sink stone went off as far as the eye could see.

"I don't know," Chu replied.

Garawin pulled off one glove and then the other. He threw them into the dirt in disgust. "How is anyone expected to cross such a barrier?" He spat out the words.

"It isn't intended for just anyone to pass." Chu's calm voice matched the quiet, broken only by the slight whistle of wind as it skipped across the barren landscape. "However, someone who has the powers of the First Key could surely find a way to pass. I believe that to be the point."

Nolan was already surveying the terrain. As the leader of the band of travelers, he ultimately had the responsibility to solve the problems arising in their path. He took several minutes looking for a solution, but it seemed only a brute show of power would allow them to cross. The Ionians of long ago had indeed set a suitable test for him. Raising his hand, he turned it over with outstretched fingers. There was a wide, flat boulder on the other side of the sink stone river, and his fingers vibrated toward it. The Earthman's concentration was fully on the stone as his fingers curled inward, forming a tight fist. At the same time, the boulder shook and then rose a foot in the air. As Nolan's fist pulled into his chest, the boulder moved over the middle of the sink stone. Suddenly, his fingers thrust open, and the boulder dropped into the stone river. It sat on the surface, but the fine powder between the stones allowed them to roll and turn, causing the heavy boulder to slowly sink. It was a slow but thorough process, taking four minutes.

Lukas's voice came from the background. "It's a sign of what will happen to us."

"Not at all," Nolan said confidently. "It was a test to see how long the boulder would stay afloat. Even though it was much heavier than the rock Garawin threw in a moment ago, it stayed afloat a little longer because the flat surface area overcomes the factor of weight."

"I'm not sure how that will help us," Lukas said in a voice that seemed devoid of hope.

"Look across the bed of gravel, and you'll see several slabs of thick, red stone just on the other side," Nolan replied. "I intend to lift one and deposit it in the middle of the sink stone. It should stay afloat long enough for—"

"—the palusas to jump from this side onto the slab and then quickly skip across to the far bank." Garawin finished Nolan's words with enthusiasm.

"Everyone mount up, and prepare to make the jump of your life," Nolan urged. He scooted back as his strong arms easily pulled Ranaa in front of him in the saddle. "After I move the slab, I might be too weak to direct the palusa. You will take me across," he whispered in her ear as he took a coil of rope hanging from the saddle and tied it around his waist. He tied the loose end securely to the pommel of the saddle. This way even if he should become unconscious, he wouldn't fall.

Ranaa didn't answer, but her grip on the reins, and the movement of her feet urging the beast backward, told him she was up to the task.

Nolan looked at each of the riders. Seeing they were prepared, he once again thrust his hand forward toward the large, red slab tilted on end along the far bank. His mind went into a trance-like state with all his focus on the twelve-foot-long slab. With its six-foot-width, the slab had to weigh at least five tons. Beads of sweat broke out on Nolan's brow as the slab vibrated. His hand shook violently as the slab didn't lift, but the tip did begin to drag slowly through the cover of loose stone and red sand toward the sink stone.

There was a short drop-off on the far bank, and when the tip of red stone cleared it, the heavy slab dropped. Instant reflexes raised Nolan's hand in the air as the invisible force of his mind caught the weight. The slab shook but continued to the center of the sink river. A sudden pull of Nolan's hand caused the slab to topple, and it fell flat into the gravel bed with a loud thud. Foot-high waves of gravel radiated from the point of contact, and the slab took up the sickening roll.

The pitching slab was an unexpected peril the palusas would have to deal with. They had to make it across before the already sinking slab was lost in the depths. "Now!" Garawin yelled.

A whoop went up from Lukas as he spurred his palusa into full flight. The beast's hooves pushed off the shoreline and easily made it to the slab. There was a slight skid as the hooves slid against the layer of dust coating the stone, but the beast was strong, and the next long stride found it on the far shoreline. The force of the palusa's strong leg muscles put the slab into a slight teeter, adding to the roll from the waves of motion rebounding off the shoreline.

There was no time to waiver. "Again!" Garawin shouted.

Ranaa went next with Nolan's arms wrapped around her waist. He was conscious, but she could tell by his fragile hold that he was very weak. The palusa did not hesitate, and with several long strides, it carried them to a position next to Lukas. Each of the travelers followed with each palusa's weight hitting the rolling slab, forming a cloud of white dust into the air. Very little of the slab was still exposed with the sink stone covering the near corner of it, but only Tok was left to jump.

He flicked the reins, but the great beast didn't need any additional urging. It saw the path followed by its fellow beasts and knew what was expected of it. Shooting forward, the hooves dug into the bank and propelled it toward the slab. The landing was cleaner than any of the others, but as its rear hooves thrust off the slab, the layer of dust built up on the red surface proved to be their undoing. The rear hooves slipped out. Beast and rider hurled forward in an uncontrolled roll, and it was obvious they would not make it to the far bank. As the red slab sank from view, the light brown and white palusa slid into the sink stone. Its eyes were wild, knowing a struggle against the slippery stone was futile. A second thud was heard as Tok slammed feet first into the soft stone. The impact of his weight pushed him down to his waist in the suffocating gravel.

Just as quickly, the travelers were off their mounts. They all moved to the bank except for Nolan who was so weak he just fell to his knees. Garawin leaned over the bank and reached out his hand, but Tok was too far away. There was a last snort from the palusa as its snout sunk under the surface, and it was gone. A momentary pang of pain coursed through the prince's bones, but he shook off the desire to yell out his grief. Tok was sinking quickly with the sink stone now around his chest. Garawin shot to his feet and held his hand out behind him. "Take it!" he yelled.

Daniel grasped his wrist, and the other travelers quickly understood the prince's intent. Each locked a wrist with Lukas anchoring the chain with his feet firmly planted in the red rock and sand. Garawin leaned out almost horizontal over the sink stones and stretched his arm forward so far it felt as if his arm socket would tear out. Tok was now up to his neck in the quagmire. The only other thing exposed was one outstretched arm with thick, blue fingers reaching for Garawin.

There was a gasp of despair from Ranaa as she saw the distance between Stor and man was still at least a foot. As Tok continued to sink, the distance grew. There was no hope.

"Further!" Garawin yelled as he let his grip slip, holding Daniel by only his fingertips. Still the gap grew.

Tok's yellow eyes were wide, but they weren't so accepting of death. They were still full of life. Surrounded by the white sink stone, he managed to let out a reverberating, raspy growl. The great war hammer broke upward through the plane of sink stone and arced in a wide circle through the air, raising a cloud of white dust. The thick shaft just under the stone head slapped into Garawin's fingers. As the prince grasped the shaft, he let out another yell. "Pull!"

And they did. Each traveler took small steps backward as their forearms burned like hot iron. Ever so slowly Tok's bulk slid from the stone death, and after a minute of exertion from all, he was laying on the bank, panting for breath. In fact, all of the travelers were on their backs, breathing deep and looking up at the clear sky. Their muscles ached from the effort to pull Tok free, but the mental drain from knowing how close they were to losing one more of the group, exhausted them.

Nolan brought them back to reality. His voice was weak and barely audible above the wind having risen from the west. "Look," he managed.

"What is it?" Garawin asked while still prone on his back, wiping the sweat from his brow with his forearm.

"I think we've arrived," Nolan muttered.

Garawin forced himself up on his elbows and looked toward the Earthman. Nolan was looking at the irregular face of rock shards making up this side of Shadow's Crag. At first it was difficult to see because the various slabs of red stone sat at odd angles to each other, leaving the face devoid of flowing lines. However, as Garawin looked closer, he saw it as well. There was a flat stone terrace at the top of three steps, and on it were four carved round pillars. The pillars supported another slab over top the terrace, providing shelter to any who might enter the dark opening visible at the rear. On the front of each pillar was a round band, and carved into it were crossed hammers and swords.

"The Soichaint mark," Garawin whispered.

"Yes," Chu said. "But long before the Soichaint, it was the mark of the Ionian builders. We've found what has lain hidden for centuries. Behold, the Chamber of the Keys is before us!"

Chapter 21

The smooth, stone wall was cold to the touch. Nolan pulled his hand from it just as he had pulled it from the other seven walls of the octagonal entry chamber. The room was large, being 40 feet across in any direction. In the center of the room was a large hearth comprised of cut, gray stone and filled with large blocks of coal. Tok, recovered from his ordeal with the sink stone, managed to light the coals. Now, two hours later, light and shadow danced across the red and silver walls cut from Shadow's Crag.

Nolan's brow lowered. After a much-needed hour of rest, the travelers had entered the entry chamber, but since that time there was nothing but puzzlement. At the top of each smooth wall was an emblem and a word Nolan didn't recognize. Between Daniel and Chu, the two men had been able to identify an ages-old emblem of each pureblood race and their written name in characters of a long-forgotten, root language.

On one of the walls was the open archway allowing them access to the chamber. Surrounding the opening were colored blocks of picture stones, each cut with a different scene, now weathered with time. Their hopes soared when they saw the weathered words above the top stone. It read -

First Chamber of the Keys

On the opposite wall from the archway was another identical archway with more faded picture stones surrounding it. However, this archway led to nothing but a small six-foot by six-foot alcove. Each of the four walls of the alcove was made of an unusual material appearing to be a mix of intermingled black metal and stone. With no other visible exit from the chamber, the group was at an impasse. Their spirits, heightened by the discovery of the chamber, were slowly spiraling downward as they failed to discover how to move on from this point.

Garawin and Daniel were inspecting the picture stones around the entry archway for the fifteenth time. Lukas, leaving the mental task to the others, was warming his hands over the coals as the sun became consumed by the darkness of night, and a cold chill wandered in from the marsh outside.

Nolan moved over by Ranaa and Chu, who were once again reading the words chiseled into the stone above the archway to the alcove. They read -

Alone with the strength he has amassed,

bearing only his wisdom,

the First Key will be allowed to pass.

"The message is clear enough," Nolan quipped. "I need to go on alone."

"Try again," Chu said.

Nolan strode to the archway and stepped in. Just as it had each of the five times he'd entered previously, the walls of the alcove awoke. Lines of silver, crackling like lightning through the stone, glowed brightly, casting an incandescent radiance within the alcove. Pushing on each wall, he felt the same sense of frustration. Nothing moved, and there were no hidden catches or switches—just himself left with a sense of uselessness. He tried to penetrate the walls with his heightened senses, but something was blocking them. He even considered teleporting to the other side, but without any sense of what was there, he risked rematerializing into solid rock.

Earlier, each of the other travelers also entered the chamber, with the same lack of results. At one point, at a loss for options, all seven members of the group squeezed into the cramped space, and again there was the same lack of results. Nolan surmised that when the alcove lit up, somehow the alcove was scanning with a technology of old, searching for something that hadn't yet been provided.

"Let me try again." The raspy voice of Tok came from just outside the alcove.

Nolan switched positions with the Stor who carried his war hammer cradled in his two wide palms. Once inside the alcove his fingers tightened on the shaft near the base. Once and then twice he swung the hammer in a wide arc before popping his elbows open. The stone head crashed into the wall opposite the doorway, creating a resounding thud with each swing of the Stor's muscular arms. Tok growled as he repeated the process on the other two walls, hitting each at least four times. Finally, putting the stone head to the floor, he leaned on the base of the shaft with one hand. He wiped his brow of sweat, and then ran his nails down each wall with his eyes closely following the trail.

Looking back at Nolan, he shook his head from side to side. "Nothing. Not even a scratch."

Nolan's chest fell as he exhaled a sigh, but when his eyes came back up to Tok's, they were a cold gray as his frustration turned to anger. "Stand back," he said. "In fact, everyone stand all the way back to the far side of the room."

After they were all by the entry archway, Nolan raised a hand and began to form a purple fireball. It consumed his hand, quickly growing to one foot in diameter. Flinging his hand forward, the fireball raced toward the alcove. A bright, purple explosion of light burst from within. Even before the sparks showering back into the chamber hit the floor, a second fireball was on its way. It hit even harder than the first, showering even more sparks back toward the group. Acrid, black smoke billowed out from the alcove, meandering upward toward the clever vent at the central point of the chamber's angled ceiling.

Nolan and Tok moved forward, waving the remaining smoke from their path with their hands. Their hopes dipped as the silver veins alit in the alcove as soon as they entered. It was confirmation of what they had already suspected—there was absolutely no damage to the walls. "Well, that proves this isn't a test of physical strength," Chu said. "It would appear the Ionians of old have left you a *mental* challenge."

Nolan and Tok came out from the alcove, and the Earthman raised his finger to the words above the archway. "It makes no sense at all. It is clear they expect me to go on alone, yet if I enter the chamber alone, nothing happens."

Daniel tapped his finger on his chin. "But something in the words doesn't make sense. It tells you to proceed alone and bring only your wisdom. It's obvious that your wisdom is part of you, so why state it? There is something we are missing here, but I have no idea what it is."

Ranaa, who had been in quiet contemplation for the most part, spoke in her soft voice. "Perhaps it isn't *what* we are missing, but *who* we're missing."

"I don't understand," Daniel responded.

Ranaa tipped her head to the side as she looked at the words above the archway. "I don't think wisdom refers to Nolan's sense of judgment because, as you said, it's obvious." Her eyes turned to look at Chu. "It seems to me we wouldn't ever have arrived here without you. There must be a reason the Ionians left all the information required to find the chamber in your head. Perhaps your reason for being here has not yet ended."

Garawin's eyes lit up. "You are many things to your people, Chu. Are you not also a wise man?" he blurted.

"Yes. I mediate disputes and my decisions are binding."

Nolan was already checking the security of his belt holding the two long knives. "It looks like we might be going on an adventure together—just the two of us." He turned back to the group and said, "If we aren't back in two hours, leave for the plains without us."

We will not leave without you," Daniel was quick to respond.

Putting his hand on his mentor's shoulder, Nolan explained, "You and I know the battle grows near. The Soichaint army is waiting for us, so if we don't make it out in two hours, move on, and we'll find a way to catch up with you."

"A few more hours will not matter," Daniel implored.

Nolan's words were soothing, but still they had an edge to them. "It's not simply a request, my friend."

There was deep respect in Daniel's eyes as he put his own hand on Nolan's shoulder for a moment. There was a pause, and then he grudgingly agreed. "It will be so—two hours."

As Nolan turned to the alcove, he felt Ranaa's soft fingers catch his. The gentle squeeze was just what he needed at this moment. He looked in her eyes, seeing the mixture of sadness and unspoken love. She raised herself on her tiptoes, and her sweet breath assaulted his senses as her lips came close to his ear. "Remember what you told me," she whispered. "Come back. Ownership is easier when you're close by me."

Nolan's face turned, and his lips brushed Ranaa's cheek in the briefest of kisses. Without delaying further, he strode to the alcove and entered. The silver veins of lightning in the stone alit once again. Chu followed, stopping just short of the archway, and his gaze looked one last time at the words chiseled in the red stone. Two steps forward and he was within. Right away, the two felt a vibration followed by a groan that could only come from stone rubbing on stone. Dust shook from the archway as the alcove began to rotate. Nolan watched Ranaa as the archway disappeared foot by foot, and then inch by inch until the line of sight was lost. The rotation of the alcove stopped, and at the same time the silver light from the alcove shut down.

After a minute in total darkness, Nolan said, "Maybe this wasn't such a good idea."

A moment later, there was a flicker of light, followed almost immediately by total darkness once again. A second brief flicker was followed by a third. The fourth flicker did not subside, bathing the two men in light. Looking ahead they saw a ten-foot-wide hallway curving off in the distance. Recessed in the ceiling were round lights every 20 feet, revealing cobwebs and layers of thick dust. This path hadn't been traveled for too many years to count.

The hallway was more clinical than the chamber they just left, having a shiny, plastic coating on the floor. Nolan looked back at his footsteps in the dust and saw it was a slate-blue color as was the arched ceiling. The Earthman swept a layer of dust from the wall, revealing royal-blue tiles shiny enough for him to see his white-haired reflection. He frowned seeing the stark whiteness had now migrated to his eyebrows and the stubble on his chin. Even his gray eyes appeared a shade lighter. The use of his powers was continuing to change him.

"We need to be careful," Nolan whispered as he took calculated steps down the hallway.

"You're correct," Chu replied. "Passing through the alcove was just the first test. I fear there are more tests and even some snares."

They continued around the slow curve, noticing the gradual incline taking them higher into the spires of Shadow's Crag. After an hour negotiating carefully along the hallway, Chu suddenly shot his arm across Nolan's chest. "Stop!" he yelled.

Nolan complied, watching Chu lean forward as he turned his head from side to side while inspecting the walls. "What is it?" Nolan asked.

"I'm not sure. My pulse began to race, and there was a great sense of foreboding that rushed into my mind." The wizen leaned a foot forward and gingerly stepped down. There was a great rumble as a ten-foot section of floor in front of them shook. Chu's arms flailed wildly as he teetered with one foot over the precipice unfolding before him as the floor fell away. Nolan reached out and caught the old man's hand, pulling him back on what was now a ledge overlooking a dark pit. The amount of time until they heard the crashing sound of stone told them the pit was both deep and deadly.

Once safely on the ledge, Chu slapped Nolan's hand away. "I would've been just fine. Everything was under control," he quipped.

A chuckle escaped Nolan's lips. "I was just being overly protective. If you would've fallen in, who would be here to warn me of the traps?"

Chu ignored the comment as he was already looking at the walls and ceiling while considering their next action.

"I could teleport across and see what continues around the curve," Nolan offered.

Chu continued to focus on the wall tiles, working his way back along one side. "No. My senses tell me moving on would be hazardous. We are missing something here," he mumbled as he inspected each tile.

Wiping the dust from one tile after another, Nolan mimicked the wizen's action on the opposite wall. Methodically, he shifted, looking from one blue square to the next. "Hmmm," he muttered as he shifted to the tile he just wiped. He had seen his reflection in every one, yet this tile was dull and reflected nothing. He ran his finger around the seam of the tile and felt nothing odd. Moving his fingers to the surface of it, he gave a sharp push, and the blue surface relented. With the sound of stone scraping on stone, the tile retreated into the wall. Nolan almost jumped out of his skin as he heard a loud pop behind him. Turning instantly, he saw a line of dust on the opposite wall in a shape resembling the perimeter of a doorway. The cleanly cracked perimeter showed them the path to follow.

"That seemed to work," Chu offered. "We need to push."

Both men placed their hands within the area defined by the cracked perimeter, and with their feet planted firmly behind them, pushed. Slowly, the section of tiles within the crack moved back into the wall. Squeaking could be heard, indicating a system of ancient pulleys and counterbalances was allowing them to move the massive weight as it swung to the side. Lights came to life, removing the darkness within the doorway where a long, wide stairway was visible, and at the bottom was a dark opening.

"This way?" Nolan asked.

"Yes, but carefully. I sense there's danger ahead."

Their tentative steps led them down the stairs until they were at another dark opening. Nolan pushed his arm in quickly, then back out. Nothing happened. He removed one of his long knives and tossed it just beyond the line of light. Again, there was no reaction from the darkness.

"We need to go in," Chu coaxed.

"It's been almost two hours. Either we go back now to reconvene with the others, or we're on our own from this point," Nolan suggested.

"Our path to the Keys lies ahead, and I sense we're very close."

Nolan nodded as his lips cut into a grim line. He put his arm around the wizen's shoulder, and together they stepped forward into the darkness. Immediately, recessed lights in the ceiling burst into life. Nolan's eyes went wide as he looked at the wall on their left where thousands of small, pointed darts covering the entire wall were aimed at them. They jumped back toward the stairs, but with a *whoosh*, a thick metal door closed the opening. They were trapped in another long alcove!

"Be careful what you touch!" Chu exclaimed.

The Earthman's glance indicated he understood. Turning, they examined the darts. The tips of some had a slight vibration indicating tension held them in place, but the deadly objects were on the verge of being released. Carefully, they moved to the front wall of the small alcove and saw words chiseled into a plaque at the top of it. They read -

Press the wrong orb, and the darts will fly.

Press the right orb, and you will be let by.

Their gaze lowered along the stone wall at the far end of the alcove. On it were glass orbs half inlaid into the stone, leaving only semi-spheres visible. Nolan counted ten in all where each was a different size.

"On this one my mind is blank." Nolan admitted. "Which one do I push?"

Chu took a few moments to look at the orbs and then shrugged his shoulders. "I have nothing. This puzzle is meant for you."

Putting his nose to the stone wall, Nolan inspected each orb but there was nothing to differentiate them other than a slight difference in size. He pulled back, crossing his arms in frustration. He paced along the length of the alcove, back and forth in front of the deadly darts. After several revolutions, he turned from the steel door and glanced at the orbs on the far wall. He took a double take. From here, further away, there was something familiar in the pattern. He could not put his finger on it, but he had seen this somewhere before. Moving to the wall, he inspected the area between the orbs. He heard Chu take in a deep breath and hold it as Nolan dragged his fingers across the stone. A look of puzzlement pressed across Nolan's face as he felt the small ridge. Moving his hand further across the stone, he felt another ridge and then a third. Using his fingers and his breath, he blew out the ridges. It took some time to clear all of them while keeping clear of an accidental push against the wrong orb.

With the task complete, Nolan took steps backward. By the time his back was at the steel door, a wide smile was on his face. The ridges were actually lines, and even more accurately, a series of ellipses with an orb mounted on each, with all circling the central, larger orb.

"What is it?" Chu asked with his curiosity piqued.

Nolan walked forward and pointed to the central large orb. "This is our sun. Each of the other orbs represents one of the planets in the solar system I come from." He pointed to another orb. "This is Venus, and this is Saturn." Nolan pressed his palm down on the third orb out from the sun. "This is the planet Earth."

Chu gasped as he saw the Earthman's hand press on the orb. He pressed his eyes closed and held his hand over his head. He was sure that in a moment he would be riddled with a thousand darts, but instead, as he pried one eye open, he heard the orb-encrusted stone wall swing away, revealing another vast chamber in front of them.

The wizen let out a nervous laugh as he followed Nolan down the two stairs into the chamber. A flame shot upward from the center of the room, throwing dancing lines of shadow and light across the walls. The flame subsided, but the coals in the central hearth, burning brightly, allowed the two men to view their surroundings. The hearth was the same as that in the first chamber. In fact, the chambers were identical—almost. Instead of eight equal sides of smooth red and silver rock, there were only seven.

"When the Ionians built this chamber, the Shang race was already extinct, removed from the face of the Athar," Chu surmised. Even their scull descendants were erased. One less race, so one less wall."

Nolan was only half listening, and excitement filled his voice. "Look around. The Keys we search for might be in this chamber."

"No, look for another doorway. The Keys will be in another chamber," the old man responded.

"How do you know?"

"Because the Kush race was also extinct at the time this was built. I suspect there is another six-sided chamber still awaiting us."

The old wizen began to make his way around the perimeter with his hand dragging along the cold stone. As they walked around the smooth walls, they looked up at each of the emblems identifying the ancient pureblood races. Other than the emblem, the walls were bare and devoid of any other features. The inspection brought them back to the wall with the archway they came through. They hadn't noticed before, but beside the archway was another dark opening, and curiously, beside that was a small gazing hole, one foot in diameter. Nolan, with the vivid memory of the sharp darts from the last alcove, quickly flashed his hand into the darkness, then back out. There was no response. He turned to the painted figures on the stones framing the archway when suddenly the small alcove lit up. He turned and saw Chu's hand within it.

That's odd," Nolan said. "It worked for you but not me."

"The alcove must have some significance for me."

They didn't step into the alcove, as there was very little room to do so. The light revealed the space filled with a wide, dust-covered chair beside a short, attached table, and the table was empty except for an open metal ring.

"This confuses me even more," Nolan muttered.

Chu was already squatting, looking through the smaller gazing hole. It was also lit up. In it, far out of reach, was a slab of stone teetering on angle from a central support, and on the higher end of the stone was a massive, round, glass vessel. At the top was a cork with a plastic tube that continued through the stone, attaching to the small table just under the steel clamp.

"I don't know what this is, but it looks dangerous. Don't go near it. There must be something else we missed," Chu muttered.

"Let's check again," Nolan suggested. He moved close to the wall and put both hands on it while slowly sidestepping around the perimeter as his eyes checked every inch of the stone face. When he came to the wall opposite the one containing the chair, an irregularity at the top caught his eye. As he pointed to it, both he and Chu focused their eyes, reading the words chiseled in the stone.

Our brother left behind to watch for one of might.

Not brute strength but the will for a peaceful fight.

If in the world of death, he should deem the Key right,

a last heroic sacrifice will send him to the light.

Nolan scratched his head. "I've no idea what this means. It almost appears not to be directed at me but to another." He raised an eyebrow. "It's a little morbid talking of death and sacrifice."

Suddenly, as he spun on his foot, Nolan yelled out, "No!" but it was too late. Chu was already sitting in the chair, and the sickening, metallic click came from the ring clamping on his wrist. Nolan rushed over just as Chu's fingers clenched in pain, then relaxed.

Nolan felt a wave of nausea come over him as the tube filled with red blood. He skidded to his knees in front of the gazing hole and clenched his teeth in frustration as he saw the small trickle of blood begin to fill the large round vessel. *The stone slab was, in fact, a lever, and when enough of Chu's lifeblood filled it, the rock would teeter over and throw a switch,* he thought. He reached in with his hand, but the vessel and stone were too far away.

"No!" Chu yelled. His voice was deep with strength of purpose.

Nolan shot up with his eyes wild. "I can't let you sacrifice yourself like this! My powers can get you out."

The old wizen smiled feebly. "This is my end, Nolan. I was born for this purpose as were my forefathers before me. My life has been spent in the hope I can serve the First Key, and help bring peace to the Athar. It was an oath between the Bantu and Ionian races centuries ago."

Nolan dropped his head. "There has to be another way. I need to release you."

"You know better, Nolan. Finding the Second and Third Keys is *your* priority. I'm nothing compared to the many lives you will save."

The Earthman wavered. With shaking hands, he stepped back from the chair and paced across to the other side of the room. He knew Chu was right. The Keys were more important than any single individual. The test must be for him to understand this, and to persevere through the torture of watching his friend die. Tears formed in his eyes as he looked across the room at Chu. The wizen's eyes were closed, content in the thought his purpose in life was being met. Nolan knew this was the only path—the one the Ionians set out for him long ago.

"Well, screw them." He spat out the words as his cold, gray eyes narrowed, looking at the vessel one-quarter filled with Chu's blood. He snapped his hand toward the stone floor. Beginning with a light breeze, the air began to swirl. Tighter and tighter the vortex churned, lifting the dust from the floor into an ominous cylinder of speeding debris. With a second flick of his wrist toward the vessel, the tight cylinder of dust rushed forward through the gazing hole, and the impact shattered the vessel into a thousand fragments. With firm strides, he strode to Chu whose eyes were wide with shock.

"You don't know what you've done," Chu managed.

"I know exactly what I've done. I've done the right thing. Enough people have died in my name." Nolan lifted his hand again, and the metal ring groaned before snapping open. Stretching an arm around Chu's shoulders, he pulled him out of the chair while his other hand pulled Chu's wrist off the table. Underneath was the ominous needle that had penetrated the wizen's vein.

The old man opened his mouth to vocalize his disapproval, but Nolan's reassuring words stopped him. "It's done. We'll speak of it no more."

Nolan squatted and looked through the round hole at the slab of stone. Again, using his telepathic ability, he focused on the stone slab, and it toppled over. Nothing happened.

Chu's voice was filled with disappointment. "You see, we're lost."

Nolan concentrated, and the stone slab moved a little further. Relief flooded through him as he heard the groan of stone on stone. Both men turned to see the opposite wall underneath the carved words slide to the left, revealing another alcove identical to the one seen in the first chamber. The Earthman strode over and caught himself just before he stepped in. He turned to Chu. "I'm not sure what to do here. In all probability, if you're in the alcove, it will not open. At least if you were supposed to sacrifice yourself here, that would be the case." He thought for a moment. "You enter first. I will follow."

"It won't work. I was supposed to be left behind. Your test was to see if you had the sense to sacrifice one you know for the greater good of all those in the Athar. You have failed."

"Nevertheless," Nolan insisted. "Enter first. I will follow."

Dejected, the old man stepped into the alcove, looking every bit as if the world was ending. To his surprise, the silver veins in the dark, stone walls glowed brightly. Nolan, with a smug grin on his face, stepped in and the alcove began to rotate. The grin turned to a smile, replacing the feelings of distress he'd been hiding.

Chu's face turned from one of dejection to confusion. "This makes no sense. I was to be sacrificed."

Nolan put his hand on Chu's shoulder. "Sometimes you think too much. What is right? What is wrong? Maybe from time to time you just have to take that feeling in the pit of your stomach, and run with it."

"The Ionians were clever. This test even fooled *me*, Chu realized. Although it appeared the test was to see if you had the strength to let me die for a greater cause, the fact the alcove is turning is proof the real test was on your conviction to follow the tough decision of right and wrong which, as you put it, comes from the pit of your stomach."

"They test my powers; they test my intelligence and they test my morality. What is next?" Nolan muttered as the alcove came to a stop.

In front of them was another hallway with the now familiar royal-blue tiles and a slate blue floor. The light in the ceiling showed the length of the hallway to be only ten feet long, and at the end was another dark opening. Nolan was curious and thought, *what test is next?* His fellow travelers, left in the first chamber, would be long gone with the two hours having past some time ago. He needed to find the Second and Third Keys soon. Surely, it wouldn't be much longer before the battle between the Toltec and Celtae was engaged. He wasn't even sure what he would do when he arrived there with the Second and Third Keys. Did people expect him to put on some type of display in the middle of the field of battle? He didn't know, but he would let the events play out. He knew, at the right time, his senses and his friends would guide him.

Nolan poked his head into the darkness at the far end of the hallway. Again, there was a strong sense of trepidation as to what lay beyond. However, there was no choice but to move on, so he stepped within. Just as in the last chamber, a flame shot up through the coal-filled hearth, revealing a chamber similar to the last. Chu had been correct in his forecast, and indeed, this chamber was six-sided. If the wizen's line of logic was correct, the Keys were somewhere within this room.

Nolan took calculated steps within the chamber, followed close on his heels by Chu. Immediately, they noticed that although the chamber was similar to those they passed, this one revealed significant differences. First, the walls were of a similar stone, but through the layer of dust and cobwebs, they could see the color was gold. On a small ledge at the center of each wall was a shelf, and mounted on each was a shiny, metal box topped with a glass plate.

Chu blew onto one of the panes of glass, shooting a small burst of dust into the air. Nolan peered over the wizen's shoulder and saw the outline of a hand etched into the surface. Each of the silver boxes had an identical pattern.

At the top of each wall was the emblem of each of the surviving races except for the wall containing the entranceway. Above this was the ring crossed with the hammer and the sword—the symbol of the Soichaint. Squinting to better see what they expected to be beside the symbol, once again words could be seen scribed into the golden rock. They read -

To stop the war a man shall need,

all brothers and sons to follow his lead.

To stop the war a leader shall hold dear,

strength of character to keep his friends near.

When they come, the Keys will appear.

"Another riddle making absolutely no sense," Nolan muttered.

Chu rubbed his chin. "The last two seemed the same, but after some thought, they were very clear. The words imply the people you lead need to be here."

"I'm getting sick of this," the Earthman grumbled as he slapped his hand into the wall. "The others left a long time ago."

"Clearly, the boxes are here for a reason. Try putting your hand on one."

Moving to the wall with the emblem of the Toltec, Nolan lowered his hand over the silver box but stopped an inch short of the glass. He turned his face to Chu as his eyes held a flicker of doubt.

Closing his eyes, Chu nodded.

When Nolan's hand contacted the glass, it glowed white, and the emblem at the top of the wall also glowed brilliantly. Nolan pulled his hand off the glass and repeated the process several times with the same result. "Come try it yourself," he said to Chu as his hand waved the older man over to him.

Chu put his hand on the glass several times but nothing happened.

The two men moved to the next box under the emblem of the Anasazi. The results were identical with Nolan's hand being able to light the glass and emblem at will while Chu's efforts were futile.

"The plates must be sensitive to me," Nolan said.

Chu tapped his finger against his chin. "Yes, but you cannot push all six of the glass plates at the same time. There's something we are missing."

Nolan turned back to the words scribed into the rock. "There must be a clue here," he muttered. He read the words over and over, and then a thought came to his mind. "I want to try something," he said. "The words say brothers and sons would follow my lead. Each of the pureblood races were considered kin, and the sculls who descended from them are often called their sons. "Put your hand on the glass plate under the Bantu emblem—the emblem of those you descended from.

To his surprise, when Chu placed his hand on the glass, it and the emblem above glowed brightly. "Very clever," Chu chuckled. "I would have had it myself in a few moments."

"Certainly," Nolan grinned. "But what now? We need a hand carrying the DNA of each of the other races here with us. I should have brought the others."

"You couldn't, Chu replied. "There's a riddle within a riddle here. The first alcove would not allow any to pass other than you and I, yet now it looks for others. Logic would dictate there must be another way into this chamber."

Nolan could not disagree with the facts outlined by the wizen. As a result, they inspected the chamber walls again, looking for some sign of a door, a ray of light, hollowness or even a fine seam. Any of these would have lifted their spirits that were beginning to dwindle.

"Perhaps there is a combination of glass plates we need to engage," Chu offered. He put his hand on the Bantu plate and it alit. "Try the others."

As Nolan put his hand on each glass surface, it lit up along with the emblem, but that was all—except when he reached the final plate under the emblem of the Soichaint. When he pressed his hand to the glass, a grinding noise could be heard coming from the far side of the coals. Although they had checked the walls meticulously, they had paid little attention to the stone floor. A section of it was swinging away, revealing stairs leading into the darkness. Both men walked carefully to it and peered over the edge, and to their surprise, they heard footsteps. With a slither of steel both of Nolan's long knives were poised in his hands. The steps came closer, and when Nolan saw the glint of light on steel below, he braced his feet in readiness and yelled, "Withdraw your sword!"

After a tense moment a voice came from below. "Stand down. We are coming up."

Nolan's shoulders sagged with relief, but his face was fraught with confusion as he recognized Daniel's voice. He watched slack-jawed as first the Bailemorian entered the chamber, followed by Garawin, Ranaa, Tok and Lukas.

"How…" was the only word Nolan could manage.

"At the bottom of the stairs is the First Chamber," Daniel stated.

Nolan's eyebrows furrowed. "But I told you to leave. The battle might be pressing on at this very moment."

"We could not leave you behind," Garawin interjected.

Nolan opened his mouth to protest, but was interrupted by Chu. "They did no different than you in the last chamber where you chose to save my life. They did what the feeling in the pit of their stomach told them to do."

Nolan could not argue the point with validity. "It's good you're here," he said to Daniel as he slapped him on the back.

"What do we need to do?" Daniel responded.

"Somewhere in this chamber is hidden the Second and Third Keys. We need to each place a hand on the glass plate under your race. Tok, you are descended from the Ionians. "Place your hand there when we are set. Daniel, you go to the Celtae symbol. Garawin and Chu, move to the Anasazi

Wyld Wynd Unleashed

and Bantu emblems." Suddenly, Nolan's face was downcast. The place under the Toltec emblem was empty. "We're short one person," he realized.

"We need to try in any case," Chu said. "It might work."

Tok began, placing his hairy, blue hand on the glass plate. White light burst from between his fingers, and the emblem also came to life. Each of the others followed and soon the chamber was bathed in white light from each of their ancestry's emblems. Nolan was the last. He looked up at the symbol of the Soichaint and placed his hand on the glass plate. He felt the warmth of the light on his palm as he watched the crossed sword and hammer glow brilliantly. Turning to the others, he kept the illusion of hope on his face, but he knew this wouldn't work. One of the pureblood races was missing.

He was right, and after several minutes with no response from the chamber, he pulled his hand from the plate as did the others.

"Perhaps if I drain some of my blood and put it on the Toltec plate, that might work," Nolan said as he walked toward the center of the chamber. He was joined there by the others near the lit coals, providing the only light for the now dim and cold room. "I didn't think that would work. The shape of a hand is significant."

"If we take some of Nolan's blood and place it on my palm, it might fool the device," Lukas said.

Tok shook his head from side to side. "I don't think that'll work. The Ionian went to quite a bit of trouble to make these chambers. They would not be so foolish as to allow the tests to be duped," he offered.

The discussion became lively with banter back and forth as each gave their opinion. They were interrupted by a glowing white light from behind them. Each of them turned and opened their eyes wide in disbelief. Ranaa's hand was on the glass plate underneath the Toltec symbol which was glowing brightly over top of her. She turned to look at the group as the white light penetrating the cracks between her fingers cast shadows over her face, hiding some of her nervousness.

Barely above a whisper, her trembling voice echoed across the room to the travelers. "In my years in the scull camp on the surface of Crann Bith, I always wondered if the men of Bailemor hunted their own descendants." Her gaze dropped to the floor. "We now know the answer."

For a moment, Nolan was embarrassed. When he first saw Ranaa with her face caste in light from the Toltec emblem, there was a moment of disdain, but it passed quickly. He needed to be a leader of *all* races including the Toltec. While spending his many months on Crann Bith in the company of the Celtae, he heard over and over the evil deeds of the Toltec race. For a moment thoughts of Deahna raced through his mind. The Toltec killed her, and now he found the woman who he deeply cared for was descended from the same race. It left some confusion in his mind.

It was at that moment Ranaa lifted her gaze to his. The look was searching. He also sensed the confusion in her mind even though it was masked with her own sudden loss of self-esteem, knowing the DNA of the same people who killed Germaine and had followed them at every turn, coursed through her body.

Nolan smiled at Ranaa. It gave her assurance, putting aside the doubt she harbored regarding his perception of her. She returned the smile. It was enough for now.

"To your places!" Nolan said, bringing the other travelers out of their own trances.

Each of the travelers once again moved under the emblem of their blood and placed their palms on the glass plates. In turn, each glowed a bright white, basking the room in brilliance. However, this time when Nolan placed his hand on the glass plate under the Soichaint emblem, it glowed brightly, but the color was a bright-green instead of white. Nolan's knees wobbled as he felt the very floor under him shake. He almost fell over as he felt his body begin to lift. Tilting his head downward, he saw a three-foot-square section of the polished, stone floor lifting. In response, the Earthman jumped from the moving stone to the floor beside it while keeping his hand in contact with the glass plate.

After a minute, the groaning of the stone stopped, leaving it three feet above the floor. Under it, the sides of the raised section were intricately carved with the figures of men and women. Their faces showed sorrow and fear while their arms were intertwined in harmony. A ring of Soichaint symbols ran around the top of the three visible sides underneath the three-inch-thick, stone slab. Nolan pressed his hand to the slab, but it didn't move. He put his feet far behind him, and with his body angled almost horizontally, the stone slab shifted an inch as his white knuckled fingers pushed the edge of it.

"It's a lid!" Nolan cried.

The others rushed over. The glow of each emblem died, except for the green Soichaint ring. Under each corner, Nolan, Daniel, Garawin and Tok each placed their fingers. In unison, they put their brawn into lifting the slab. It rose an inch, and the men moved it half way off the raised section before the weight forced them to drop it down.

Nolan's heart raced as he saw a small chamber under the slab. *Surely the two remaining Keys lie within*, he thought. "Again!" he shouted as his voice cracked with excitement.

Once again, the four men lifted. This time the slab was removed from the stone chest and laid on an angle against the side of it.

Nolan leaned over the edge and looked in to see a piece of black felt laying across the top. With his fingers shaking he pulled it aside while being almost afraid to see what was underneath. A blue glow was the first thing he noticed coming from a two-inch-diameter column at the back of the chest. On the top was a small dome glowing a light-blue, and on it was inlaid the etched pattern of the ring crossed by a sword and hammer. Around it, soft white, down feathers filled the chest half way to the top. Gingerly, Nolan slid his fingers into it, waiting for the feel of an object, but with the first pass there was nothing except dust as the centuries old feathers fell apart at the slight touch. He repeated the pass again, and each time a handful of white dust was strewn on the stone floor beside the raised chest. Each time he sifted the feathers his motion became more frantic. Over half the feathers were removed, and he found nothing. The other members of the group looked over his shoulders as he continued his search while the blue light cast an eerie glow on his features. The movements of his hands became wilder as they swam through the feathers, leaving a continuous trail of white dust flowing over each side of the stone chest.

Eventually the chest was empty, so Nolan's fingers dug at the corners at the bottom. "There must be more!" he cried as his nails scraped the stone, and blood dripped from more than one scored finger.

His fingers moved to the sidewall, and there his fingers touched leather instead of stone. His eyes were wide as he pulled the thin, leather-clad book under his gaze. He blew the white dust from the cover, and inlaid in gold letters on the blue leather, it read -

For the First Key

A shaky hand pulled open the cover, revealing a single white page within. Nolan read out the words inscribed on the page in a soft voice as sacred as the ancestors who wrote them.

"Your resolve is the First Key.

Your courage is the Second Key.

Those who follow your vision are the Third Key.

There is no more.

The destiny of mankind lies in the empty hands of men.

You need nothing else.

Believe this yourself, and others will believe in you.

Go. The Athar awaits."

Nolan thought the thunderous beating of his heart would press it through his chest. He leaned over the edge of the chest, clamping his eyelids shut to keep the tears there from flowing freely down his cheeks.

It isn't possible, he thought. He couldn't do this alone. Everything was a test—a test of his strength and courage, and now the greatest test lay before him. He felt more alone than he had in all his life. In the minds of the ancient Ionians the fact he was here reading these words was the proof he was worthy of being the First Key and the leader of the Soichaint's quest for peace. His shoulders slumped even more even though he felt the hands of more than one of his fellow travelers on his shoulders in an effort to reassure him.

Thoughts bounced through his mind. *What should I do now?* The tension in him built and built and his whole body shook. A vibration built deep in his stomach, moving up to his chest and filled his lungs. It was uncontrollable. A deep growl moved to his throat, and the guttural yell brought forth by his deep, natural instincts of animal and beast leapt from his wide-open lips. At the same time his hand sliced down to the blue glowing emblem of the Soichaint at the top of the column until his palm slammed into it. The yell grew even wilder as he felt the instant pain and smelled the burnt flesh. He tried to release his grip on the column, but it was held fast as a beam of light-blue light burst from around his fingers and shot upward through the vent hole in the ceiling. Nolan closed his eyes, and he saw the Athar in his mind's eye. He saw the familiar red and yellow markers, but now he also saw the beam of blue light move across the panorama of thought. As it crossed it left bright, blue markers spotted amongst the yellow and red. More and more blue flooded his mind until he could take no more. It was as if his mind exploded with color.

Then all went black. His hand slipping from the blue orb was the last thing he remembered before he thankfully lost consciousness, slumping to the floor.

Chapter 22

"Nolan. Nolan!"

The calm bliss of the quiet blackness in the Earthman's mind left him. He heard the voice drawing him from the peace of a still mind, free of the troubles of the Athar. Even before his eyes opened, he called the Athar back into his mind's eye. He took a deep breath and held it, wary of the explosion of blue remembered from what seemed only a moment ago. However, the vastness of bright, shocking color was not there. But the Athar was indeed different. Light blue markers now mixed in with the red and yellow that had been the norm since he first invoked the vision almost two years ago. It sent a wave of fear through him, knowing things would never be the same.

"Nolan. Nolan!"

He pried open his eyes and saw Ranaa looking down at him as her fingers softly tapped his cheek. Holding his head, numb from the mysterious blue wave, he sat up and gave her a reassuring smile. As his gaze passed over the room, he saw Chu and Tok helping Garawin and Lukas regain their senses, but Daniel was still unconscious. He realized the wave of psychic energy must have passed through all of them. Lukas looked over to him, and he could sense the fear his blue-haired friend held.

"This isn't right," Lukas whispered as he slowly shook his head.

"The Athar has changed for you also then?" Nolan asked.

Lukas's head nodded up and down.

Nolan turned to Garawin and his head was also nodding up and down, indicating the vision of the Athar in his mind was changed in the same manner. Beside him, Daniel regained consciousness through the tapping of Tok's wide, blue finger on his chest. Nolan didn't have to ask him the same question as the answer came through the confusion seen in his blue eyes.

The pain in Nolan's hand brought him back to the events just passed. The keys were nonexistent. There was only he and those who followed him to bring peace to the Athar. The task, seemingly impossible from the beginning, was now redoubled with doubt. He looked at the dejection on the faces of his fellow travelers and knew it fell to him to give them cause to remove it. If he had hope, they would have hope, and if they had hope, who is to say they couldn't still lead the Soichaint to victory?

"Put the Athar from your mind," Nolan said in a firm voice. "We have business to attend to on the plains of Kaleel."

There was a response from the others, but it was slow and lethargic. Nolan sprung to his feet, hiding the wobble in his knees as best he could. "Quickly now!" he yelled, and the reverberations echoed through the chamber.

The others immediately hastened their actions. In moments they were all on their feet, striding down the stairs leading them back to the first chamber. Just outside, the palusas awaited with their snouts dancing in the air as they smelled the scent of a new day. To the traveler's surprise, beyond the beasts, the sink stone river sizzled and popped. As they moved closer, heat hit them squarely in the face. Garawin picked up a large stone and threw it in the center, and it bounced across the surface before settling on top of the hardened configuration of stone and dust.

"It would appear the Ionians even gave us a way out," Tok said in his raspy voice.

"But the surface is hot. It will be some time before we can pass," Garawin added.

Nolan pointed to the sky in the distance. "It won't be that long," he said. The black clouds tumbled toward them with the wall of pummeling rain underneath. It took only another five minutes for the heavy droplets to fall on the melded, sink stone surface, resulting in a high-pitched whistle of steam. The travelers held their hands to their ears as they watched from the protection of the stone awning covering the entry to the first chamber. Great clouds of white steam curled upward only to be beat downward by the rain. The ebb and flow of light versus dark continued until finally the heat relented. When the rain stopped, a thin, two-inch layer of crystal-clear water lay on top of the once deadly sink stone river. As far as the eye could see in each direction, the water reflected the sun's light, giving it a mirror finish.

Nolan, having already mounted his palusa, coaxed it to the bank where the short drop to the sink stone held the glass-like surface in place. The beast bent its front legs, and a hoof touched the water. Uniform circles flowed out, causing the surface to hypnotically undulate. The second time the palusa pressed its hoof down, it made contact with the stone surface below. Feeling the solid resistance, it carefully walked out into the shallow river. The others followed, awed by the beauty of the water which not so long ago held only the likelihood of death. They left the chambers of the Three Keys behind them and hastily left Kilean marsh by the same route used for their arrival.

Three hours later at the roadway, Nolan asked, "Which way?"

"We need to proceed quickly, following this road until we're past the north face of Shadow's Crag," Garawin offered. "From there, we can plunge directly across the land. The palusas are strong and can manage the canals, field and forest." The prince pulled one eye into a squint as he said. "In four hours we should be on the plains of Kaleel."

For the next three hours, there was no discussion as the beasts moved at a steady gallop, first north and then west across the Iswan countryside. The hooves of the great beasts hammered into the water of the shallower canals while they showed their versatility, swimming strongly across the deeper ones. The softly undulating fields were not a challenge nor were the forests where low-hung branches whipped across the skin of beast and human alike.

As the horses exploded from a line of trees, they were pulled to a halt. Just ahead, five men on palusas were talking amongst themselves as they surveyed the ground. As the two parties sighted each other, the five drew their swords, and their palusas were slowly sidestepped toward the travelers.

"Who are you?" one of the men demanded.

Garawin spurred his palusa forward. He looked at the blue and silver uniforms. A red crest covered with a silver bird in flight having great, sharp talons, drew his gaze. "I have not known the personal guard of King Lothar of Savantee to be so rude," he said as his cold stare moved to the eyes of the bold, young soldier.

The palusa danced lightly back and forth as the soldier responded. "My apologies, but war is upon us, and we search for Prince Garawin and the First Key."

"Then you have found him," the prince bellowed in response.

"Thank god!" the young guard said. He removed his round, chrome helmet adorned with a tuft of white fur protruding from the small metal spike at the top. "I am Taluk Bar, Captain of the King's Guard. He sent me to hasten you to the field of battle. The initial forays have been going on for a day, and soon the battle will be fully engaged."

Nolan skipped his palusa forward next to the young captain. "I'm Nolan Harrison and these are my fellow travelers." He held his hand out to Taluk Bar.

The young captain held his hand out, and it shook as his fingers grasped Nolan's forearm. "You—you are the one," he stammered. Taluk Bar could not help but stare at Nolan's snow-white hair and eyebrows, but he dare not look at the First Key's eyes that were gray with the whites now colored a very light, pale blue.

Nolan was confused. The captain found his goal, yet he saw the fear in him. "What is it, Captain?" he asked.

"There is talk the world is ending," Taluk Bar blurted. "The purebloods say the Athar has changed and will never be the same. Yesterday, every one of them fell into unconsciousness, and when they awoke, they wailed and cried. Many held their heads like children as they knelt on the ground in shock. Fortunately, the event slowed the battle, but it didn't take long for both sides to renew their hate, thinking the other caste was responsible for the monumental change."

Nolan thought the same thing the rest of the group did. *The change in the Athar with blue added to red and yellow changed in every pureblood throughout the Athar.* He was not sure what he had unleashed from the chest. Was it a weapon or was it a sign of their destruction?

He gave a reassuring smile to the captain. "Fear not. The purebloods were given a sign from the Soichaint. The power of peace was sent as a signal to all of them, and it is the first step in our victory this day."

"Then we need to fly our beasts. My king has demanded I bring you to him with all haste." The young captain put the helmet back on his head, and the fear in his eyes was replaced with resolve. He spurred his steed to speed, and the rest of the group did the same, following the dust trail of the determined captain's mount.

"Who are they?" Julian asked as he pulled the binoculars from his eyes and passed them to Theron.

Theron, the Vice-Prime of the Kre nation, pulled the binoculars to his face and looked across the sloping plain to their right. Squad by squad, the Soichaint army was forming at the far end of the valley. On the crest of the hill, where the Soichaint army waited, a group of riders had appeared. They were on fine, large mounts, and their presence was creating a stir amongst the soldiers.

He counted. Through the binoculars, he could see the odd group mounted on the rare beasts he had come to know as palusas. There were four men, one quite old, a woman and one Stor who he assumed was a servant to the others. His gaze was drawn to the rider in the lead. His unusual white hair stood him out from the rest of the Soichaint followers.

"I suspect your First Key has arrived in spite of the measures you told me would not make it possible," Theron said with a disappointing sigh.

Julian recovered the binoculars from the offered hand of the Kre and looked across the field for a second time. He focused the lens on the man with the white hair, turning the dial to increase the magnification to maximum. Reviewing the face in great detail more than once, he finally whispered, "So we meet again, Nolan Harrison and Mister Daniel Dupuis."

"You've met them before?" Theron asked.

"Yes, on his home planet. He escaped then, but I'll not make the same mistake again."

Before Julian's words were complete, there was an area of the Soichaint hill where the tall, yellow grass fell over. The air above it turned opaque, and he couldn't see through it. Colors formed in the swirling shape, but as Julian watched, they moved into a semblance of order. He could begin to make out the shapes of legs and arms carrying spears. A few moments later, the teleportation was complete and eight thousand warriors were added to the Soichaint numbers. He handed the binoculars back to Theron and asked in a curt voice, "Who are they?"

With the binoculars held to his eyes, Theron said, "They are Anasazi—Outriders to be exact."

"Those are some of the deadliest soldiers the Anasazi have to offer," Julian mumbled.

Another two areas of the Soichaint hill turned color. The same psychic event they just witnessed, happened again in each area. When it was complete, ten thousand Anasazi soldiers from Bolirax and another five thousand from Snowshold stood beside the Outriders of Rivenloc. "I believe the Anasazi have arrived," Theron said.

"How many soldiers do the Soichaint have in all?" Julian asked.

"There are now close to 50 thousand in total."

Julian closed one eye as he performed calculations in his head. "There are only 23 thousand Anasazi in that number. Let's face it. They're the weakest of the remaining purebloods. Even with this mythical First Key—" He chuckled as he said the words "—they're a threat we need not worry about any longer."

Turning to the army across from him on the far slope, Julian considered their numbers. "There are 80 thousand Celtae there, and that is where our focus needs to be. However, let's see if we can draw out the First Key and see what he is made of." He snapped his fingers over his head and yelled, "Jelan Tulis, to me!"

The big man was beside Julian in an instant. "Yes, Commander," he said.

"Take a message to General Tyril. I want him to send a detachment of Malagar's finest foot soldiers forward for another probe. I want this one to be the deepest yet, and I want to see damage to the Celtae front line."

"Right away, Commander!" Jelan Tulis snapped a salute and was on his sakcaj in a moment. The creature was large for its species and carried Jelan well. After a few moments, all that remained was the dust cloud kicked up from its three-toed hooves.

Nolan Harrison rode in front of his fellow travelers as they passed each group of soldiers comprising the Soichaint army. Each had a different custom in greeting, but the joy and smiles on each of their faces was a common theme. Some raised their weapons in cheer while others yelled, and more than one group dropped to one knee, taking up a reverent pose. The Soichaint army's spirits were lifted by his coming. In each of the soldier's minds they were convinced the prophecy was true, and any true god must surely be on their side.

Having finished reviewing the army, Nolan turned his mount to the group of tents at the highest point on the hill. There, he found the kings, regents and leaders of the lands providing the soldiers to the cause. One man stepped forward. He was old with a white beard, but he wore the armor of a warrior, and from the way he moved in it, the message not to underestimate the long sword hanging from his belt, was clear. He dropped to one knee, but with his strong eyes still looking up at Nolan, King Lothar of Savantee said, "Our welcome to the First Key. We, the Kings of Iswan, and the other leaders of our allies, greet you and turn over leadership of the Soichaint army. We are in your service." Steel rasped on steel, and Lothar's sword was out from its sheath. He placed it on the ground in front of him. There was a great metallic din across the field as first each king also went on one knee and pulled out their royal weapons to symbolically put them on the ground in front of the First Key.

The action passed across the field of warriors until every fighter was on one knee with weapons offered to serve Nolan, a once simple man from a plane called Earth, but now the unquestionable spiritual and military leader of them all.

Nolan pulled a leg over his palusa and jumped from his mount. He pulled each of the kings up to their feet. The army, seeing this, arose also and went about their duties as the Earthman went about addressing the kings. "I accept your charge, and thank you for your allegiance. From this point on, you'll not serve me again by kneeling. Rather, your service will be on your feet, wielding your weapons and using your mind's power to ensure that at the end of the day, the death we will both hold and inflict will result in peace for all, and the sacrifices we each make will not be in vain."

There was no response from the Kings of Iswan. They stood in front of Nolan in what appeared to be an uncomfortable moment.

"What is it?" Nolan asked.

"Forgive us, but you're the First Key and you've seen your effect on the spirit of the army, but we need to show the Toltec and Celtae we have all Three Keys. That will break their resolve, and quite possibly bring many over to our side before any blood is let."

"In life, things aren't always as simple as we would like them. The Second and Third Keys as described in folklore aren't as some might hope." Nolan saw the spirit in the eyes of the king's immediately fall. "The keys to stopping the bloodshed lie in each of you and in each of them." He pointed his finger at the troops cascaded in groups across the hill. "They have the courage to be here to fight for what they believe is just. No object or device can compare to a man's will to do what is right so that when he goes home to his family, and he looks in the eyes of his children, he sees the pride they have in him."

"These men will have fear when they hear they are on their own," King Lothar said.

"They're not alone!" Nolan replied with a voice seldom raised. "All are here together. Call them gods, the creator, or visions of our forefathers— they are all here with us." Nolan continued as he weaved between the kings. "Yesterday, did you not see every pureblood on the field drop into unconsciousness? Have you not heard how the pureblood Athar is changed? Have you not seen the fear in their eyes and the hesitation in their step? My destiny was to be here on this day and ensure the purebloods who would continue to kill for the sake of killing, know it was I who did this. I sent the wave of energy felling every pureblood, not only on this field, but also throughout the infinite Athar. They know I'm here, and they'll be sorry to test my resolve."

Daniel raised an eyebrow as he looked at Nolan. The Earthman had not altogether lied, but he had certainly embellished the events leading to the blue markers in all their minds.

The kings appeared more relaxed as the nervous fear left their eyes. They just met Nolan, and Daniel could tell they were impressed by the young man's character.

The discussion was interrupted by a trumpet blaring in the background. Nolan turned and watched with the kings as a group of five hundred warriors broke in a steady gait from the Toltec line. They moved in a slow loop away from their position, curling downward toward the Celtae front. Half the men carried square shields almost as tall as their height, colorfully adorned in yellow and red-striped lines of dye.

"It's another probe sent forth to test the Celtae defenses," Lothar said. "There have been many in the past two days."

The horde broke into five groups and rushed forward at full speed down the gentle slope. The men carrying the shields were in the front with the remainder close on their heels. They made quick time. They were a third the way up the far slope toward the Celtae when a shout was heard from the enemy line. A long row of Celtae warriors dropped to one knee, and the archers behind them let loose a volley of arrows. At least a thousand deadly tips arced toward the oncoming Toltec. The men carrying the shields stopped and jammed the bases of the shields into the earth. The carriers huddled underneath as they angled the large curved surface, leaving enough room for their partner to fit into the cover of each shield. The arrows ripped into the attackers. Most arrows ricocheted off the shields, but some found human flesh.

The group sprang to their feet, leaving their fallen behind. Another 50 yards at a full run, and the twang of a thousand bowstrings sang through the air. Once again the warriors huddled under their shields as the arrows brought death to those exposed. However, this time, after the arrows had dropped, the men down on one knee slung their shields to the side. Their comrades behind them bolted upright, and hundreds of glowing balls of energy were released from their fingers in unison. They hurtled toward a common point at the center of the Celtae line. In response, the warriors there huddled together shoulder to shoulder with the two rows of warriors just behind pressing forward until they were all in a tight pack. Their green, psychic shields flared into life just before the orange wave of energy hit them. Bodies flew tens of feet in the air as the two energies collided. Celtae dead were strewn on the ground, but more soldiers from the ranks filled the gaps.

The process repeated several times with the Celtae archers attempting to time their arrows to when the Toltec men were throwing their volley, and of course, the Toltec tried to release their attack in between the deadly flights. Slowly, the Toltec moved closer, ten yards at a time. As each yard of ground was gained, another ten Toltec lay dead in the long grass of the valley.

Nolan watched in disappointment at the carnage with dead bodies littering both sides. The disappointment was heightened when he saw another horde of five hundred Toltec begin their swooping run to replenish their fallen dead.

Nolan turned to Daniel. "I need to send a message."

"What do you mean?"

"The Soichaint need to have faith in me, and the warriors in the valley need to understand there are options to war. Even they have heard the rumors of my coming. They need to see I'm here," Nolan replied solemnly.

Before Daniel could argue the point, the Earthman's figure stretched and curved momentarily before disappearing from view. Looking toward the field, he saw Nolan's resulting teleportation complete in the middle ground between the remaining Toltec forces and the Celtae front line. His shield flared a bright-green, and his white hair swung off his collar as he threw two purple fireballs at the remaining Toltec shields. Metal cracked and bodies flew with the impact even as a thunder of arrows rattled into his back. He turned and lifted his hand with his fingers clenched in a tight fist. As he sprung them open, three large boulders were levitated into the air and then hurtled toward the line of archers. As the men turned and ducked, the solid rock crushed them, leaving many dead with broken and twisted bodies.

The First Key turned again, expecting an assault from the Toltec, but they were in flight after dropping their shields to allow them even more speed. The second oncoming horde stopped in their tracks, and amongst the blaring of horns from the Toltec rear, they retreated back to the safety of their lines.

Nolan raised his hands to the air and focused. The message could be heard in the minds of every pureblood on both sides—even those Anasazi in the Soichaint forces.

Join us. Peace is at hand!

Nolan's vision blurred, and then he was once again right beside Daniel. The entire event only took three minutes—three minutes forcing chaos into both sides of the battle. Murmurs grew to loud discussions and yells as arguments broke out. Each army was in disarray.

Julian Morenz couldn't speak for several minutes, and his face was red with rage. He saw how easily Nolan Harrison dispatched an elite group of troops from Malagar. The First Key made a point of using several powers. Teleportation, the energy shield and telekinesis, long forgotten with the extinct races, had all been used with great skill. It was no wonder his army was awash with confusion and doubt.

Julian turned to Jelan Tulis and said, "Bring a white flag. We're going to parley with these Soichaint and see what they really want."

From behind Julian, General Kouros cried, "Are you sure that's wise? He could kill you with a blink of his eye!"

219

Turning with his eyelids narrowed, Julian surveyed his generals. "Theron and Tyril, you'll come with me. Jelan, see to General Ramos on the east flank. His soldiers are restless. They're the closest to the Soichaint forces, and they must hold their position. If any waver and move to the peace movement, they're to be killed. The rest of you, go to your men, and get them in order. Move!"

Jelan was on his sakcaj in an instant. He spurred the beast to the eastern flank while Julian, Theron and General Tyril mounted their beasts. Julian, on his white and pink albino, led them to the bottom of the valley. Not to be left behind, it didn't take long for a group of men to break from the Celtae ranks. A moment after that, five palusas began their noble gallop down from the Soichaint line toward the base of the valley.

Julian had a sneer of disgust on his face as he recognized Daniel and Nolan under his white brow of hair. "It is unfortunate we meet again under these circumstances," he said once the larger palusas came to a halt.

"You know these scum?" Jerric, the leader of the Celtae forces, growled in front of his three captains.

"Once, and they escaped, but they will not be so lucky this time," Julian said to the Celtae before looking up at Nolan on his tall steed. "Your magic show was quite impressive. Perhaps you can also juggle some balls or pull a coin from behind my ear."

Nolan sighed. "Many of your people and the Celtae lay dead on the field of battle. If you don't pull back and remove yourselves from this world, many more of you will die, not only at my hand but by the hand of those who follow me."

Leaning his head to the side so he could see around Nolan's palusas, one eye squinted to block out the sun. "I see only 50 thousand soldiers," Julian said. "I alone have 80 thousand expertly trained, pureblood warriors at hand."

Julian lifted his head and smiled smugly at Nolan, but it didn't last long. In the distance over the eastern hill, a rumble could be heard. It became louder and louder with a mechanical, droning beat. They all looked in the direction of the noise and saw a sea of blue break over the crest of the hill. At least ten thousand Stor warriors rolled over the long grass at a slow run with the feet of each moving in unison. Each time their cadence of feet hit the ground, they tapped the head of their mighty war hammers against their brightly-colored shields.

Tok, mounted on a palusa next to Nolan, gave a raspy chuckle. "Stirm has arrived."

"As have the tribesman," Chu added. He lifted a closed fist in the air, and a shrill, high-pitched sound came from his mouth. In response another deep sound, as ominous as that from the Stor's, came from the cliffs bordering the western edge of the valley. It sounded like thousands of giant birds flapping their wings against the air. "*Hoooo—hooo—hooo*." The sound echoed off the rocks and circled the field of battle. As the group searched for the source of the sound, dots of yellow appeared from between the crevices and from behind the rocks at the cliffside in the distance. More and more became visible until there was more yellow than gray.

"Nolan, here are another 15 thousand wildmen of Kaleel at your disposal," Chu said proudly.

"Enough of the theatrics," Jerric screamed. "I count 70 thousand who will try and stop this battle, and between the Toltec and Celtae forces, there are 160 thousand pureblood fighters. You peace activists are right. We don't care who we fight." He pointed at Nolan. "We will fight you just as well as the Toltec."

Jelan Tulis watched the group at the base of the valley. He watched in amazement as both the army of blue creatures and the savages in the rocks made themselves known. The pieces were quickly falling in place. He owned one of the last pieces—the one he had been waiting to play almost all of his life. The surgical change in his face, the lengthy time he spent in prison waiting and the service to this imbecile Julian, all led to this moment. It was time for his piece to be played.

Jelan arrived at the table set out at the rear of the Kaezzar military forces where fully 20 thousand soldiers were at the disposal of General Ramos. As Jelan jumped from his mount, the general and his two captains rose to their feet.

"What news?" General Ramos asked.

"I have orders directly from Supreme Commander Morenz. Explicitly, he states you are to follow them to the letter," Jelan replied.

"Out with it then," Ramos said as he circled his hand as if it would draw out the orders faster.

"The cause is lost. The Toltec have decided to join the peace movement. You are to take all 20 thousand of your men, and take your place on the open space on the northern flank of the Soichaint forces."

Ramos's jaw dropped, and his hand stopped in mid-circle. "You can't be serious."

"I'm very serious."

General Ramos's face went white, and confusion clouded over his eyes. "This makes no sense," he mumbled. "A move to peace? It's something many want, but we're soldiers here to fight our sworn enemy." He paced back and forth in front of the table with his fingers clasped together behind his back.

"You need to follow your orders," Jelan repeated in a voice devoid of the emotion screaming through his veins.

"The orders are treason," Ramos said as his eyes went dark. Just as quickly, they opened wide and glazed over. "But if I don't follow my orders, that *also* is treason." His voice trailed off into the wind.

"If I might, Sir." The voice came from the captain next to the table.

"What is it, Captain Sherman?" Ramos asked, thankful for an opinion of any type.

Captain Drew Sherman rubbed his bearded chin, remembering that under the stubble was the long scar along his jawline. It was one of many remembrances from the ongoing war. After completing his assignment for Julian on Earth, he was recalled into the general military, and as a result of some careful planning by Adrian Korlis, here he now stood in a crucial moment for the peace movement. This was the time for him to play his part and engrain his will on the young general, just as surely as the emblem of the Soichaint was emblazoned on his chest.

"You're a leader of these men, General," Sherman said. "Look at them! They're young and confused. Half of them want to bolt to the Soichaint even without the order from you, and many are little older than children. They don't want to die uselessly on a field on a foreign world."

Ramos starred at Sherman as hesitation lingered in his eyes.

"Think of the roar of life which will flow across the field as you give the order to join the Soichaint. You'll be a hero forever remembered in our history books as the one who broke the delay. Your courage will leave a statue of you on the far cliffs and also in front of the military headquarters back at home on Kaezzar. You can do this."

Brightness came into General Ramos's eyes. In his mind he envisioned his face chiseled onto the far cliffs above the monument that would forever carry his name as the one who propelled the pureblood races toward peace. "Rouse the troops!" he yelled. "We are joining the Soichaint. Peace for us all!"

There was a great roar from the Toltec division. Julian turned his head to see his suddenly boisterous Kaezzarites as they threw their caps in the air. On mass, 20 thousand loyal troops ran east, up the incline of yellow grass, and filled the open piece of plain on the Soichaint's flank. "No!" he yelled. "It's not possible!"

Theron, calm as he always was, said, "Its best we go and try to recover your troops."

Julian was already bouncing up and down on the rump of the sakcaj as he spurred it toward his command center at a full gallop. He never learned to ride the beast well, so he looked foolish on the virginal beast as he made his way back to his depleted forces.

Back at the base of the field, Nolan clicked the reins, and the palusa picked up a casual gait back to the Soichaint lines. His comrades followed. Half way up the incline there was another roar from the Celtae lines. The Akkadian blue-swords were easily recognizable by their midnight-blue uniforms and the plume of tightly-wound, light-blue feathers strung from the back of their helmets. As they cheered, 25 thousand men broke from the Celtae mass and took up position on the southern flank of the Soichaint army.

Daniel had as wide a smile on his face as Nolan had ever seen. "What is it?" the Earthman asked.

"Do you see the man at the front, leading the Akkadians across the field?"

"Yes," Nolan replied.

"That is General Kato Corrowin, my bond brother," Daniel stated. "He is as good a man as you will ever meet."

Once Nolan arrived back at the tent that also served as the command center of the Soichaint army, he grouped together his fellow travelers and the leaders and kings of all the participating nations. Twenty proud men stood in front of him as he began his address.

"Look behind you," Nolan said.

The heads of the leaders turned to look at the valley. The far flank of the Toltec army was rolling down into it on the opposite slope. The Celtae forces were performing a similar move, until the edges of the two armies touched. Well over a hundred thousand men formed into one huge army facing the Soichaint forces.

"Welcome to those who have joined us," Nolan said. "We'll need your added strength and resolve. Even though our ranks have swelled, we're still outnumbered. The Toltec and Celtae across the field appear to have their minds set on a battle, no matter who the foe is. However, I can't ask you to sacrifice more of your lives. The Soichaint have made a mark on the Athar today. It is time to negotiate rather than attack."

A murmur passed over the leaders and they shifted more from restlessness than nervousness. "I for one do not agree." It was the strong voice of King Lothar of Savantee.

"Nor do I—nor I." More than a few leaders vocalized their agreement with King Lothar.

Nolan waved his hand in front of himself. "There has been enough death already today. It's time to negotiate."

Tok pushed through the other leaders so he could be heard. To the surprise of more than a few, he spoke his thoughts. "The enemy is not staying to negotiate, Nolan. We need to finish this today. Indeed, there will be bloodshed, but finishing it today will avoid even more bloodshed in the future."

His face was red with frustration as his arm shot out, and a finger pointed across the valley. "They outnumber us!" Nolan yelled.

"Only in pure number of soldiers," Garawin replied. "However, in conviction and the spirit coming with it, we have the greater advantage. When they see this, they will easily be discouraged and broken."

Nolan looked down at the ground. "I cannot ask you to do this," he repeated.

King Lothar chuckled. "I might be old, but my memory does not yet fail me. You did not ask me here or these others. We are here because we believe in an ongoing peace. With all due respect—" He paused for a moment, his eyes bright with pride "—we're here with you, not as subjects but as equals, and as your equals, our vote is to finish what we began today."

Nolan's face lifted, carrying a less than convincing smile. The words were spoken with a hush, but as he continued, they became deeper and louder with conviction. "Then, as your equal, we shall finish this. When the sun sets over this land today, a flag bearing the crossed hammer and sword will fly proudly over this plain. Victory will be ours!"

There was a rousing cheer. Through it, Lothar yelled, "What is the plan of attack?"

Nolan's eyes turned to Chu. "Send a runner to your men in the cliffs. Tell them to harass the rear of their forces, and keep them looking over their shoulders. Hit and run! Hit and run!"

Kato Corrowin spoke. "The two flanks should attack and spread their forces thin."

"An excellent thought, Kato, but they've enough soldiers to react and defeat the attacks. Attacking the flanks is indeed what they will expect, and we'll comply with that, but as their forces spread to the flanks, the fastest detachments we have will thunder to the center. The wildmen of Kaleel will do the same from the rear, and when our forces meet, we'll turn and divide their army in two. Then we will have the advantage of numbers." Nolan finished with his fingers clenched into a tight fist in front of him.

There were murmurs of approval from the group.

"Go now and prepare. In ten minutes, with the blast of two horns, we begin!" Nolan said.

Nolan finally found himself caught up in the excitement. As arranged, when the two long trumpet blasts sounded, the Stors marched forward from the right flank with their war hammers beating against their shields in unison to the beat of their feet. On the left the Anasazi forces, led by the Outriders carrying their short spears, moved forward in a slow gait. With the center of the Soichaint line fixed in position, the rest of the line curved with the movement of the flanks. It was sprung like a bow with the center ready to explode.

Sure enough, soldiers were seen running in the back of the enemy's line. Some detachments moved to bolster the flanks where they expected the first blows to land while smaller groups battled the forays of Chu's kinsmen at the rear. How unnerving it must be for the Toltec and Celtae! Dealing with the black-skinned men, wearing yellow animal furs and covered with striped war paint on their faces, was causing the enemy's fighters trouble. They would spring up from the tall grass, 50 wildmen at a time and stab at the rear of the line, kill five to ten warriors and then depart just as quickly.

Julian was immature, cruel and less than wise in his personal decisions, but he wasn't a stupid man when it came to warfare. He was brought up in its shadow, and he was a student of the history of many epic battles. Having studied many of them in the history books on Kaezzar, he was suspicious of the Soichaint movements. He barked out his orders. "Move men to bolster the flanks, but Theron, keep your Kre in the center. I need strength here to hold us together.

The remaining generals still allied with Julian and General Jerric, nodded their heads in acknowledgment. Whispers were heard as the orders were sent back to their subordinates, followed by the pounding hoofs of the sakcajs as they took their messengers to the troops along the line.

It didn't take long for the ploy to reveal itself. When the flanks of the Soichaint forces were almost upon the line of Toltec and Celtae, Nolan yelled out the order to attack. As if they were released from a cannon, the Soichaint center thundered forward. The Kaezzar troops led by General Ramos and the Akkadian blue-swords led by Kato Corrowin rushed forward. In front of them, five thousand men and women from the mixed armies of the provinces of Iswan rushed across the field. In front of them, Nolan and his fellow travelers, with their weapons held high, led the charge.

Julian saw the ploy and was ready for it. He ordered the Sillians and the Kre forward to meet the attack. The Sillians, who were experts with the long pikes they wielded, were at the forefront. General Jerric ordered two divisions of his Gwyneddmen to follow close behind, reinforcing the charge from their own lines. Both armies hurtled toward each other, quickly closing the half-mile gap between them.

The wind blew lightly from the north, but a new, fresh breeze came over the cliff face to the west. It rolled over the sharp rock and bounced off the yellow grass dotted with tall, blue flower stalks growing through it. The wind grew in intensity, rolling up the gentle hillside and sweeping across the

Soichaint encampment. The tents rippled as the strong wind, growing in strength, almost blew them over. Wild in its movements, the wind accelerated up the far hillside before rolling back on itself. It then whistled down the slope toward the very center of the valley where the two armies were about to meet.

Fixated on the battle to come, neither Nolan nor Julian noticed the wind until its front began to boil and pitch. White clouds rolled from a wide circle, and the area between became translucent, then solid with mixed colors. Now many of the warriors did notice, drawn by the wind as the howl turned to an all-out shriek. Since they were in their battle frenzy, it didn't stop them even as the first white-clad warriors burst through the translucent colors.

In a full gallop, one close after the other, groups of mounted warriors thundered through the rift that had appeared in the wind. Five abreast, the warriors were donned in silver with blue trim at their belt and a crossed harness supporting their swords behind their backs. Light-blue fur hung in a tight braid from the back of their silver helmets, and flowing from their backs were capes of light-blue trimmed in yellow. However, the most noticeable characteristic of the mysterious riders bursting from the wind was their hair. Each of them had long, flowing hair blowing in the wind, and it was as white as the purest snow Nolan had ever seen.

The rift did not close before five hundred warriors, each riding a great ferocious beast, thrust through the seemingly mystical opening. The creatures were also stark-white and stood at least 12 feet tall. They were marked by legs that appeared to move slowly, but their long length bore them down the hillside at great speed. The beast's long necks reminded Nolan of a giraffe, but it didn't appear so docile as its snout was adorned with two curved tusks.

Although there was some hesitation, only five hundred riders wouldn't deter the many thousands of warriors thundering toward each other in the heat of the anticipated blood bath. A white rider in the middle of the front line of five pushed ahead of the others. A gloved hand was raised and thrust forward. The natural elements were at his beck and call. First it was only a vibration, but quickly the whole field shook, and more than a few of the oncoming warriors and steeds fell. However, the mass was not deterred and continued to press forward.

The shaking grew more violent, and then suddenly stopped as a line of rock and dirt flew upward from the center of the field. In its wake, a great ten-foot-wide crevice split the field of battle between the two armies, from one end to the other. It took a great effort for the momentum of both armies to stop. Pushed forward by the numbers in the rear, a few soldiers screamed as they were pressed into the crevice, but the armies did eventually stop.

The long line of white warriors split in two with half running parallel to either side of the long, narrow fissure at the base of the valley. By now many of the warring soldiers had turned and run for their encampments. Only a very few, including the leaders of both armies, stayed at the edge of the crevice to meet the mysterious white warriors. Nolan watched as the warriors on the great, white beasts slowed to a gait. The battlefield was now quiet, leaving Nolan, his fellow travelers and the Kings of Iswan on one side of the crevice, with Julian, Theron, Jerric and the other generals on the side opposite to them.

Julian looked up at the white warrior who had parted the land and yelled, "You have no right to intervene—whoever you are! Leave now before we…"

The white warrior raised his hand up in front of his chest and pushed his finger and thumb together in a quick snapping motion. Julian's lips kept moving, but his voice was gone. He tried over and over for the words to continue, but there was nothing but air expelled.

Jumping off his unusual steed, the white warrior moved to a position directly between the two groups of leaders. "His voice is gone forever. It was the only weapon he could truly wield when need be, and now it is no more. Now he is harmless. We show him both pity and mercy."

The onlooker's eyes were wide in shock, but they dared not interrupt the man. "I am Rhuarc, Prince of Tolardsaxe, sent here to represent Ionia."

Garawin's words stumbled. "Ionia? The Ionians have been extinct for centuries."

There was something calming as the man laughed. His white hair matched his white eyebrows, and his pupils were fair, surrounded by an electric-blue tint where there should have been white.

"The Ionians are not extinct," he said. "Centuries ago, as your three races continued to press all your efforts into war, we Ionians put that energy into technology and science. We found within the multi-dimensions of space another level out of synchronization with what we purebloods call the

Athar. The skill to travel into it was learned and then harnessed. We have kept ourselves hidden from you for what must seem time on end, so you could ply your trade of war while we grew in our quest for life with the powers of all the races."

"It's impossible," Lukas mumbled.

"Look in your own minds for proof if my men mounted here in front of you is insufficient. The blue dots on your view of the Athar are the Ionian markers added to those of red and yellow," Rhuarc added.

"Why now?" Nolan asked

Rhuarc laughed again. "Because we were called!" he bellowed. "We left an opportunity for the remaining races to prove there is a hope they are worthy enough to join us. Are you not the one twice marked, Nolan Harrison?"

Bringing his finger first up to his white hair, Nolan opened his palm and then brought it in front of his gaze. The ring, crossed with a sword and a hammer was burned into his skin and matched the small emblem on the front of each of the Ionian warrior's helmets.

"You have proven the worth of humanity," Rhuarc continued. "We are of the same blood, you and I, yet I could not have the courage and perseverance you have shown. You have passed all the tests set out before you, and now you are here to lead the Toltec, Celtae and Anasazi, along with the sculls of the infinite number of planes, into a future of peace."

"It is a daunting task," Nolan replied.

"These men, my brother and I are here to help you."

"Your brother?" Nolan asked.

There was a movement from the other side of the narrow crevice. Theron, Vice-Prime of the Kre, lifted his hand over his head. With fingers outstretched, he pulled his hand down over his body. As he did so, the black and silver changed to white and light blue. The long tail of hair turned from black to snow-white and the scars on his face disappeared. The missing arm was again whole, and he smiled wide as he looked every bit as Ionian as those mounted on the large beasts. "I have waited for you for a long time, brother Rhuarc," he said.

Rhuarc responded to his brother with a warm smile and then brought his gaze back to Nolan. "So, what say you, regent of all the peoples—pureblood and scull alike? We are your personal guard to assist you with our lives if necessary. Do you accept your charge?"

Nolan Harrison, once a simple man of Earth, looked at those around him. Garawin would always be close to him. Daniel and Lukas would be his eyes and ears toward the Celtae. The man he met long ago named Drew Sherman and the one he just met named Jelan Tulis, would be his emissaries to the Toltec. Including Chu and Lothar, these would be his council. They would assist him in governing a lasting peace across the Athar.

Nolan pulled the two long knives from his belt. At another time he would have raised them over his head, but this time it was more appropriate to lay them on the ground in front of his feet. Once he righted himself, he turned and looked at the leaders on both sides of the crevice and the soldiers who had slowly returned to the front line.

"I accept the charge!" he shouted. "We move on in a life of peace!"

There was a great roar. It thundered from the lips of every man who stood on the field. As Nolan heard the support, a slight breeze broke through the throng of men and nipped at the hair along his collar. It would have sent a chill down the spine of most men, but it sent a warm sensation into the core of his being.

It was so much for Nolan to take all at once. Being the First Key was an insurmountable, mental task as it was, but now he was being asked to take his place as the leader of all men and maintain a peace with the support of the Ionians. He raised his gaze to the heavens as if he was looking for a sign or some kind of additional support for the monumental task. When he lowered his gaze back down, he looked at his friends, but it was what he saw behind them that brought a wide smile to his face and relief to his anxiety. He spied a small figure on the far hilltop. Ranaa sat on the ground with her knees drawn up while her arms clasped them close to her breast. Nolan loved the woman and the love would be relentless as long as his heart beat with life. He knew he would lead well with her by his side.

Dear Reader:

Reviews are important to every author. We are thankful that many readers take a few moments to return to the purchasing website, in this case, Amazon, and leave a rating and a review.

If you could do so for this story, it would be much appreciated. Keep in mind, a Hollywood style review is not needed. Even a few simple words would be great.

Thanks again, and I hope you enjoyed the story.

Peter Sandor

www.ingramcontent.com/pod-product-compliance
Lightning Source LLC
Chambersburg PA
CBHW051242250626
47155CB00009B/3128